mush

mush

KATHLEEN KIIRIK BRYSON

First published 2000 by Diva Books, an imprint of Millivres Limited,
part of the Millivres Prowler Group, 116-134 Bayham Street, London NW1 0BA

A catalogue record for this book is available from the British Library

ISBN 1 873741 46 4

Cover illustration and design by Andrew Biscomb

Printed and bound in Finland by WS Bookwell

Acknowledgements

I would like to thank my agent Tricia Sumner and my editor Helen Sandler for their immense support, advice and belief regarding *Mush*. I would also like to express my gratitude to Gillian Rodgerson, publisher of Diva Books. Special thanks as well to Michael, Clive and Hélène, all of whom read earlier drafts and contributed valuable advice and comments.

Simone Stumpf also read and advised, and deserves special mention: Simone, I could not have done this without you. Thank you for your belief in me back when my ideas were scratches of ink on the back of college assignments, and for your wonderful love and laughter since that time, as well.

I would also like to express my thanks and love to my parents, who not only instilled in me an appreciation of libraries, but also moved up to Alaska from Southern California several months before I was born, thus enabling me to grow up in a unique and beautiful state – a state whose environment even now is threatened by commercial interests and industry; a wilderness that I hope is preserved for future Alaskan generations so that they too might grow up in the full dazzling splendour of the Great Land.

For Michael & Carlos

look out as they did here,
(you don't remember)
when my soul turned round,

perceiving the other-side of everything,
mullein-leaf, dog-wood leaf, moth-wing
and dandelion-seed under the ground.

– H.D.
from *Sigil*, XI

i. inside

Prologue

Across the saltwater bay was a range of volcanoes. Some had the same cratered tops as the volcanoes in children's dinosaur books but, like any of the other peaks, these were said to be as dormant as mountains. This all changed the winter Lady Julia rained dirt and ash down through the air, the flakes falling like funeral confetti onto the crisp of pure clean snow below. There was no snow ice cream that year, no combined tastes of fresh snow, vanilla extract, evaporated milk and cocoa powder. But there were other compensations for a child – the prehistoric spewing across the inlet and the excitement of the jet-dark snow that endured until early April, when the melt of it revealed twisting patterns of its grit on the damp ground beneath.

The girl was already stirring this volcanic dust into designs. She squatted on the beach in the clustered melting snow and, with her finger, traced her name softly in the ash. And though the sun was shining and she could see the sea-grass was green in places, when she touched the snow she was old enough to remember the violent frigidity of winter – when people freeze to death in forty minutes – spelling over the months from October to March. This memory had been enforced by the conversations of adults around her, by their constant references to past and future winters. And when darkness came back so intensely in October, inhabitants of the small town always forgot the midnight sun of only months before. When the sun sparkled on the snow in winter it was beautiful, but the light lasted only a few hours before it would begin to darken into lush purple again. The frost tightened even in the normal lubrication of one's eyes; even the air could be murderous. Such details were not forgotten. Even a six-year-old child could remember.

She looked at the strokes she had made in the ash, ash which had melded onto the coastal ice. She had only learned to write words other than her name a year before, and even this familiar spelling had required concentration. But she was satisfied with it. She put her hand in her pocket and squeezed her fingers round something else she had discovered on the beach today, a rough and peculiar stone. She had made towers of smooth small rocks all along the beach and once she had found this special, spongelike stone, she had left the other ones behind her. They no longer interested her, but the porous stone she had found was full of secret, textured holes, a hundred tiny dark caves smaller than her pinky. One hundred was the biggest number she could count to. Still squatting, she managed to see past the crook of her elbow to a figure approaching her along the beach.

"Nicky?" Her uncle now stood beside her. She rose and looked up at him. "What have you got in your hand there?"

The little girl released the puckered stone she held and offered it up to her uncle, the rock greasy with sweat from her small hand.

"That's a vesicular igneous rock, Nicky. Do you know what *igneous* means?" She shook her head. "Do you remember when the volcano exploded?" She nodded. "Well, *igneous* means that this rock came out of the volcano. It was hot and soft as chocolate syrup at first, and then it turned hard." Nicky looked at the rock her uncle now held. She didn't understand how it could have been chocolate, but her uncle never lied. He knew a lot.

"Can I have it back?"

Her uncle laughed and returned the rock. "Come on, we'd better make a move. Your mom will be worried." He picked her up and sat her on his shoulders, even though she had nearly grown too heavy and too old for it. She held on to her uncle's neck with glee, as he slowly and laboriously walked up the trail that snaked over the cliffs.

"Can I come stay with you in the cabin this summer? Can Susan babysit me?"

An odd expression flickered momentarily on her uncle's face. His daughter probably needed babysitting herself, he thought, not sole responsibility of an active child. But Susan had reached that difficult age of fourteen, and he found himself increasingly bewildered as how to bring up a teenage daughter in the late seventies.

"Can I?"

"We'll see," he said, balancing the little girl carefully as he picked his way up the bluff. "We'll see how Susan likes the idea of babysitting a kid cousin for a couple days."

"She will."

The uncle smiled at her self-assurance. "Alright then."

"Hurray!" Nicky kicked her heels against her uncle's chest and, though he swayed, he managed somehow to keep his balance and stop them from tumbling down to the beach below.

She laughed, delightedly. She was fearless.

The town in which she lived was set high upon these very cliffs, and at its far end the community sloped down to the mouth of a wide river. It was here that the river's mouth opened onto the inlet, so the water here was mixed, sweet and salt at the border of the Pacific Ocean. Several drowned every summer in both the river and the sea; it was nearly impossible to fall in either and survive unless there was immediate rescue. And even barring likely hypothermia, there was no chance of survival at all without a life jacket to keep neck and head above the bold current and strong tides.

Perhaps an hour after the uncle and niece had left the beach, an older girl happened along the same stretch. It wasn't until she passed by the third pile of pebbles that she began to be intrigued, and search the beach ahead of her for a sight of additional heaps. She wondered what type of person would lump these rocks together; what kind of code was meant to be read. Was it a child collecting stones of a similar shape, or a secret message from one lover to another: *Meet me up on the cliffs. Not until later, my husband is watching.*

Ellen stared at a pile of the stones, curved and clustered as dark grapes. They reminded her of moose droppings. Recognising the evidence of moose – and bears, too – was easy, whether their tracks and spore were fresh or old. Most kids knew their shit: bear patties were just mush, no prettier than the excrement of cow or dog. But moose droppings, locally called nuggets, were shaped pellets, uniform in colour and, yes, similar in size and shape to grapes. They were often collected and shellacked, goggly eyes and little legs added; shit made cute and palatable for tourists.

She looked at her Snoopy watch; she'd better walk back to town and find the others soon, or they would be waiting angrily at the bus for her. It wasn't often that she was given a 'free day' from the children's home, and it would take her nearly an hour to walk back to the bus. She was supposed to be learning responsibility, and had been given the watch to encourage this trait. She didn't want to disappoint anyone.

She walked up from the incoming tide now, and spied at the top of the still-snowy beach what must surely be the last of the rock piles. *Number seven*, she counted softly to herself. And there was a name this time, N – I – C – K – Y, scratched into a flat slab of merged ice and volcanic ash. It was already melting away, and the inevitable disappearance of the sculptor's signature made her feel rather sad. And the water was coming in now, too; she hoped that whoever the message was meant for had had a chance to read it.

Rather than taking the trail up the cliffs, she made her way up the dirt road to the state highway. There, she saw a cluster of parked cars of teenagers who jerked away when they saw her coming, then relaxed back into their seats when they saw the passer-by was only a twelve-year-old girl. One of the boys even waved a joint out at her, a friendly and slightly sleazy gesture, and a girl with bright red hair peered out the half-drawn window of the same car.

"You want a toke?" the girl with red hair asked.

"Hey, come on, Susan," someone shouted from inside the vehicle, "that's my *stash*, not charity for jailbait."

But Ellen shook her head anyway, for she had to get back; she had to get back to the bus in time, back to town, and the red mop of hair withdrew back into the car, out of sight.

Back to Little Novgorod, incorporated 1792. A distant colony of Mother Russia, a settlement in the wilderness far from the gilded domes of St. Petersburg until 1867. Then a mere outpost of a remote U.S. territory until statehood in 1959. Less than ten years later, oil would change everything for Little Novgorod. Still, the town was not so young as not to be old, as people had lived there as many as ten thousand years before. But in the minds of Westerners it had only been an entity since the Russians came and slaughtered and mated. Thus it was nearly two centuries from reckoning as such, which still meant quite an old town by the standards of the state. When counting correctly, it turned ancient. It was made up, mostly, of white people who had moved up since the advent of the oil pipeline and also of Indians and Aleuts with Russian names and blood. There were few Inuit, either Yupik or Inupiat, or people of African or Asian descent; in many ways it was a small hick town like many other North American towns. But its history was different. Its scenery was different. When one had the time to look closely, and most people had a lot of time, the subtle details were different, too.

As Ellen walked along, she glanced up. The sky was light grey; the sun had made an appearance earlier in the afternoon, but it was gone now. The sky in this town often veered from brilliant blue to smoky grey, regardless of the season. Spring, right now, was unremarkable. But particularly when winter came the sky would turn purple. It would be quiet. The snow crunched beneath feet while walking through the woods, she remembered this. That would be the only sound she would hear within the hush, unless a dog howled from far away or a moose was walking nearby. When a moose was in the vicinity her attention had turned to other things, so noticing the purple sky or the hush was difficult.

But in the absence of the threat of moose – when she was truly alone in winter – she made her narrow human tracks in the white snow, leaving a trail of dark pods behind her. If she brushed against a spruce tree laden with drifts then, the falling clumps made new and tiny marks themselves on the white fluff, tracks from a sea of nervous small animals. If she looked up then, she'd still see the purple sky. It was specific to winter in this town; the hue never appeared in summer, for example. And now in spring it had already faded to the colour of an insignificant bruise.

"Hey," the red-haired girl was running up to her on the dirt road, dust skimming behind her. "Hey, what's the time?"

"It's almost five." Ellen stared at the girl's hair, as red-orange as poppies and caterpillars.

"Shit," the red-haired girl said, and turned to run back to the car. Then she called back over her shoulder: "Hey, nice watch. Thanks."

Ellen looked down at the Snoopy watch again, the dog's racket eternally slapping at the floating tennis ball of the second hand. "You're welcome," she said, and continued walking up the hill.

She made it to the bus just within the hour. There were no houses to speak of in the centre of town: just a handful of small businesses, the Mall, the main high school, the chamber of commerce, the court-house. None of these buildings meant much to her, with the possible exception of the courthouse in which she had previously participated in a series of foster-care hearings. She wondered why it was always so quiet here, but figured this was because the houses were diffused, spread out along the edges of the community. She was glad she lived out in the woods, and not in this dull and quiet town.

There were many reasons, she thought, not to live in town. For example, if there were to be an earthquake, the first to go would be the enormous redwood oil-money houses on the bluff, if not by a tsunami then by their frail rumble down to the beaches below. The poorer houses and the trailer parks were set further back in the woods. People living there didn't have a great view; they couldn't step out the evening and look over the inlet at the red sunsets rimming the volcanoes, nor see the white hides of the belugas peeping from the water that tourists wondered at every summer. But in the event of a tidal wave, their homes would not be the first into the sea, unlike the houses of the rich. The children's home was far out in the woods, miles from the coast. Still, Ellen thought, there were other dangers than tsunamis. Ones from which she was not sheltered. Ones that emerged from earth, woods and air itself. Earthquakes. Bear attacks. Freezing to death.

She looked along the parking lot of the Mall. A few stray cars for weekend shopping. She longed to see normal children her own age with normal parents, but saw only kids younger than herself, hanging on their mothers' hands. One boy her age exited the Fish & Game store, but she didn't talk to boys and, anyway, he was guiding a small child himself ("Hurry up, Carol, you stupid little bitch," she could hear him saying). They both had bright white hair, and it made her think uncomfortably of her own straight boring hair. Why did everyone seem to have these brilliant colours of white or red, whereas her own was as dark as wet earth, as dark as dirt? If she had had prettier hair, or been a more attractive toddler, perhaps she would have been adopted by a nice normal family years ago. But again, there were things which couldn't be foreseen or directed, she considered, moving her thoughts back to her inventory of local dangers.

The '64 earthquake had come and gone, leaving Little Novgorod relatively unscathed. The tsunamis did not wash over it as they washed over other towns not so far away, in the vast relative terms particular to the state. 'Not so far away' could mean neighbours hundreds of miles away. No, the tidal waves had not hit the dirt cliffs of the town nor the houses perched on these cliffs, but ever-present in the minds of the inhabitants, and even in Ellen's mind, was the Big One. A '9' at least on the Richter scale, predicted ever since the '64 quake. So when the trembling started, she and the other kids at the children's home were still taught to crouch under their desks, to stand in doorframes, to cover their heads, to avoid electrical wires, to wait and wait and wait for what could be aftershocks if they were lucky or, worse, mere preceding tremors of the Big One...

It didn't matter: living in town would be still worse, she thought. The Big One would drown the townspeople all like puppies, gagging on salt water when a tsunami made it over the cliffs. And that was certainly a possibility in the event of the Big One; living in Little Novgorod meant living right in the violent jewel of the Ring of Fire, the seismic chain that linked tectonic plates all the way down to Mexico.

"Glad to see you made it back in time, Ellen," the team leader flashed an enthusiastic grin at her as she grew closer to the parked bus, "guess that watch was an investment after all."

Ellen glanced down at Tennis Snoopy, forever batting the seconds just out of reach. "Yeah." She could see time moving; she was looking forward to summer when she had been promised even more free days away from the group. She liked to be on her own.

Carol and her brother Brett left the Fish & Game store.

"Did you get the guns?" Carol was jumping up to see what her elder brother was holding in the plastic bag.

"They're not guns; they're bullets," her brother said, with more than a hint of superiority. "Ammo."

"How come they let you buy it? You don't have a gun." She was still straining to look more closely at the bag, but Brett was walking too quickly, telling her to speed up. They were alone as they strode across the asphalt parking lot, except for a scraggly girl up ahead of them who paused to glance down at her watch, then hurried on.

"'Cause they've got Dad's details and they know me. Now shut up." The older boy was aware of his responsibility in this mission, and all he wanted to do was carry the bullets back home to his father and wash his hands clean of them. They made him nervous. But he couldn't admit that to his dad; he knew it was a privilege to pick up the order for his father. He couldn't admit he was scared of the shiny, lethal little things. He wasn't a sissy. Still, he was secretly relieved that his six-year-old sister had wanted to come along too, because then he could impress her with his elevation to being a real man of the house.

"You've got to be careful with them, see," he said, as they finished their long trek back to their house, through the sparse neighbourhood and near the woods. "They're not something you should take lightly." He made his voice gruff; there, now he sounded more like a man. It sounded like something his father would say. He sneaked a look at his sister to see if she was impressed. But her gaze was darting on ahead, to where their mom and dad stood by the car, waiting to take off on the trip to the moose range.

"Took you long enough," his father commented.

The boy sighed inwardly; they had walked as fast as they could. But he steeled his face and voice: "Carol was dragging along, otherwise I would have been here a lot sooner. Don't make me take her next time, please."

His father gave him a wink and clapped his shoulder. "Nature of the game, sport." He turned to his wife. "You hear that, Linda? Now we got us a bit of protection, thanks to Brett, here." He ruffled Brett's hair and the boy grinned, despite himself.

"Did you bring my bucket, Mom?" Carol piped up suddenly.

"Yes, but honey, you know the only blueberries you'll find this time of year will be frozen mush."

"But you brought it, right?"

"Shut up, stupid," said Brett, "you're out of luck."

Carol's mother exhaled slowly. "I remembered, Carol. Yes."

Brett elbowed Carol. "You should be glad," he whispered, "because there'll be less bears around if it's not berry season. But maybe they'll eat *you* instead, 'cause they'll be hungry."

Brett knew there was a genuine fear of attack. Most families owned at least three firearms, and these would be toted along when walking in the marshes on the moose ranges. There had been a fire in the forties or fifties in this prime picking area, where officially it was illegal to pick since it was federal land. The guns would ensure a chance against an attacking bear; the guns made families feel they had a chance against fear. It was considered foolhardy and *cheechako* – greenhorn – to go camping, hiking, overnight fishing, backpacking, even berry-picking without an instrument that could kill.

"Can Nicky come berry-picking, too?" Carol asked her mother, just as her father put the key in the ignition.

Her parents exchanged a glance overhead in the rear-view mirror. Her mother cleared her throat. "I don't think Nicky's at home today, honey. I spoke with her uncle earlier when I walked by the house, and he planned on taking Nicky to the beach for the afternoon. And I don't think your chances for getting any blueberries are high, peanut. It's just too early in the year."

"Nicky's mother's an old drunk," Brett stated from the back seat, "that's why her uncle has to take Nicky away for the day."

"That's not kind, Brett," said his mother. But she did not contradict him.

Carol folded her arms, pouted and looked out the window. She wanted to go berry-picking with Nicky; it made it much more fun. And now Mom was saying there weren't even any berries! She didn't want to go walking with smelly old Brett, nor admit to him that she was afraid of bears. That was why they had to go get the bullets, wasn't it? And Brett hadn't even let her see the bullets before he handed them over to Dad. Brett was selfish. So she would be, too: she would eat all the blueberries she could, and no one else would get even one. And she'd run to the car if she saw a bear or moose. Even though she knew that was the worst thing to do.

Both bears and moose could kill, and Carol was never sure if the man's-scalp-torn-off-but-still-survived bear stories her brother told her were true or not. She knew that if you began to smell a cattle scent while in the woods it was a very bad sign.

There were tricks to avoiding bears: talking loudly, or singing while hiking. A moose with her calf was to be avoided at all costs, too, as the cow would occasionally charge unprovoked. Moose might be funny-looking but, like bears, they were also huge. Children such as Carol were given the comfort of folk-wisdom on what to do if they were charged by moose while waiting for the school bus; they were supposed to stand still. They were never supposed to run. The same with bears, one never ran. But the advice varied: was it best to play dead with bears, or best to scream and shout and threaten bears away? Nothing was ever perfectly clear except for the inviolable fact that one never, ever ran. Bears sensed fear. And they sensed food: once Carol had left a trail of M&Ms behind her, like Hansel and Gretel, and had gotten spanked for it. And they even sensed gore: perhaps it was a misogynist myth, or perhaps not, but it was thought dangerous to menstruate while deep in the woods.

Brett would hint darkly at this to his little sister, but Carol didn't even know what the word period meant. The bears smelled blood, Brett said.

Moose were worse, Carol thought, that was what her parents always said. Moose were primarily lethal through their confusion; it was common that they walked into speeding cars and this was almost always fatal for the moose and often for the driver, too. And roadkill could not be salvaged for the freezers. It was always confiscated immediately by officials to be distributed to poor families, her mom had told her.

Even now as the family turned onto the state highway, it was necessary to slow down in order to get past the obstructing corpse of a young bull moose, encircled by a crumpled green Dodge and the red-blue flash of several police cars.

"You can't eat roadkill," Brett whispered to his sister in the back seat, "even if it killed Dad or Mom. You have to *need* the meat."

The family car passed quickly through the town centre, and was shortly on the road heading towards the enormous moose range, government land. This was where Carol's parents liked to go walking, at least once a month – *to stretch the legs a bit*, as Carol's father would say. The whole vast space of it was relatively untouched, but then most land in the state was still untouched. In most other places on earth where humans live, the land has been conquered and worked over. Sifting dirt through fingers means that another human has sifted it once, too. It is likely that some other human is *in* the dirt, the years passing corpses through them in an efficient recycle of earths. In most places, in all directions where the eye meets the horizon are buildings or farmland or ancient-tilled fields turned deserts and forests. But here in this place, a town of two thousand people became the exception: only a small comma in forests which had never been felled and regrown, mountain ranges never been scaled, lakes never fished nor swum, rivers and streams never forded. All of it was for the first time. This held true for most of the state. The effect was open and big, nearly operatic. The world that surrounded the town was too big. Both of the children in the back seat felt this, as the car whizzed down the gravel road, space to both sides.

The family arrived at the intended patch, parked the car and settled down to pick for several hours. No bears appeared, which made Brett slightly sulky. Despite his fear of firearms, he had been looking forward to proving his manhood, maybe rescuing his family single-handedly. Maybe he could have taken the gun from his dad and shot the bear himself. Then he would be a real hero, and he could take the teeth to school to show around. Of course, these guns killed people, too, the boy thought; sometimes you had to kill people if they were mean enough.

Along the same stretch of the federal moose range through which the car had sped were any number of murdered bodies, often brought to light and justice ten years after the fact. By then the tragedy would be too old for townspeople not directly involved. The Benktsson boy had been missing at least fourteen years before he turned up again as rot instead of escaped convict. Even family members sometimes preferred the illusion of a precipitous escape out of state to a half-decaying, half licked-clean corpse. Still, the bodies did turn up from time to time. Even more side effects of freely obtained ammunition existed:

children killing siblings and friends by accident, gory aftermaths of domestic violence, trespassing disputes gone wrong.

But, thought the boy, well-schooled in a culture that loved guns, sometimes it was necessary to kill.

The berry-picking was not fruitful. Carol rose from her chosen clump to show her mother an entirely empty pail. Her mother noticed several purple stains at her daughter's mouth, from ingesting old berries that had frozen last fall and now had thawed. But she smiled and didn't comment on the fact.

"That's okay, pumpkin," she said, as Carol headed grumpily back to the car, trudging through the bits of snow and the cold moist lichen. "It's still spring. There'll be more blueberries later, in a couple of months when summer comes."

"Can Nicky come next time?" The little girl pressed her head against her mother's thigh.

"Sure, honey." Of course she can, thought Linda Flanagan, anything that gets her away from that mother of hers. It was absolutely disgraceful: passed out on the front couch, and Nicky herself had to call her uncle for help. The man should take his niece for good, not just for the day. Or Nicky's father could come down from the platforms up north. Or something. She glanced down at her daughter, and felt relief flood her heart at the sight of her own child's activity and happy liveliness. "Race you to the car?" she suggested.

"Okay!" Carol ran, her pale hair streaming out behind her, and slapped her hand on the hard metal of the car. "I beat you! I beat you!"

"You sure did." Her mother looked behind her, where husband and son were still plodding along. It was nearly eight in the evening and, though there was plenty of daylight, she wanted to get going. They'd had a nice walk, but it was chilly, and indulging her daughter about the berries had been a silly whim. They would come again in summer, when blueberries would bubble up like little plums through the bushes, and she would eat as much as her daughter and still fill all the pails.

*

At last spring turned to summer. In summer it was not, as many from Outside supposed, a neolithic tundra riddled with ice-pools but instead was verdant, green and lush. Cottonwoods and overgrown sick and spindly spruce would wave high into the sky, and underfoot was the swarm of tangled life. The devil's-clubs thorning out like malevolent and tearing cannabis; the bright pointillism of cranberries and currants dotting through the brush. Aspens stood at middle height, halved between cottonwood giantesses and the sprawl of the living weave underfoot. The scent of the air was warm and over-ripe. Mulch and rain and the haze of sun-ripening process, cordialling the tarnished green of aspen leaves and the amber sap dripping on the grey-mottled spruces.

The ground was sticky with plant resin, the insects mossed and mossed, all creatures sat still and watched the trees thrive. Anyone could come to the trees and finger their lichen. Some trees lay dead; but they also lay organic, the decay working itself out in a thousand other types of life. They had mossy organ ways of showing them- selves, these trees lying deep in the sex of the green woods. In the trees, it was said, there were spirits. They would work themselves into a person's head, too, if one paused long enough in the woods and merely breathed and watched the secret rot unfold. And a person's thoughts would go blank when these spirits were found; when the tree religion hit, then thoughts were always nothing, one was opened by the fungi, by the soft wood turned teeming paste. A person could feel the green weight of the trees. It was something that would stay in the head for a long while after.

Linda Flanagan stepped outside her house, sniffed the air and thought immediately of blueberry-picking. The berries would be ripe now, nearly purple. She felt her mouth water as she thought of the sweet and slimy white insides of the berries. She would make blueberry pan- cakes tomorrow morning. Her kids would want pie, she knew, but it was tiresome to make and she preferred pancakes herself.

She called out to her daughter, who was playing with her new life-size baby doll and an old party wig near the swingset. "Carol! We're going berry-picking today." She paused and then added, "Do you want to run over to Nicky's house and see if she wants to come, too?"

"She's playing with Susan today. She told me she was going to. Her Uncle Joe is coming over, too."

"Well, ask Susan and Mr. Barber if they'd like to go pick berries with us."

"Okay." Her daughter dropped her doll and the wig in the mud, and took off running to her friend's house four houses down. Her mother stroked the little gold cross on the fine chain around her neck, and then walked over to the swingset, picked up the mud-splattered objects, and brought them back in the house to carefully dab at the dirt in the kitchen sink.

She was just patting the wig dry with paper towels when her daughter came back, trudging through the kitchen door and glowering. Her mother noticed the mud she dragged in on her shoes, but she bit her tongue. She would clean it up later; she didn't want to nag. It was more important to grow up happy and carefree for a while, than to grow up tidy.

"Is Nicky coming?" she said brightly, with a fresh smile for her child.

"No." Her daughter made as if to kick the leg of the kitchen table, then looked at her mother and thought better of it. "They already left. Her mom said I just missed them. Nicky's gone away for a whole week and her Uncle Joe is babysitting her."

"That's nice," said Linda Flanagan. "It will be good for Nicky to be able to play out in the woods." She untied her apron, folded it, and then placed both the dry clean doll and the wig on the table. "We're going to be leaving in about twenty minutes, Carol."

"No!" The little girl stomped her feet. "I don't want to go now that Nicky's not going, too."

"Carol," her mother admonished, and then switched tactics: "I'll make a blueberry pie tonight." She had been looking forward to tomorrow's pancakes. Maybe they'd pick enough berries for both treats. She felt exhausted suddenly, thinking of rolling out the pie crust and stewing down the berries. "With ice cream."

Carol considered this. "Okay," she finally agreed, walking over and picking up her doll from the kitchen table. "But next time Nicky can come, right? Are you playing dress-up too, Mom? How come you took the hair inside?"

"Next time," her mother promised, answering only the first question. She pressed the tips of her fingers to her temples; she felt the stirrings of a headache. "Be ready when I call you, Carol. And tell your brother we're going, too." It really was a shame the little Barber girl couldn't keep Carol company. The two of them got on so well, and when they played together it meant she had to devote less energy to Carol's entertainment. But she shouldn't be thinking like that. Again she gave a cheery smile and for a moment laid her hand softly on her child's shoulder.

Nicky waited for spring to pass and for summer to come back. And when it finally happened she was deposited by her relieved mother at her uncle's house far back in the woods. Her cousin came down the path to meet her.

"Bye-bye, Nicky. Be good." Nicky didn't answer her mother; she was staring with excitement at the woods and, further along the trail, the cabin. Susan was going to babysit her. She hoped Susan wouldn't pinch her when she was bad this time. Maybe she would even get to sleep outside in the hammock, just like Susan did.

"Hi, Nicky," her uncle called a long way off, in the cabin. "Are you coming in or not?" Susan stretched out a hand and the little girl gripped it, walking on the trail towards the log house. Her cousin's hand was warm and friendly, and the little girl could smell the spruce pitch in the air. Everything is growing, Nicky thought.

They walked into the cabin. "Hi there, Nicky!" said her uncle again, as he gave her a hug.

"Hi, Uncle Joe."

"So here she is," interjected the teenager. "I'm going to take off for a while, okay? Go out for a walk?"

She looks so sullen and her hair is uncombed, her father thought. It was a tangled red mass. But all kids her age go through a dishevelled phase, he reminded himself. He reached out for a moment; wanted to make a tender gesture, stroke her hair, pat her arm or something. He wished they could get along better. "Okay," he said. "I've got a group of students coming around in about a half hour for a nature walk, and it would be nice if you could watch Nicky then."

"Can I go with Susan on her walk?" The little girl appealed to her uncle.

"No!" Her cousin turned on her, her hair a flaming circle as she whirled round. The dozens of flowers hanging upside down above Susan's head were quivering from the movement. Some looked freshly picked; others were colourful but crispy, like the dried blood on a scab when Nicky fell down and skinned her knees. She knew that Susan liked to pluck them and dry them out, although Uncle Joe discouraged it. He liked the flowers to be alive instead; Nicky had heard them arguing about it the last time she was here.

"I think Susan wants some time alone, Nicky. You'll have plenty of chances to play with her the rest of the week." He hesitated. "You'll come back within a half hour, Susan?"

"Oh, sure." Susan gave them both a dirty look and then walked out, slamming the door behind her.

At least we're in the middle of nowhere, her father thought dryly. There's no place to go in a tantrum except to walk it off in the woods. "Okay, Nicky, let's sort your things out a bit. You're going to want to take a sweater and a raincoat with you, because you're going to be out the rest of the day, and it's not a warm one."

It had turned from a sunny summer day to a particularly chilly day, and it looked like it might rain. He busied himself with finding a cot for his niece and a place to put her little travel suitcase, and tried not to think about his daughter and her recent moodiness. She would have to work it out for herself. When he had finished sorting out the cot and making sure the six-year-old was bundled up in warm clothing with a waterproof jacket, he went outside the doorframe and called out: "Susan!" There was no answer. "Susan! Nicky's ready to go!"

His voice echoed all the way down to the lake below. Irritated, he shook his head. He would have to look after the girl himself now, and here was the schoolbus from the children's home, pulling up to the driveway in a fine example of bad timing. He looked down at Nicky. He liked this part of his forest ranger job, showing the kids from the home around the lake and interesting them in new species of flora and – he hoped – an appreciation of the wilderness itself. But it required a great deal of his attention.

He kneeled down to his niece's level. "Listen, Nicky, I'm not going to be able to talk to you much when I'm showing the brats around."

"Brats?"

Her uncle's eyes twinkled. "Brats, orphans or delinquents, take your pick. Matter of fact, I was once a delinquent myself." He said the term with affection and, though unsure of the word 'delinquent', the girl giggled. "But even delinquents deserve some attention. I want you to stay close to me, and if you're quiet, I'll show you how to make flutes later."

"Flutes?"

"That's right, Nicky, flutes. If first you stay close and sit still. "

Nicky smiled, and he took his niece's hand and headed down the trail to the driveway, where at least a dozen teenagers and pre-teenagers were spilling out of the bus labelled MCALESTER'S CHILDREN'S HOME.

She sat quietly on a stump in a wet clearing near the lake, while her uncle showed the group of mildly interested students and their chaperone the correct technique when digging for the coiled, snail-shaped roots of the fiddler's head fern. There were pink and blue flowers all round the glade, ones her uncle named as fireweed and lupine and bluebells. Earlier, her uncle had showed everybody the safe way to build a campfire, but he'd also shown them how to douse it with lake-water and sand, and now it had become wet, cold sludge. Nicky could still smell smoke everywhere, though. Out of the corner of her eye, she saw one of the students slipping away into the bushes on the other side of the clearing, a short girl with straight, dark brown hair cut in sharp bangs across her forehead.

She wondered if she should say anything, but her uncle had asked her not to interrupt him, and she wanted to find out how to make the flutes. *Plip-plip*. She looked up; the grey sky was beginning to drip. She was glad she was wearing her yellow raincoat. She liked the sound the drops made as they hit the bright plastic, and so she sat quietly.

Ellen had sneaked away from the group and now stood at the lakeside, looking out over its expanse and listening to the loons. The sun displayed itself momentarily in the grey sky. It is beautiful, she thought, and was glad that she had managed a few minutes on her own. The forest ranger's talk was absorbing enough, but she doubted she would ever need the wilderness survival skills he was showing them, doubted that she would ever be desperate enough to make a fire with no matches, or have to dig for mushrooms, or roots of ferns. She just wanted a couple minutes on her own. Around the edges of the lake, the sun was now sparkling on flowering lilies, their rain-moist petals waxen and yellow. Small concentric circles were forming in the lake, thin edges of fading hoops and rings, and she looked up in the sky. It was starting to sprinkle and the short interlude of sunlight had ceased.

She walked back to the shore again, stepped off the dock and into the bushes, so she could see the lilies more clearly. They were floating right there, directly in front of her. Some of the flowers were white, not yellow. What would have caused that, she wondered? Maybe the water was different here? Perhaps the forest ranger would know.

The water was moving again, stirred by something more momentous than raindrops. Not far to her left – past the dock, but shielded by a group of trees, which was why she hadn't noticed this at first – was a person wading out into the water.

Ellen sucked her breath in; she wasn't sure if she should call out or remain silent. Perhaps this person was only swimming. But no, the figure continued walking out, past the group of white lilies and further out. Only a pair of shoulders and a head remained above the water, and Ellen realised with a start that she had seen this person before; she recognised the traffic-stopping red hair that hung down over the girl's frail-looking neck.

She should say something, but any moment the red-haired girl was going to glide into a breast-stroke, or a crawl, and talking would destroy the calm of the lake. The blazing patch of hair disappeared beneath the water, and Ellen felt her tongue freeze up. Several bubbles rose to the surface. Surely she would come up now, surely she would come up for air soon. Her own mouth felt numb, her tongue had become goo; she couldn't cry out. Any moment the red hair would rise up, and the girl would turn grinning around at her, saying *I remember you from the beach*. Any moment now.

Ellen felt a scream rising in her throat and she tried to open her lips, but a hot itch was rising in her, flooding her chest with blood. She looked at the spot where the girl went down. The lake was still and not even rain was marring its surface now. Ellen fell to her knees amidst the spruce trees on the bank. The moss swelled wetly over her jeans as she sank into the bracken. She pressed her hands on either side of her head. Something was inside her skull now, and she couldn't get it out. *Listen.* No, she couldn't. *Save me.* She hadn't.

At last Nicky's uncle came over to her. She had been waiting patiently, and she knew from his smile that she had done well.

He was carrying a long dead tube of a withered stalk in his hand.

The students were with their chaperone; he had made a small assignment for them collecting different berries and felt he ought to spend a couple minutes with his niece. He wished his daughter had shown up, but he couldn't disappoint the child further.

Nicky looked at what he was holding. "Is that a carrot?" She had heard him identify it earlier for the others, but it wasn't orange; it looked more like a stick.

He looked surprised, then smiled. "I see you've been listening. It's called wild carrot – you can eat the roots, like real carrots. This isn't the root part, though – this is the stalk. The plant is also called Queen Anne's Lace."

"Is it a flute?"

"It will be." He broke off a length of it, and then with a pocketknife carved out several holes. He blew out a high-pitched warble. His fingers wiggled on the other holes, and a little melody came out. "Do you want to try making your own?" he asked.

"Yes." She grasped the tube and, under her uncle's careful instruction, carved out a minute, perfect little mouth-hole. She held it up to her lips and pursed them as she had watched her uncle do. A sharp sound came out. Neat! She would show Carol when she got home. She turned to her uncle to see if he would help her with the other holes, but he was looking past her, to the edge of the clearing where the bushes were moving. Nicky saw the one who had sneaked away earlier re-emerge.

"Someone's fallen in the water," this dark-haired girl was saying to Uncle Joe.

Nicky's uncle was terrified; he had been assured by the chaperone that all of the students would be watched carefully – "What?! Sit here, Nicky, don't move" – his mind was already racing through resuscitation patterns, whether there were enough warm blankets up at the cabin –

"A girl with red hair. She wasn't with us," Ellen added, but the forest ranger was running through the bushes to the lake.

And so Ellen ran after him, following, she could maybe show him the exact place where the girl went down.

She still sat on the stump, holding the half-finished flute in her hand. Had Susan fallen down? Susan was the only one she knew with red hair. Nicky squeezed her knees together. It was starting to rain again and she had to pee. A feeling was creeping in on her; and she let fear wash through all parts of her body as she sat there. She wet herself; her jeans went sticky with hot urine; there was a sharp scent in the air, of piss as well as smoke. Things were shifting, changing, forming into danger. In a minute her uncle would return. She gripped the flute tight, her fingers crushing its holes in its frame so that it was only a broken mass of plant fibres, its openings hidden forever.

Already she could hear her uncle screaming, but she sat perfectly still, just as he had told her to. The rain was coming down hard now, wet and violent on the hood of her raincoat, but inside it her head was as dry and immobile as a preserved wildflower, the kind Susan liked to hang upside down to dry and then shellac with a shiny, brittle glaze.

1. Nicky

Nicky lived in the skirt of the woods near the trailer park, far back from the cliffs and the inlet views. There, the trees whispered and whistled in codes of wind and slow sprouting. The house was empty and large. Her dad was rarely home as he worked hard, very hard, her mom told her, on the oil platforms up on the Slope in northern Alaska. *He pays for all this*, her mom would say, her speech careful and precise as she spread her arms to indicate the wooden deck, the shag carpet, the mirrored plywood walls. *He pays for this*, her mother would repeat, weeping this time. She would forget to make her speech careful; she would set her vodka down too clumsily on the built-in bar in the kitchen. *This is what you get, Nicky*. Yet it wasn't what Nicky wanted. *I want a sister*, Nicky would say, *or a little brother. Or a puppy.* But her mother would keep her head in her hands on the bar, and in the mirrored hallway wall Nicky could see the reflection of her weeping mother even as she left the room to play Legos with her friend Carol.

She was seven when she started pinching her friends. She had tried before with her mom, but didn't get the reaction she got from her playmates in the neighbourhood: slaps from her mother, but deference from other children. Nicky pinched them deep into their soft, usually pink skins. Most would cry and hate her, but afterwards they looked at her with new respect. Nicky was in charge and a limited few of her neighbourhood playmates would even be drawn to her mild viciousness. Perhaps they thought she might protect them from other, more dangerous bullies. The more her fingernails cut into Carol's tender arms, for example, the more it seemed Carol liked her. Carol lived only four houses away, right next to the forest, but her house was much nicer. She had a big brother who laughed; a huge Lego set; a Baby Alive you could feed until it pooped and, best of all, Carol's mom didn't cry like Nicky's mom. She was nice and gave Nicky cookies to take home. In fact, she had already baked chocolate-chip cookies this very afternoon. They smelled wonderful: of burnt sugar and melted butter.

Nicky set aside the tall Lego truck she had just compiled and carefully placed her fingernails against Carol's flesh. If she twisted hard enough, she felt sure she could frighten Carol into asking her to spend the night.

"Ouch!" Carol tore her arm away from Nicky, but an expression of confusion and slight fear passed over her as she rubbed her arm. Nicky could tell that Carol didn't want to lose her as a friend; Carol was too weak to stand alone. "Nicky?"

"Yeah?"

"Do you want to stay over?"

"Yes."

It always worked. Later, just as Nicky had hoped, she was sitting on Carol's stairs, spending the night at the Flanagan house. Carol's mom and dad were having a party, but she and Carol sneaked down to watch through the stair railings. Nicky could see Carol's mother speaking right now as they leant over the banister to watch the bright crowd below. Carol's mother was pretty with her twinkling eyes and surprisingly hearty laughter. She had brown eyes and her eyebrows went up and down as she spoke. *what it would feel like to be kissed and hugged asleep by Carol's mother, a kiss, a kiss, a soft kiss sinking into your cheek, the lips going through, fluid, passing down to warm your heart wonder* Nicky's own mother kissed her asleep sometimes but it all went wet and wrong and she smelled funny, and then sometimes she would start to cry again. Nicky would always fake herself asleep on those occasions.

She didn't want to go to sleep at all tonight; she wanted to watch the party at Carol's house until she grew so tired she wouldn't realise when she nodded off. Because then she would wake up in the morning and would have missed the night and the murderer, too. Carol's mother's hand fiddled with the gold cross around her neck. She was, after all, a church-going woman, that's what Nicky's mom said, anyway. Now Carol's father approached his wife with a possessive arm around her waist, now – oh, no – Carol's father saw Nicky and Carol and was heading up the stairs to put the two of them to bed.

He tucked them in, his hands warm and dry, his kiss comforting and kind on Nicky's forehead. Then he drew away, the door clicked and he was gone. Nicky's own dad was never there to tuck her in, not even when she couldn't sleep. *You can't sleep.* Nicky couldn't sleep; the murderer would get her. *strangled. knifed. steely through the door of flesh on the chest, irritating itch of fibres distracting from the hold around the neck. Wake up.* Nicky woke up. Carol was asleep beside her. Nicky could feel her heart racing; she was the only one awake in Carol's bedroom. Had the murderer been in the room? Had he crept in from the woods? She had forgotten to pull the covers over her head. She had forgotten to pull them over her head and put a pillow where her head ought to be. Now she did exactly this.

If she did it right, the murderer might think the bed was empty and miss her when he came into the room. He would take Carol instead – which was too bad, since Nicky liked Carol – but Nicky planned to survive the murderer's attack. Yesterday in the newspaper she had spelled out the story about the murderer from Oklahoma. He killed three Girl Scouts sleeping in a tent. *eyes closed claws of a dread man ripping flesh knife and rape and blood blood blood a trench a trembling inch of a pulse a rip* She remembered the words from the newspaper, and her mind was mixing them up, blending the words together in her head.

Nicky was a Girl Scout, just like those girls had been. Sometimes she went camping and slept in tents, just like those girls had done. The police hadn't caught the murderer. He got on a plane and escaped. Nicky knew exactly where he went – the state which was the biggest to hide in and the furthest away. He flew here after murdering the Girl Scouts and got off the plane in Anchorage. Nicky's town was only a twenty-minute plane ride from Anchorage International Airport. *Wake up. Wake up. Wake up.* And she woke up into the next day.

Light streamed into the room, through the glass, through the grid of the mosquito screen.

"Get up, Nicky and Carol," said Carol's mother. "You're sleepy-heads, both of you." The murderer hadn't come after all, so Nicky politely watched Saturday morning cartoons with Carol until lunchtime. Then she headed off home, picking her way through the rain puddles. In fall, she liked to stamp on puddles and break the ice. But now in summer she avoided them with some care. There were big black bugs jumping around in the puddles, but Nicky hadn't managed to catch one yet.

"Oh, it's you," said Nicky's mother when Nicky walked in. "I thought it might be your father." She was in her bathrobe with a glass in her hand when she tried to hug Nicky, but Nicky dodged her. She was smelling funny again. Nicky went upstairs and looked out from her bedroom window at the forest and the houses on her street. It was a small town and it was dangerous. She had heard visitors commenting on its breathtaking beauty, on the obvious visual pleasures of white-tipped Alaskan cotton or the caribou or the skies which turned so extremely red and violet and pink and orange and yellow in the sunsets. But they couldn't feel the sheer restless uneasiness of living in a place which was active, living, moving, as Nicky did. They didn't know it was a dangerous place to grow up.

And there were other things than murderers to worry about. Nicky knew this for a fact. Danger was everywhere; it had been dangerous ever since last summer. For starters, the forest itself: she could never make out what exactly it was that the trees quietly wailed at her when she stepped outside her house; whether their phrases were comforts or threats. But, like her, they were laid open to violence. Her uncle, who was a forest ranger, had once pointed out to her a field of black stumps and white-grey crippled and stunted half-alive trees. It was caused by a campfire, he said. Be careful. Be safe.

She was surrounded by flammable trees; the trees knew this and they hissed this fact openly outside the house and even through the open window, through the screen's countless tiny metal squares. *We are vulnerable*, the trees hissed at her. The trees could all catch fire all at once. Once Nicky's mom had caught fire when she had fallen asleep with a cigarette. The trees swayed threateningly outside. They could all catch fire, too. *Crackling, horrible, skin bubbling, teased along into charred flesh. A flame eating up an arm.* If trees could catch fire, then houses could, too. What if there were a fire while she was sleeping? There could be a fire. Nicky would escape through the window, down the metal fire ladder, and run to Carol's house but... she didn't know what she would do if she had to run out naked. Her mother said it didn't matter in a fire.

Nicky looked out along the line of houses. If she squinted, she could just make out the shapes moving within the windows of Carol's house. And there was also the Devil to worry about. Last summer before it happened, her cousin Susan had told her all about him. *A slash man. A slash man with eyes of razor blades and horns. The terrible, all-knowing Devil. Yes, the Devil,* Susan had said, and had detailed for Nicky the scary bits of a movie called *The Exorcist. You must be careful,* Susan had told her. *You must keep safe.* Yes. Keep safe.

People died in real life, too, not just on TV and in the movies. And last summer Susan died in water. *dripping soft flesh in silent bubbling water* Nicky thought for a while that Susan would climb out from the lake in the forest and into her window and get her like the zombie movies on TV, but her mother said that was stupid. But then one day when she was playing at Carol's, Carol's big brother Brett said that vampires could climb in, even if zombies couldn't. And maybe Susan was a vampire now. A vampire was like a mosquito, but worse. Nicky had pinched Brett hard but he had only laughed at her and didn't seem to care.

After that, vampires had kept climbing into the very window she now stood at. Every night for a month she slept on her right side (the bible said, I will seat you on my *right* side) with her arms crossed. She had heard a story about a boy who died in his sleep but went to Jesus because his arms were in a cross, and Carol said that crosses and onions worked against vampires. Nicky had learned the dying boy story in Sunday School; her mom would take her sometimes when her headaches weren't too bad, but she wasn't a church-going woman. One night Nicky screamed away the monsters with the thick long teeth until her mom came up to her room. The vampires never came back again after that, but she had continued to sleep with her arms in a cross.

For several seconds longer Nicky stood at the screened window listening for the trees. Though the trees were usually quiet in the day with hisses and whispers, at night they roared – *Wake up.*

Later that summer she went camping with Carol's family. Her mom always gave her permission. *It stops you from whining,* she said. Nicky ignored her mom, because she was quietly removing a box of Tic-Tacs from her mother's purse. She was just beginning to forget about Zombie Susan and her scary devil stories, the vampires and the fires. But at the campsite she could smell the black-ashed campfire. *slash ash* She could touch the pale bluebells and fireweed growing by the water, the crooning rich trees by the cliffs. *Bubble-drowned flesh.* The flowers reminded her of something she wanted to forget.

Once they'd pitched the tents quite close to the bluff, Carol's father took the two girls hunting for firewood. The sloping cliffs, said Carol's dad in a teacher voice, would sometimes shatter and re-form according to the quakes which shook the area through the years. Sometimes wind carried pieces of the bluff away. And sometimes rain soaked through the reddish dirt of the cliffs to create mud that slid and slid. All of this was called *erosion.* Nicky already knew there was not a season in which the rain would not come, so dry days were a cause of gentle internal celebration. Nicky felt happier on dry days. Today had also been a dry day, and the tents would be comfortable to sleep in.

She and Carol had the mosquito-surrounded pup tent to themselves that night, but Carol's brother Brett crept in to tell them ghost-stories. Nicky sneaked glances at Carol while he talked. Carol was pretty just like her mom and her eyebrows went up and down too, as Brett told the scary stories; her white ringlets standing out *electric shock* from her scalp. Nicky felt herself grow scared. Unsafe. Nicky told Carol and Brett the story that had scared her, all about the girls in Oklahoma. They were killed with a knife in a tent. But Carol and Brett just laughed and Nicky grew cold inside her skin and pulled the sleeping bag over her head so the murderer would miss her. *scratch pinch rip* But she was already scared. She remembered how earlier that day, when she had touched the bluebells near the inlet, death had echoed back because *face it.* The Girl Scouts had died. Susan had died. Her uncle dragging up the limp body, her cousin's flesh sodden and grey and soon dripping away... No. *a soft kiss for* Brett returned to his own tent; Carol drifted off, and Nicky couldn't get to sleep.

"Carol, are you asleep? No?" Nicky unzipped her sleeping bag and climbed into Carol's bag to give her some of the candy she had stolen. The small white Tic-Tacs at the edges of Nicky's eyes didn't stop her from worrying about the Girl Scouts. *Carol's hair so pretty, like white cotton candy.* The pale pellets were sticky in Nicky's hand. Carol pulled down her underpants and showed Nicky what she called her pussy. Nicky thought it looked like a seed, there was something there she had never before seen. There was a special design between a girl's legs with a hidden seed and a star pattern.

Carol's mother served them instant hot cocoa and instant oatmeal cooked over the campfire. Shortly after breakfast, Brett climbed down the bluff and came up shouting, his face flushed with discovery and excitement. It transpired that someone had secretly hidden the most beautiful candy in the world in the cliffs, candy even more desirable than peppermint Tic-Tacs. Carol's parents tried to hush up what Brett had found buried in a crevice halfway down the bluff, but Nicky and

Carol found out anyway when Brett told them. In the orange dirt of the cliff, he said, he had found a mass of coloured candy with drugs inside, set there by some man – Carol's parents said – to lure children into eating it. Brett told Carol and Nicky that it stank like sour milk or sour butter, when he dug the whole lot up. Poison. Drugged. A murderer. Beautiful candy.

Nicky had seen some of the candy herself before Carol's parents took it away. Some of it was rocket candy. Rocket candy looked like clear rainbow candy-popsicles, all different colours swirling to the tip. Drugs made a person go to sleep and dream for a thousand years, like Sleeping Beauty. *Go to sleep.* It was swirling and transparent and beautiful and drugged. Nicky knew it didn't stink. She knew it smelled and tasted wonderful. She wanted to taste it. Just a little bit. If she had found it before Brett, maybe she could have gotten Carol to taste it first. Nicky gripped her hands round her rehydrated cinnamon instant oatmeal, her palms too hot against the sides of the plastic bowl. For a moment, all she could see was rainbow candy. The world around her seemed to be caught up in a moving, coloured, jingling mass of chaos. Then everything righted itself and Nicky was once again sitting on the steady tree stump by the cliffs, her tummy warm from the food and the cocoa. But for just a moment there had been no masks and no edges. The blur had filled Nicky's eyes and throat; the mass of colours had been indistinct. The candy was filled with rat poison, Brett said. Beneath beauty, poison.

"Come on, Nicky, let's look for shells. Forget about what Brett says." Carol was already running ahead of Nicky, barefoot and dodging pebbles, towards the trail that led down to the smooth sand by the water. *Wake up.* Afterwards Carol's parents took Carol and Nicky aside and discussed why young children should never eat any candy they find. Carol's parents spoke in careful, serious tones, but oh Nicky wanted to eat some. She had never tasted a rocket candy stick, but she wanted to now, and this candy was drugged and mystic and evil. It meant seductive death or worse, unspeakable things. She knew of another example of dangerous but sweet beauty. Pop-rocks were the candy grains you placed in your mouth that immediately began to bubble and froth. Every kid knew the story of the boy who had eaten ten or twelve or twenty packets at once and then drunk Coca-Cola and his stomach had exploded.

*

After that, the trees were quiet for a while, but six years later the whisper in the trees came back again. When Nicky turned thirteen her summer job was babysitting for her parents' friends, who had a fishing site. Riding in the back of a pick-up on the beach, she saw weathered shacks on withered stilts lining the edges of the cliffs. Those who owned the shacks also owned the water spread before them. They owned the cold waves and any fish they caught beneath. Because Nicky liked these small fishing houses, she was slightly on edge in case one day a tidal wave came and destroyed them. She rode with her charges in the back of this truck, which was dwarfed by the rocks they passed by on the beach. Bumping over the smaller rocks and with the truck dodging in between the house-sized rocks. At the foot of the huge rocks was always a pool of sea water and on the low underside of the rocks were the brilliant sea anemones and sea cucumbers. The ride took Nicky all the way to these pools, where tide animals and sea cucumbers rolled too quietly, she thought. If she stepped in salty liquid and poked a finger *trembling soft purples with yellow stripes* they retracted themselves.

The cliffs had lush vegetation, had what people called sandstone but what was actually limestone or sometimes splintered shale. Nicky knew this because her uncle had once told her. The sandstone stuff was difficult to climb. It crumbled away when Nicky placed her foot on it, and there were small jagged rocks there as well, but you could carve messages that stayed for a long time: *I love Deanna. Sindy + Will. Mike '74*. There were tiny waterfalls that trickled black rust pools down the cliffs. A jungling strong green when she looked up the cliff *an amount of tungled undergrowth.* Nicky's gaze was as careful as a cat's as she stood on the beach and looked up, up to the trees on the cliff. Most likely no one had been that far up the cliff yet. It would not be her, either.

She sensed a disturbing mixture in the air, a persistent and perturbing mix of saltwater, rot and campfire smoke. The boats came back at lunchtime for pop and roasted hot-dogs, and she watched the fire as well as the kids. Her charges loved to try to climb the cliffs, and often brought down armfuls of bright fireweed and Queen Anne's Lace. She waited below as the fire soaked pink deep into her eyes until the flames were as lurid as the bouquets presented to her by the children. When she closed her eyes, sharp forks of pink fire still trembled against her lids. Towards evening, heading home, she shared the back of the pick-up with a lot of fish, and still the colour flashed against the fragile skin of her eyelids when she lowered her lashes. At home, the scents grew foreign on her clothes again in the domestic environs of her normal life. It was sharp and tangy nutmegs she was breathing; all her clothes reeked of ocean spices, of ash, and when she licked her lips she tasted the smoke and salt. The sharp of it was caught in her mouth. Sharp.

She spread herself out along her bed and listened to the radio playing 'Burning Down the House' by the Talking Heads. This reminded her of the possibilities of fire, but she knew that even if the whole block went up in smoke, she would not be able to move until things went right in her head again. "Watch out," David Byrne warbled, "You might get what you're after." Finally, the pink needles in her vision began to fade.

"Nicky!" her mother called up. "There's the phone ringing. Can you get it?" Nicky walked slowly to the telephone, rubbing at her eyes. There was a whisper sound emitting through the window from the woods, but she ignored it.

"Hello?"

"Hi, it's Carol. Do you want to go camping for a week with us?"

Nicky thought for a moment. She could barely remember the last time she'd been camping with Carol's family. She had been just a little kid, but something weird had happened; she felt tentative about going again. She thought of babysitting the brats at the fishing site again, which she no doubt would be obliged to do if she didn't go with Carol, and the strange thing that had happened to her vision at the site. And then she thought of spending the week alone with her mom, the uncomfortable silences every evening after she returned from babysitting, and that decided it for her. "Okay."

"Don't you have to ask your mom?"

"No, it will be alright." Nicky was pretty sure her mom didn't give a shit if she was there or not. As long as she had her favourite Five Star brand of vodka.

"Great. We're going to hike out to the State Park." That was right near where Nicky had been babysitting. She could still taste the smoke in her mouth from the fire. However, she'd get to see the cliffs and tidepools again, and she wouldn't have to babysit the children with their disturbing armfuls of dead flowers.

Treading along with the whole of Carol's cheerful family, Nicky brooded over why the last-minute invitation, why Carol had started to ignore her at junior high right before the school year broke up for summer and why she would blanch when approached by Nicky in the hallways. Maybe eighth grade would be different. Carol had been part of a seventh-grade clique that all dressed alike: matching miniskirts and legwarmers. Carol's group all wore mood rings and they would take turns making translucent glass candy at home – blue and red and brown, all from food colouring – that was flavoured with root beer extract, or maybe vanilla, cinnamon or peppermint essence. They'd bring it in to share during breaks between classes, their fingers sticky from the jagged pieces. Nicky was included in none of this. This homemade confectionery was as beautiful as shards of stained-glass windows to those to whom it was not offered. But Nicky was diverted from her thoughts when she noticed that Brett had joined her. She smiled weakly up at him; Brett lingered behind to talk to her and the others continued on ahead.

"You've got something stuck on the back of your shirt, Nicky," said Brett, slipping a hand beneath Nicky's backpack and leaving it there, warm against her flannel shirt. Nicky had looked up at him. A memory was surfacing from somewhere: sweet poison. Rat poison. And then the memory disappeared. She tasted smoke. Brett was nineteen, strong and used to rugged camping.

"What is it? What is it? What's the matter with my back?" Nicky whispered rapidly. This was it, now, something was going to happen, this was the horrible thing that she had been waiting for all her life, she realised stupidly. The unknown qualities of vampires, murderers, the Devil, poison candy, the things that whispered in the trees were going to hit her all at once. A drip-shot of panic swung down her spine. Brett was looking at Nicky strangely. He withdrew his hand.

"Nothing," he said quietly. He loped on ahead. But an hour later he lagged behind again. "I'll have to see you sometime, Nicky, without Carol," he said this second time. Quietly, for Carol hiked along only several steps ahead. Nicky's face flamed red; she pretended to ignore him. She would concentrate on efficient, monotonous hiking. She could smell a thick scent emanating from the birches by the trail, like butter on the verge of going rancid. One foot in front of the other – left, left, left, right, left.

"There's something you should know, Nicky," he said, whispering in her ear. He was close beside her again. Nicky halted. She balanced on one foot, then the other, her backpack swinging against her rump. Carol had been walking near to Nicky, and so she stopped too, and stood by closely and protectively – while Nicky's prescient heart kept thumping and bumping and humping away. She was powerless in front of Brett; she had never been able to pinch him enough to bend to her will. She felt her face turn quickly from the efficiency earned from satisfactory hiking to despair.

But Brett said nothing and would not reveal what he knew, which just made Nicky queasy. Again he walked on ahead, leaving Carol and Nicky quite a distance behind.

"What did he say to you?" Carol asked, curious.

"Nothing," Nicky said. Her stomach was churning.

"I think he likes you, Nicky." Carol said. "Weird, huh? I think I've lost my mood ring. Have you seen it anywhere?" And though they searched for a good quarter of an hour and even backtracked, they could not find Carol's mood ring. As they gave up and hiked up to join the others, Nicky found the thought of it secretly lying in the woods, winking up the colours of its moods irrespective of its owner, slightly disconcerting.

She settled down for the night in a tent on her own; she slept until the sound of Susan's voice calling for her woke her up. Nicky went out of the tent into the ashy night of the lagoon near which they had camped. The ends of the lagoon met the sea and Susan was standing in the crotch of the water, holding an armful of cut spruce branches and calling. *Nicky, Nicky,* her voice was cool and high and when Nicky walked over to Susan her feet went smoothly and quickly over the trail. In a glide Nicky was near Susan and Susan was leaning over, leaning over and whispering something to Nicky. But maybe Nicky didn't hear her right, because Nicky woke up cold and cramped and someone was in the tent beside her and it was still dark night, not even dawn yet.

Then in the tent Brett pawed at Nicky's crotch, clawed, and all the while Nicky thought of ways to put him off, to delay, to not let him suspect Nicky knew what he would try to do. "Later," Nicky said. "You can do that later."

"Okay, Nicky," Brett said; he yawned and went back to sleep and for a moment Nicky felt some relief. But several seconds ticked by in the night and Nicky started worrying compulsively where Susan had disappeared to. But Susan, her cousin Susan, was nowhere to be found. Susan was not in this tent or any other.

Then it was light, cold morning and Brett crouched in the tent – Nicky thought he was intending, eventually, to go out for a pee, but this calls for pluck since mornings can be so cold; it is the case of a full bladder versus the relative warmth of the tent. The light shone through the tent's plastic in red-orange glow. Brett told Nicky to clean up a tube he held in his hand; it could be a pipe of Queen Anne's Lace or a vacuum cleaner he held, the hose grey and ridged with circles. Nicky looked inside it and saw all the bloody pieces of Susan – her toenails, small joints and drenched wads of hair. Her hair still smelling of lake, the dank scent of wet flesh. He had chopped up all of her with a knife, even the limbs and managed to fit her in the basin of this hollow flute. Susan was definitely dead.

She woke up the next morning finally on her own, and Carol's cheery parents were calling for her, calling her a lie-a-bed. For a moment Nicky lay there with her eyes closed; thought of the night that had passed. None of it seemed to make sense. It wasn't *sharp* enough. But for the rest of the camping trip and the rest of summer, she avoided Brett, unsure if it were her nightmares warning her away, or worse. And still the trees held their tongues.

The following school year passed her by as quickly as the summer, leaving just vague recollections and the hollow curve of diluted memories in her mind. There was nothing there but she sometimes afterwards felt that if she could only reach her fingers in the dip, she would pull something out from it, gingerly fish out a stringy trauma, painstakingly and resolutely pulled like a smoke-darkened knot of phlegm from her nose. Something which could explain why she couldn't remember whole sections from the preceding summer. After school let out each afternoon, Nicky would return home to her huge house with its fake-wood panelled interior, her father gone, her mother passed out on the couch, and she would have to stare into the glass eyes of her father's many mounted trophy heads. Except she didn't think it possible that he could have shot them all himself, because he had never gone hunting in her memory. The eyes would stare back at her. *You are lonely,* they would say, *you are not popular like Carol is. You have terrible dreams. You do not have many friends. That's because you pinched them, Nicky. And they all secretly hated you for it. Even the ones you cowed into being your friends. And now you just have us. You just have us and the trees.* Then Nicky would go to the upstairs window and look outside, as she used to do when she was younger. And even the trees remained mute.

Her loneliness stemmed partly from the fact that Carol, just as Nicky had suspected she would do, had attached herself to an entirely separate crowd in eighth grade – with few more concessions to their former friendship than a passing nod at the lockers. With no new companions, Nicky would lock herself in a toilet booth and weep until the bell rang signalling the end of lunch. And removed from Carol's protective social influence, a crowd of near-enemies moved in on her. The last day before Spring Break, a so-called friend gave Nicky a piece of pizza to eat which had been found in the garbage. Carol observed the incident but said nothing to the perpetrator; moved silently away with her snickering clique. That day Nicky waited for school to be over and for vacation to begin. *Sun through the shutter wonder if mom would wake up for her dinner wonder* She waited through her classes, her throat pounding. Around two o'clock, with an hour and a half left of the school day, with Algebra 1 looming before her, she couldn't take it anymore.

Easter Vacation always coincided with break-up season, right before proper spring. Break-up was the type of weather where snow begins to melt slowly and smaller children run screaming out of doors to play in the mud and let it drip through their chubby fingers. And right then, as she broke all the rules and sneaked away from impossible formulae she would never fully understand, even if the x she'd inserted in the $x = y + 2x$ homework turned out to be right, the relief of approaching spring flooded Nicky's flesh, liberating her from the stilted rituals of junior high. She went off campus and no one thought to stop her. In April the ice was still there; but it was melting-ice weather. The sun was already starting to set late, late, and the carnival had come to town the week before and set up its Ferris wheel in the parking lot of the Mall. And all the while the ice was melting in Nicky's veins and she was skipping school. The sun and the ice mixed together in her bloodstream as soon as the school was out of sight; she felt like running alone down to the beach and rubbing her face in the melting water and the sparkling snow-encrusted icebergs and raising her hands up and whirling around. The smell was of sun-warmed dead grass, of dog-shit, of water.

A wintry day with melting snow and then the pre-spring sunlight melting this snow down to the musty rotten leaves. Nicky stepped off the road from the school and ran into the trees. *Faster, come on, faster; mush.* The ocean was straight ahead; the school was right behind; she stopped where she could see neither. Only the elongated spruce trees and the sprawling branches of the birch. She heard the screams of trees, the wild whirling in her head. In the snow, sitting in the roots. Sitting and her skirt was wet. She clutched her forehead and started to cry. And eventually the whirling stopped. All that was left was a weird anticipation. My god, she thought, what's in store for me? A piercing, exciting, biting, maybe hopeless life. The snow was cold, it stung her skin. She was still, but she had to take big breaths. For some reason the image of the lake near where her Uncle Joe lived flickered into her consciousness. But then it disappeared, and Nicky didn't chase the memory. Instead she was left with the image of a forest rather than a lake, and she let this remembrance sift away as well. She had the impression of bluebells and fireweed, and then almost nothing was left of the recollection. Almost nothing. *The soft white hairs on Carol's arms.* The shadow reflection of someone else's wet red ringlet.

pale hair and knots of flesh, the blood-taste of metal and spoons, of a wet tongue frozen to a signpost, of the thermos of warm milk poured to loosen it, to melt, dissolve, flesh-knots becoming mush in sharp and icy winter, remember,

Nicky sat crouched under the tree. The wet snow crunch-crunched under her feet. Then she looked up between her fingers. The sky was overwhelming, the clouds went slowly by the sun; they took their time and time was slow. An airplane went buzzing overhead. The sound, droning and peaceful, calmed her heart, took the pain from the inside. The screaming feeling: the winds blew so perfectly and the sun sparkled on the crust of the snow. Nicky clutched the rotten leaves in her hands as well as the snow but it was the snow that stung her fingers. Cold. Stung.

Go to sleep, forget about it, her head told her. *You can numb it. It doesn't have to be sharp.* Sun-drenched stones poked out from the water. *Doesn't have to be sharp.* She remembered, despite herself. She remembered only too well. The lake where her cousin died. The day of flute-making with her uncle. The day it all happened. She wished she'd been somewhere else that day, that Susan had been somewhere else. She had once overheard Carol's mother telling her own mom that they had planned on inviting them out to go berry-picking the day it happened but had asked too late, and for a while this used to make Nicky angry with Carol. But that was when she was a kid, now she could see that it hadn't been Carol's fault, either. But she had pinched Carol terribly when she had found that out, pinched her until she cried. Sometimes she got so angry with Carol. Sometimes Carol still made her feel vicious: sharp and nasty.

Nicky's lips were close to the moss; all she could smell was earth and wet and old stumps, just like that day so long ago. It was the end of Break-up. Spring had finally come. She got up and ran again. She thought she couldn't see the beach from here, but if she looked hard, there it was, between the trees. The sun shone on the water. No, *No.* The sweat ran between her small breasts. She tumbled on wet grass, rocks; birch-bark scratching at her cheeks. The trees began to whimper to her again, *where are you, Nicky, where?* Would they help or harm her? She slammed herself down against the trunks of a group of spruces growing near the bluff. Light glittered unsteadily between the trunks, reflected off of the pulling, pushing water.

The trees had finally got her, good or bad; she was going to fold herself into them and become numb. Mush. Fuzzy. She pushed herself against the trunk. She saw herself with her heart torn out; there were roots which went directly from the ground to her limbs. But to her surprise, as a tree things became clearer and more defined. She felt secure and, nearly, safe. She sat there for a long time trying to feel what it would be like to live out her life as a tree, with no worries or treacherous friends. As a tree she was bound to the earth; she had to look at the gristle of moss at her feet; but she could also look out at the enormous sun-drenched rocks on the beach below. The watery sun burnt straight into her. Her heart began to slow. She remembered the warmth of Susan's hand round hers. And for the first time in her memory, keen beyond her panic, she began to feel and not just fear. She curled herself in the roots of the trees; she fell asleep.

*

The trees woke her up again four years later with their snarling and growling. *Fire,* they whispered, *fire.* At the age of seventeen, she woke up to the smell of smoke. The forest is flaming, she thought. But the fires were not yet visible. She couldn't feel their sharpness or their warmth, but she did feel something imminently smouldering. A boy with an earring and big black boots had called her late at night the week before. He had asked Nicky, was she wearing a bra under her T-shirt? She felt herself getting wet but even at the time she thought she might like Carol more than him and besides, her mother was straining to listen in the other room. She couldn't whisper back what he wanted to hear from her. But Carol could.

Carol had gotten prettier, it seemed to Nicky. Of necessity, Carol had bleached her hair pale – its natural colour had darkened to a dirty blonde – and Carol had sprouted stiff dark nipples. And, most significantly, in the spring of their junior year of high school, Carol began to date the boy with the earring and the big black boots.

The boy had Carol to whisper to him, Carol with her tiny waist and large breasts Nicky stared at when the three of them smoked pot together. When had Carol grown those? Carol, she realised, was complicated. Once ensconced in Little Novgorod Central High School, Carol had lost her universal junior high popularity. She shattered her goody-good reputation, bleaching her hair, wearing thick makeup, dating *him*. The popular, nice girls who were her friends began to avoid her but, for Nicky, Carol's new-found sophistication only increased her mystique. Once Carol showed a grapefruit-sized bruise on her arm to Nicky; said the boyfriend had given it to her after they'd had sex in the dugout of the municipal baseball field. According to the rules of the in-crowd, she now counted as a slut. Nicky wasn't sure if this was true, but in return for Carol's renewed friendship she kept silent all the strange dark secrets that Carol was confiding. Bruises. Hickeys. Insinuations of coke and speed ingested when Nicky wasn't present.

But even though Nicky was quiet, the jealousies between the three of them would fester. Her nose and throat filled up with the smell of smoke, like a warning that something had to give soon, or her head would burst into flame at any given second. Carol suspected – Nicky was only slowly growing aware of the fact herself – that Nicky wanted to fuck her boyfriend. This was partially true. Nicky was Carol's closest girlfriend once again; Carol didn't have many these days and Nicky's loyalty was easily accessible. One time, smoking pot in Carol's bedroom, Nicky felt herself growing horny. She went to the bathroom, locked the door and fingered herself, half-thinking of Carol. Carol turned her on. And at the same time Nicky could hear them moving in the other room. The boyfriend knew how Nicky felt about Carol. Nicky knew he knew about things like that. When Nicky returned from the bathroom, her hands scrubbed and smelling faintly of soap, he watched her staring at Carol's pretty, made-up face, and Nicky watched him register her gaze in his thoughts.

Nicky stared across at Carol as the boy grudgingly handed over the smoking pipe. Carol's face was smooth from thick foundation, and Nicky couldn't rightly remember if she had acne scars underneath – maybe that's what the heavy build-up of makeup was for. But for whom it was intended, she had no clue. Makeup was something Carol's boyfriend professed not to like, though he couldn't keep his hands off her; he made fun of makeup, said Carol caked it on, put the mask on with a frosting-knife; he mimicked the curve of Carol's long, regal nose with his hand movements and called her Pinocchio; he was so damn sure she was doing her whole look for him, all that plumage for him, all for him... but really, the look was something girls liked or, at least, something Nicky liked, for girls could be nasty to Carol, too. But Nicky was convinced that when these girls weren't calling Carol a slut, they all wanted this particular Barbie Doll to dress up and over-feminise, just as they pleased. It was envy that made them cruel. They wished they had the guts to be so obvious. Carol was the lady three-year-olds pointed to in the street, said *Look, Mommy, she's pretty*, while their duller mothers hustled them away from Carol, thinking *God, that woman was trashy*, doubting their children's future taste and morals. Nicky sucked in a pungent, harsh hit of marijuana, then passed the pipe along to Carol.

A very young woman instead of a girl, a *Penthouse* and *Hustler* of a woman, Carol was all men's versions of perfumed prettiness come back to scare them in one parody, one vagina dentata, one drag queen, artificial blow-up doll of a woman who still managed to be Pretty. She played their game, Nicky realised, and she beat them at it. At the same time she found herself uncomfortably siding with the boys: to be feminine was to be weak. And to revel in femininity meant to revel in weakness.

Nicky watched Carol and her boyfriend lean into each other, softly kiss. Carol's eyelashes, as she closed them coquettishly, were beaded with dark mascara. When Carol was alone with Nicky, she would reveal the dark, violent things she and her boyfriend did together, but when the three of them found themselves in the same room, Carol tilted her head flirtatiously; looked at her boyfriend out of the corner of her eyes, her attention solely on him. Nicky needed Carol to reassure her that the fakery was an elaborate joke on boys. That there was strength beneath her mask, not just a weirdly erotic submission. But instead Carol, the boyfriend and Nicky drifted on in a sterile and vague threesome.

Carol owned a car. Sometimes Nicky would sit in the back of it while Carol drove both Nicky and him home, but it was always Nicky who was dropped off first. *Say: I want to fuck you. Say: I want to fuck you. Still do. Never would, though.* There were lots of things Nicky never said to Carol. She no longer dreamed of burning trees, but her dreams turned so violent she suspected she was going crazy. But maybe it was just the dream residue of what Carol told her during walking hours: *and then I hit him where it hurt. And then he shoved me on my – And then he put his hands around my –* It was affecting Nicky somehow, hearing those kind of things. Nicky dreaming *Carol strangling* Nicky dreaming *him strangling* Nicky dreaming *fucking both him and Carol separately dreaming fucking dreaming strangling* until pleasure and fear weren't distinguishable the way they were before. Her nights weren't getting any better; she knew the weird build-up of dreams meant something.

Worse, the boyfriend always had a way of knowing, too. He told Nicky *he knew she wanted to screw Carol.* Nicky began to dream that this was true, and deep in these dreams Carol said *over my dead body. strangle hold pinning pale hair pinch pinch* Or worse, what if Nicky did want to sleep with Carol, and the boyfriend found out that she wanted it for real? He'd rape Nicky. No doubt in Nicky's mind. She had heard enough bad stories from Carol not to doubt this. And then he would kill Nicky too, of course. Slash. Sharp, like a proper murderer. But probably not. Occasionally Carol's face flickered in her thoughts in the midst of masturbation, and Nicky was unsure what that meant. Maybe it meant that the boyfriend was right: she wanted to screw her best friend. Simple as that. It was a terrible fascination, but she couldn't break free of Carol and the boyfriend.

Perhaps uncertain as to Nicky's role and nervous concerning Carol's confidences with her, the boyfriend once drew her aside at school.

"You're keeping your mouth shut, right, Barber?" Nicky had stared at him, frozen and unblinking. He released her and shoved her several feet away. "Just mind your own fucking business." Nicky didn't answer, but kept her head down and her eyes from his as she scuttled away. He was making sure she knew his capabilities: he was six feet tall and held an advanced belt in karate and liked guns a lot. But this was obvious to Nicky, she didn't need to be reminded how powerless she was.

When in the summer Carol broke up with him, Nicky didn't know whether she was relieved or heartbroken. *pale hair and danger danger danger* There was glass on the floor when she came to Carol's house to comfort her, and the detritus of a thrown cocaine fix. Her nostrils picked up the scent of smoke; there it was again. The sharpness of the scenario made her freeze for a moment. Razor blades, spilled powders and a broken mirror – all those edges and disorder. Because though she appreciated the clarity that often accompanied it, disorder and the unexpected fundamentally bothered Nicky.

"God, Nicky! This is awful." Carol threw herself in Nicky's arms; Nicky felt her own heart beating so rapidly she thought it would drum a tattoo right through her ribcage.

"It's okay, Carol," she said uncomfortably, trying awkwardly to stroke at Carol's pale hair. She surveyed the scene before her. Edges and disorder, disorder and too-sharp edges. She closed her eyes; heard Carol's breathing slow down and become regular.

Two days later Carol left the state to go live with relatives for several months. Nicky was relieved, she was ashamed to discover. She no longer had to worry about Carol strangling her or the other, more erotic dreams. Now she had only the boyfriend to worry about.

The worst thing was, Nicky felt herself growing sick with fear and lust for him. She wanted to fuck someone who was dangerous. Unsafe. *And you want to fuck girls,* a voice said in her head, before she quickly pushed it back. Her head was filled with the word *fuck*. She could taste smoke on the tip of her tongue. She would wake up with a knife in her throat. It would be him. But probably not.

Four days after Carol left, he grabbed her aside again at school. "I hear you've been making up things in your drugged-out, lezzie mind." Nicky never took drugs except the occasional hit of grass and she doubted strongly she was as crazy as he suggested. *Say I want to fuck you.* And as far as the lezzie mind went, she told herself she wasn't sure.

She did not tell anyone she felt danger coming off the boy like radiation waves, danger so thick and bestial the thought of it made her choke. Who could she tell, anyway? Her drunken mother? Her few safe, sheltered acquaintances at school? Carol was the only one she could have told, the only one who had the power to protect her. And Carol was gone. Danger. When she woke up. In her house. Out of it. The next week he called up and said *fuck you* in the phone. *Fuck you, too,* Nicky said, and hung up. Her hands were trembling round the receiver but something twisted in her. Her guts turned hard, gaining edges. She wasn't going to be a bit afraid of him. If he came for her she'd get her dad's gun and she'd shoot him right in the balls, in his tight little pants. No, she'd shoot him straight in the face. To be shot in the face by a girl – that would really get to him. He couldn't even touch her. Yes. She *did* want to fuck his girlfriend for herself, with lust, and she wanted to fuck him, too, to have his hands on her nipples, on her tits, but only *to feel the power feel the power of watching him weakening beneath her.* Because she would be: *a fuck that would get to him.*

Nicky felt herself now turning as sharp and as hard as she was ever going to be. Her guts were solid metal. Sharp. Strong. Clear. She could weaken and remember how she had felt towards him all those times in the back seat of Carol's car. The fact that he probably wasn't all that dangerous anyway. That maybe he was just as frightened by all these new dark feelings coursing through the blood as she was by her own strange sentiments. She could remember the gorgeous flame of trees behind her eyes. The almost-relationship the three of them had had together. Or even the clit on her whenever he got near enough to see her breathing, but he would use that against her – her lust, her compassion – wouldn't he? So he wouldn't get it, because she'd learned a few lessons and could not be foolish anymore, not for him, not for Carol – *say: I want to fuck you still do never would though.* It would be a hot fuck with him, she had to admit, but never quite as hot as the thought that he'd never get it from her. *Sharp, Nicky. Remember.* Those fucking trees. Those fucking trees were never silent, these days.

Then Carol came back. Nicky saw her first at an outdoors party at the gravel pit, autumn in their senior year, but Nicky had already heard the news from her mom that Carol had returned. A fire had been built at the pit and its coals were red-glowing and illuminating; Nicky could see, out of the corner of her eye, Carol furiously making out with him all over again. They had gotten back together all over again. Nicky felt her jaw clench. A girl beside Nicky began to dry out the pot leaves on the hot stones circling the campfire, and passed round a pipe to smoke them in the fire-dappled darkness. Carol slipped her hand on the crotch of her boyfriend's jeans. Within seconds, Nicky poured her Coke on the fire to douse a few of the coals and started walking quickly away, leaving Carol and him to it. She felt deceived, but she wasn't quite sure why.

"Hey, where are you going?" A male friend, tolerable enough, followed her. The gravel pit was inundated with condoms, limp plastic ghosts of rubbers were spewed all over the moss in the clearing. The colours were translucent pastels: pale-green, pale-pink, cloudy white.

As if on cue, she and the boy took off running. She didn't exactly know why he was running, too, but she knew in her heart of hearts that she ran from Carol and the boyfriend. They ran off the road into the woods at the right, hurdling the dark moist stumps of trees and sodden moss, *come on, faster, mush, mush* running through the wet branches dipping low above them, drenching their jeans and not stopping to check and see what they could hear behind them. Nicky felt the rush of the trees in her head and said a silent prayer of thanks – for once she could appreciate the rustle of their whispering. They filled her and she felt she understood them. She knew the dips and rises of the woods. The dips were filled with fragile black old leaves and ambitious bright new mushrooms and she and the boy barged through these as well; *mush,* their feet so cold but they did not care. The woods ended long from where they started running, they stopped and felt how out of breath they were. Time passed quickly, for they had run for nearly half an hour. They were in the back alley behind a pizza parlour, the one that never closed until two a.m., so they went around to the front.

When they entered, breathless, they saw Carol and the boyfriend in the far booth. He was sitting next to Carol, his arms around her. Nicky's stomach fell momentarily, seeing him shake his bright tongue onto Carol's lips. Still, she slid into the circular booth alongside them, a wide fake smile stretching her face out until her teeth ached. They ordered extra pizza, and later that night when the boy, her friend, was kissing her, and she was trying to figure out an excuse to tell her mom in the morning about why she didn't come home, in case her mother asked, which she probably wouldn't, Nicky felt relieved that this anonymous, convenient boy's warm hands were holding her face and that her warm tongue was in his warm mouth, slow and not in a hurry in the slightest. She had managed to get away from something, something dangerous, a feeling of

the sounds of water and breaking ice down on the beach in springtime
the code of the words from the trees

Whatever, Nicky said, shaking her head. It passed. Or at least it usually did. But that autumn it went on and on.

It was a strange last winter at home. There were parties at which both Nicky and Carol were present. They had avoided each other since

Carol's return but some conversation was inevitable.

"Are you sober?" Carol would always pose the same question with an expression that mixed concern with a certain drunken politeness. Nicky would be dizzy; would have been drinking her two beers really fast to avoid feeling whatever it was inside her. At the parties she would have looked over at Carol, who would be laughing good-naturedly at the time it took Nicky to respond. She never answered Carol, but instead would smile courteously and slowly turn away. Inside at these parties it was always hot and bright. Once Carol enquired after Nicky's sobriety while they were both in a Jacuzzi together, surrounded by several others as naked as they were them-selves. The water of the Jacuzzi hot. Nicky had been hot, too, blush-ing even before Carol spoke to her. But before she turned away, she'd seen Carol looking back at her. Turning, but still seeing Carol's dark nipples reflected in the shiny fogged-up mirror, Carol's hand resting on the wooden side of the tub. The grain of wood yellow-orange, with dark brown lines running alongside each other.

Outside it would be pitch, pitch black at these last-year parties, with towering spruce trees weighed down with dark snow. *Listen.* Snow which came all the way up to the deck, the large framed frosted window a television to the rest of the world. It would have showed Nicky and Carol the world outside while they made their stilted, polite one-sided conversation; would have showed them the dark snowy wilderness while the party stayed warm in a smoke-smelling cedar house. In a carpeted bright room with other people. Nicky ought to feel safe, but she never did. She felt like her throat was dry, her heart racing, a slow panic beginning to pulse its way through her. People shouting drunken jokes and laughing. The spin-the-bottle game to the left becoming even more intricate and involved.

She would tell herself to calm down, to look away from Carol. She would notice the sweat reflected off the flushed skin of the spin-the-bottle players at these parties. Not vividly reflected; not spiky. Just dull. She would try to concentrate on other things. She would note the pink glow of her own forearms, the window in this room four feet by four feet, showing the driveway, the snowdrifts, the cars parked outside.

But the parties of winter were forgotten, as was the customary exhilaration of spring and, though Nicky listened for the trees, there were no more secrets rasped for her. Summer came and Nicky's cannery job would be starting in several days. She hadn't seen Carol since graduation, but hoped that they'd be working in the same cannery. Nicky had worked the last two summers for money, whereas Carol's parents usually insisted that Carol work in order to build character. It was a given that most local teenagers would work the canneries regardless of family means and income. But today she walked through a mall rife with backpacking Austrians and boat-workers come in off the docks in scrubbed-clean rubber boots.

She bought a vanilla cone in the town's single shopping centre, known only as the Mall, one with raspberries on top and chocolate sprinkles. The ice cream had a curious intensity. The raspberries nestled amongst the soft ice cream like over-ripe salmon eggs; the dark squiggles of chocolate looked like rejected meat squiggles from a grinder. She took a mouthful and tasted the biting sharpness of the raspberries; she tasted the syrupy chocolate fragments; she thrust her tongue down into all the soft folds of ice cream. She ate it slowly, experimentally tasting every mouthful.

She shook her head; she had a headache despite her deliberate moderation, and she continued walking through the Mall, passing the flower store. Flowers were the unnecessary aspects of vegetation, she thought slowly. Decoration and no roots.

Frivolous. *Soft.* The store looked cool and even unnecessarily air-conditioned. Hoping for the kind of heat which required artificial cooling, Nicky thought, was slightly over-optimistic for Alaska. She looked in through the florist's window. She saw roses of every colour, the petals whirled around themselves: peach-coloured roses, red roses, white roses, pink roses, pale-green roses, purple roses, friendly yellow roses. They had all been cut, or at least contrived. The only flowers here were dead ones, drying out – or fake ones. The colours reminded her of the pale old rubbers at the gravel pit: artificial, synthetic. A smooth confectionery of soft and candied rainbows. A memory stirred in her. *Beneath beauty, poison.* She saw all the colours right for a moment, twisted into solid hues, bright blocks of colour. She felt her face go hot for a moment. Her thoughts flitted inexplicably back to Carol's bright face in the Jacuzzi last winter. Maybe she had seen Carol right for the first time at that party, too. *all that plumage blonde and gilded pale, soft and pretty show me your pussy too, Nicky no*

They were placed at the same cannery by the job agency, but Carol was with her boyfriend more and more often; him disapproving of Nicky, Nicky telling herself she didn't care about the two of them anyway. In summer she could convince herself she was distracted, for the small fishing town was full of seasonal distractions. Even on the warm days there was the cool forest and the ocean nearby. The salty air and the scent of fish. During the summer fishing period, a large proportion of the town's teenagers, both male and female, would eventually lose their virginity to college workers from Outside – California, Oregon, New York.

Last summer, Nicky had debated several times losing her virginity to charmers from Montana and Virginia – psychology majors, political science majors. But to all of the boys she decided ultimately no, supposing that she would have ended up being just one more local girl they screwed. And so far this season she was as yet untouched. And a week into the cannery work, it was clear that Carol still was screwing *him* exclusively, although Nicky watched the college boys looking at Carol speculatively. Nicky watched them look at Carol's chest, her hips, her quick movements as she spoke.

Still, Carol sought Nicky out at break-time and said: "I'm moving Outside at the end of summer, going to drive down. You want to come with me? Down through Canada?"

"Yeah," said Nicky. "Yeah, I do." A small flame of happiness burst in her head. Smoke on the tip of her tongue; she touched her fingers to her lips. *Wake up.* She did want to come; it meant she could leave Alaska, finally. And maybe it meant Carol wanted to leave, too, wanted to leave him. After this tentative plan, they didn't talk at the ten-minute break and kept a certain distance from each other. But Nicky could sense Carol moving about out of her range of sight, flirting with the college boys. It was an old familiarity which linked them, the familiarity between friends who had grown apart.

Nicky thought about this new arrangement as she stood at her post on Butcher Crew. If she went down to Washington or Oregon, maybe she could make late registration and enrol at one of the state universities. Then she had to pay attention, for she held a knife in her hand, and Butcher Crew was hard work. She'd been working double-shifts, fourteen to twenty-two hours in a row since it was peak season, usually with only four hours of sleep. After the lunch break passed too quickly with no more communication with Carol, and after the dinner break passed, and the next coffee break, at around sixteen hours all Nicky could hear was the drone of machines and the *click! click!* of the head-chopper, sending rows and rows of decapitated salmon down to her, and then she gulleted, or gutted, or split and stripped the bloodline, and sent the hunk of dead meat on. *Down through Canada. A new life outside.* The words weren't real; the cannery was the only thing that was real. It became a blur. Death after death passed her, packaged into a dense parcel of fins and scales, and she stripped the deaths numbly and passed them on to others behind her, who transformed and modified the parcels further.

A butcher-line job was good in some ways, she thought, because she could talk to the people standing next to her. It was much worse working alone. There was one job which consisted of separating salmon eggs from the innards and putting the eggs down a chute. She had sat at this job yesterday; the fish-insides had kept rolling towards her on a chute, never seeming to stop. She had to separate quickly and she had to always keep her eyes strained, always keep them alight for the pink marbles coming down the chute. Earlier in the day, in the shift right after Carol had brought up the possibility of the trip, a boy doing eggs suddenly started screaming and ran out. He had been doing eggs for eighteen hours straight, seven days a week for three weeks. On the next coffee break, people had whispered that he told the foreman that he was seeing things in the eggs; the foreman gave him a three-day break to recover. That made Nicky nervous. What kind of dark designs did one see in a basket piled full of pink, smoothed-over salmon eggs? Had he seen things moving in the eggs themselves?

A new life outside. Away from all of this. It was tempting. In her dreams of the last few weeks she had become the fish she slaughtered and, though bordering on the nightmarish, even these dreams were much preferable to what her violent dreams of Carol and her boyfriend had been. Even this morning she had woken up with her hands aching with tendonitis, but the cannery kept her head full; the finning, slicing, gutting kept her from thinking about other things. Twitching silver, wiggling tail-ends of greenish dreams. Fish were out there in the open; they were obvious. Fish were not decorative. You could see them coming for you and you could prepare yourself.

Only five or six more hours left, people were whispering further up the butcher line, and the gossip travelled down the assembly line. Only fifty totes of fish left. There would be a momentary end to it. Only last week Nicky had written to the convenient boy who moved Outside, out-of-state, on a postcard: *What's it like there? Are the girls cute? Do you have a girlfriend? The cannery's the same, of course. There was frost this morning. Yesterday someone on the night shift got their finger cut off. You're not missing anything. We had a kegger last night so fun we had a bonfire & got stoned. This is the last summer I do this Are you still coming back why don't you write don't forget your roots Carol's always show within six weeks* Carol would get pissed off if she knew Nicky wrote that. Carol was sensitive about the fact that she had to bleach her hair. But Nicky liked it.

The foreman's voice ripped into her thoughts. "Barber! Your turn on the machine." Feeding the fish into the cleaning machine was a loner's job. The machine to the right of the cleaner was vibrating all the time. Nicky took her turn at the cleaner, and immediately remembered reading a book about how the factory girls of the 1800s would press themselves up against their sewing machines and receive orgasm after orgasm, even though they didn't realise exactly that they were masturbating and that that was what it was called. But of course they knew, thought Nicky, of course they knew. She tried pressing herself to the contraption now before her, but could only stand with the top part of her right thigh and part of her crotch vibrating. Not really enough. But she stood there for two hours, never really coming. She wished she had never begun. Fifty totes left; now surely only twenty-five. *All the way through Canada to Outside.* Fish. Sewing machines. Machines.

At the break she took off her rain-gear and her gloves and went to the bathroom and masturbated, with great sexual frustration but also great relief. She hoped no one heard her; she was almost through by the time the others came in. She was almost sure they couldn't see the vibrating shadow of her hand on the wall from the bathroom stall. Was this perverted? Did other girls do this in public? Would she get caught? It was not the most sexy of atmospheres – an outdoor toilet, pictures of fish and blood-stained yellow rain-gear in her mind.

That made it even less arousing, and even more necessary that she masturbate to a climax instead of just giving up and stopping. *Faster.* She desperately rammed her fingers on herself. It was far from satisfying when she came, and somehow seemed so sordid. She washed her hands under the cold water faucet with a sliver of cracked, dirty soap. Her fingers would be chilled when she re-sheathed them in the cotton gloves and the final prophylactic rubber-glove layer that kept the tote-ice and blood from seeping through. When would Carol notice she was alive? Something had gone awry, had gotten stalled, and she wanted to feel free again. But things seemed too fuzzy: her memories, her emotions, her life. She wanted to somehow touch something which felt right and good and clean again; she wanted to know if the honed smell of burning leaves would ever make her catch her breath again, if she would ever get back the sharp feelings from the trees which whispered, hissed and swayed. For the remainder of the summer Nicky wondered if she would ever get back the feelings she used to have when she was younger. *Hone yourself, Nicky,* the trees said. *Sharpen. Remember. Sharp. No mush.* But it was difficult to make out their words now when she stood trapped inside the cannery, outside the edges of the forest.

There were four of them in Carol's car Seattle-bound: Carol, Nicky and two Californian cannery acquaintances of Carol's whom Nicky didn't know. The road trip was starting out fine; they kept the car windows open and could smell the smoke from burning autumn pyres. The trees on the road which twirled down to the coast were so towering; the birch and the aspen leaves were red and gold and brown. The car rushed down the road towards the valley filled with the autumn trees, and late August felt as spooky as Halloween. Carol put a hippyish Windham Hill tape into the car stereo, music full of chimes and flutes. Somehow, it was appropriate. Nicky was excited: she knew there was more out there in the world for her; she had managed to wait till she graduated from high school and soon she would get entirely away from this place. Even these last traces of home – changing leaves, burning compost – seemed drawn-out, intermediate.

At one point up the coast on the way to Anchorage, the four of them made a short detour halfway down an incline and drove on a dirt road for a while until they parked the car. They left the doors open and the stereo on, so they could hear an old Sting cassette even as they walked around the forest and kicked the piles of dead leaves that carpeted the ground. The other two walked on ahead. Carol was taking black-and-white photos of the trees and the silence was not often broken as she and Nicky walked around. Nicky was filled with a terrible longing which she could not explain. All around her was the forest. A terrible longing, she felt happy right now, but there was an anticipation on the inside which hurt, *the sunlight moves through the dust, almost making a mist in the summer sunlight* and she couldn't even figure out why. That fact that Carol had asked her to come along made her feel special; she was flattered. *You can see through the sun-rays, though, you can see the mountains and the glow of the early sunset although it will stay* She could not explain this feeling that she had inside herself. Thought-fragments were spinning through her: glimpses of a future that was years or minutes away. The song 'Russians' played; Nicky whirled around in the leaves, jumped up, threw the leaves in the air. Carol was gauging her uncharacteristic behaviour from several feet away.

"Come here." Nicky beckoned to Carol.

Carol walked up closer to Nicky. "What is it?"

She kissed Carol on the mouth. And waited. Neither said anything, and then they walked off in opposite directions, their feet crunching in the leaves.

"We're leaving in ten minutes," Carol called out as she drew further away.

"Okay," Nicky answered. Her face was hot and she did not look back. Oh my god, this was unsafe. When she turned and walked back into the score of the sunlight, she smelled dust that was settling on the road after a truck had driven by. The sunlight moved through the dust, making a mist in the late summer sunlight. Nicky could see through the rays, though; she could see the mountains and the glow of early sunset; yet it would stay light for several more hours. It was only nine in the evening but it was so quiet. If it was a dream, then she wouldn't wake up.

And maybe there were things and feelings one simply couldn't retrieve. The summer would go on, into late September, and then winter would follow, as it would, and the days were already getting shorter. It was starting to rain regularly now in fall, but today was an exception. Soon Nicky would get back in the car with Carol and the other two and they would all continue their drive down to the Lower 48, Oregon or Seattle to live, cannery money safe in their wallets. Nicky took a short walk through the leaves, delaying the inevitable embarrassment of seeing Carol at the car. Here in woods like these, she thought, here I ran through the brush under the stars late at night. Here is where Carol lost that mood ring one day when we were camping. Here in woods like these I escaped a day of junior high and rubbed myself against the earth. I saw the Northern Lights in skies like these, glowing green across the frozen sky. It can get so cold here it hurts to breathe. Will I remember these kind of things? These almost-magic things? She sat down on the grass and dust by the side of the dirt road and her fingers sifted through the gravel on the ground. Over there in woods like these is the great forest of my dreams, she thought. There, the trees are shouting now; they bellow for me not to leave. She looked down at her fingers. They looked like small greasy antlers. She spread and closed her fingers and looked at the spaces in between. All it took was the strength not to give in about the stuff about Carol, she felt. Strength and stoicism.

She hugged herself. The evening had become noticeably cooler. The sun was setting in a gold dusty dusk. The mountains stood as they had always stood. If she were to stay here then bit by bit she would see less of the dust as the sun-rays lowered to ankle height, the beams running across the grass, making it shine gold-green. Then the sun would set and a red glow would remain. Nicky stood up.

Walking back to the car, where Carol and the others were waiting, she passed a rain-puddle, coagulated in a ditch. She could see herself reflected in the water and her reflection was smiling; behind her, also reflected, were many tiny globes of white light, lights strung up through branches, disguised as raindrops and reflected as many suns in the muddy water. She wasn't sure of these distortions. The ebbing sunlight shafted down. She had a lot of excuses ready for Carol. *I didn't really want to; it was just something I did – I don't know why, I was just in this mood...* She stomped on the water in her leather boots; when she was a kid she used to stamp the frozen puddles in fall nearing winter at the bus stop, now it is nearing autumn instead and she is finally on her way out of Alaska with Carol, and the water is wet, not frozen, instead. And she is an adult, not a child anymore. Instead.

They were all waiting for her by the time she got back. Carol was already in the driver's seat. Nicky got into the car next to one of the Californians. Nicky looked up, and her eyes met Carol's in the rear-view mirror, just as their eyes used to meet in the Jacuzzi at all those winter parties. Nicky looked out at the woods again, the car door still open, her hand hesitating on the handle.

"Are you sober, then?" Carol said, as she always used to ask at the parties.

"What are you talking about? Of course she's sober," said the Californian in the back seat, a Natural Foods-type of girl who wore sturdy hiking shorts and no makeup.

Nicky swung the door shut, and then glanced up at the rear-view mirror again. For a split-second, before she looked away, she thought she saw Carol flash a smile, her teeth as white as Tic-Tacs. Something exciting rippled through Nicky's body then, something she had never felt before and therefore could not name. Then Carol turned the key, the motor growled, and they were on their way.

ii. outside

2. Carol

You squirt it on your pussy, which sort of burns now. The sting of perfume always makes you squirm. You have lipstick in your travel bag, too, a shade labelled WINE. You remember how you wanted to put some on when you were walking up the hill, and you take it out now, unscrew it and paint the areolas of your nipples. They stiffen immediately around the colour. You start to sing 'Paper Moon' to yourself. You rub just a taste of the lipstick on your lips to tint them; you don't want someone to refuse to kiss you because of lipstick plastered on your face, it's happened before.

Stop. Goes your brain. Stop. But your mouth keeps going in song – the truth is, you can't imagine what Nicky will say when she comes back from her walk.

It is a strange, dirty little hotel room where you're now waiting for Nicky, in a building set high up the hill in a neighbourhood above downtown Seattle. You think hard about Nicky. She looks great now that she's got her hair cut properly. Just how you like it, a really sexy bob. It suits her. You wonder if Nicky is pleased with the fresh bleach job you did on your own hair – it's hard to know, Nicky rarely tells people what she thinks of things, even you. She measures her words and the words themselves always surprise you. She's a thinker, alright. She's always been like that and you suppose that at one point you just got used to it. Usually you even guess wrong if you try to guess what she's thinking. That's why people think Nicky's so weird – because she's so hard to read.

It's been about five days since Nicky kissed you in the woods back home. That was a wonderful day; you took your camera out and snapped a few shots before she kissed you. Now you're pleased you took photos of that particular day, because it might well be a momentous one. It might well be the start of something good, and the photographs will be a souvenir of sorts. Nicky hasn't tried once to kiss you since. You've known her forever but lately, since the kiss, you've been looking at her in an entirely new light. You wish she'd try to kiss you again. You'd close your eyes; her mouth would be soft and sexy, like the skin of a ripe apple, like that favourite lipstick colour of yours, *Wine*. Nicky's lips stay perpetually red; she doesn't need lipstick like you do. Maybe Nicky loves you. But you don't know, she hasn't said anything about it.

This is what happened earlier: in the morning, you dropped off the other two who had driven down the Al-Can with you. The four of you had driven shifts straight through the Canada nights and made it here in five days. Then it was just you and Nicky. There were no local parking places, so you parked the car in a pay-lot at the bottom of the hill and then the two of you walked fairly slowly up the incline to the hotel. You kept trying to catch her eye, but she wasn't playing. Guys whistled at you from the cars that were zipping past. You felt yourself tingle down between your legs as your calves stretched with each new, happy stride. You hadn't felt like this since Mark, the one Nicky hated so much. True, he turned out to be a bit of a jerk, but sometimes you would go even further and make up things just to watch Nicky's eyes narrow. God, she was so possessive. She used to pretend she couldn't remember his name. It really got to you sometimes. You walked up the Seattle hill, wearing a tight white tennis dress, ponytails on either side of your head. Guys really go for the little girl look, you thought to yourself, taking care to put one foot in front of the other and, just like you had heard, it seemed to make your hips sway. You wondered if Nicky liked this look, but she was staring straight ahead, ignoring you as you walked. Maybe you would do that Marilyn Monroe trick soon and cut off one of the heels to give you just a bit more of a wiggle. You saw the birthmark on your left thigh with each step, each step bringing you closer to the hotel.

What is lesbian sex like? you wondered then. Probably just lots of cunnilingus. Maybe girls putting their fingers up each other. That would be okay with you, you like that. You like it when boys' fingers get all wet, you're such a tart, they say, look at you, you're such a tease. And then you squirm and put your finger in your mouth and look up at them with big eyes. They like that, too. You wonder if Nicky would like that. Maybe Nicky doesn't like you at all in that way, maybe she's not a lesbian at all, the way you suspect she is.

Maybe you'll have to kiss her first. You can't do that. Maybe you're the one who's gay, really, not Nicky. That's why you've been thinking about the kiss for five days straight, when obviously she forgot about it since it was just a joke. Usually when you start to think like this you go and put some more lipstick on or go flirt with a boy – because that way people won't be able to tell that it's really you who might be gay.

The two of you kept walking up to the hotel. You wondered what Nicky would do when the door of the room shut behind the two of you. Would she grab you and kiss you now that you were finally alone together? If you were to kiss her first she might think you were disgusting, too forward. Sometimes in the past boys have said that to you when you try to kiss them first. But Nicky's not a boy. Sometimes she acts like a boy, though. She won't wear makeup and she won't laugh right.

It felt strange just walking along up the hill with Nicky, being away from your parents and in a big city. You'd never been on your own, without adults before. You thought: I can go eat a couple pints of ice cream now, just because I can. But this freedom also meant there were no rules… so you *could* kiss Nicky, couldn't you, if she wanted to kiss you, too. You're both thousands of miles away, nobody knows you here. Several cars beeped their horns at you. You smiled, wishing you had put on lipstick so that you'd look even prettier. Nicky seemed to graciously acknowledge that the attention from the cars was for you alone, not her. It was your due.

But once you got to the hotel, Nicky turned weird and cold and said she was going for a walk. So you took off all your clothes and checked yourself out in the mirror. You wished your hair was longer, just a few more inches and you could sit on it. You reached your hand behind you and pulled on your hair in front of the mirror. You pretended it was Nicky pulling on your hair. Knock, knock. Who's there. It was hot in the hotel room.

You went to open a window. Your breasts brushed against the sill as you forced up the stuck window. Off in the distance, nearly two blocks away, you saw someone you thought was maybe Nicky, walking back towards the hotel already. You wondered whether Nicky liked big breasts, the kind you have.

You thought: maybe I should put my clothes back on. Maybe not. Your heart started beating quickly. There was a haze in the room, a sunlight haze, but it was already darker here in Seattle than it would be at this time back home. They have dark nights here. That's what you had remembered about Seattle and the rest of the Lower 48, that it was generally hot and dark at night. You looked out the window again and saw that the approaching figure was Nicky for certain, but she had only progressed about a block. There was about another block to go. You grabbed your perfume from your travel bag. It was a really decadent, heavy, trashy scent – *Paris* – and you knew it never failed to turn Mark on when you wore it. But maybe Nicky would recognise it. Maybe she was sick of it.

This is what's happening now: the perfume is still stinging slightly. You put the lipstick back in the travel bag, go to the bed and sit down on the edge, crossing your legs and facing the door. You've stopped singing. The rouged nipples make you feel powerful and now you feel confident of the situation. A little bit of colour has perked them right up; forget that ice-cube shit you once read about. You don't know why you have this little catalogue of sex tips in the back of your head and you don't know where the catalogue comes from, but you know it serves you well. You are hyper-aware of your protruding scarlet nipples; you put your hands behind you and wait.

Nicky opens the door. She just stands there in the doorway, looking at you. She appears shocked. Maybe you've made a mistake. You look down at your sluttish-on-purpose nipples and again you feel a burst of courage. Without raising your head, you look up at her from underneath your eyelashes. "Hi," you say, "come in and shut the door."

"I've just been out walking," says Nicky. She closes the door, pulling it until it clicks.

"Your shoes are wet," you observe.

"I walked through a sprinkler."

"Mmm." You can be as cool and casual as you want because in the end it is going to be her who makes the first move. Maybe she doesn't think this is shocking. You will mention the nudity. You'll draw her attention to it, so she has to notice even if she doesn't want to. "It got so hot in here I couldn't help myself," you say. "I had to cool down." Nicky looks nervous. Is she gay or isn't she? Most guys would have been all over you by now. But you've been naked with each other before this, for chrissakes. You've known each other since you were kids, after all. Maybe she thinks you actually *did* get too hot. Maybe she thinks this is all perfectly normal. But you aren't. You're perfectly abnormal.

"Just a second," says Nicky. She walks over to the thermostat. "Well, no wonder it's hot," she says. "It's turned way up to ninety degrees." You do hope that she didn't read last month's *Cosmopolitan* with that little trick. Of course not, who are you kidding, she would never read *Cosmopolitan*.

"Come over here on the bed," you say. "I want to talk." Nicky comes over and sits some distance from you. She's trembling. So she *is* nervous about you after all. Now you know what to do. You swivel your upper body towards her, keeping your pelvis where it is. There, that can be a bit of a tease. You're not giving her everything at once. You absent-mindedly look at your hand, then let it brush across your tits; her eyes follow your hand, as whose wouldn't? But you are talking to her, "I'm scared," you're saying. "I've never lived Outside before."

"That's not true, Carol," she says. "You left for a while the summer before our senior year. When you used to have those fights with... him."

"Yes," you agree partially, "but that was only an extended vacation. Just to let things cool down for a while." It had been your mom's idea, anyway – she thought your relationship with Mark had gotten too intense. Living in a suburb of Seattle for a couple months with your great-aunt wasn't exactly your idea of big-city life. Not like now. Now was different. "But now we're living down here, Nicky, and it could be completely different. Maybe they'll think we dress funny. Maybe they'll think we talk funny."

"That's also not true, Carol," says Nicky. "We talk just the same." She's so literal. You look at Nicky until she breaks the gaze and then you let your eyes fill up with tears and spill over. Nicky looks at you again, "Oh, Carol, don't cry," she says and she tries clumsily to hug you. As soon as she touches your flushed skin you know you are going to win this one. Your lips and Nicky's lips are so close that she kisses you quickly on the mouth again, just like she did in the woods that time. She pulls away and starts to apologise, but you give her your brattiest and most charming smile, the one she couldn't resist from you, even when you were kids. She looks stunned and then smiles back and pulls you to her, like James Dean, even though she's a girl. You close your eyes and imagine James Dean kissing you. Then she starts taking off her clothes while you put your hands behind you and lean back on the bed again watching her. You will remember this moment. There are points of time you remember clearly for years.

There are points of time you remember clearly from before you were locked up, details of nature, such as the snow. And you loved the hard spruce needles of the forest. It was a forest with thick canopied leaves like pale green lace. And if you touched it, so it trembled, the lace fell down delicately. But now you're removed from nature, and when she reaches the place where you sleep, her hand moves into your bed and coldly on your neck.

Nicky puts her mouth down against your pussy, and you move your hand onto her neck, but she doesn't lick or probe any further. Your body towers over hers, the kneeling body. *can she smell the Paris* You are turned on. You smell like sweet water and you taste just as good. You know it. Then Nicky begins to lick you just outside of your lips, but working towards angling in, if you catch the meaning. At first it feels good and while she does it you run your hands up and down the designs of bone on her spine, up and down. You let your hands rest on her back for a moment, like you are doing that laying-on thing in church, and you look up at the ceiling. You imagine what you look like sitting there, your head back, your hair brushing the bed-frame behind you. Your face is tan, a fact of which you're well aware, and it probably looks very beautiful. Then it starts to feel bad, it hurts when Nicky spreads your pussy far too tightly, and even though Nicky now has her tongue up you and then on your clit and even though you are getting wetter, it hurts. You don't know the right way of telling Nicky how bad the pain is. So you stand the pain. You grip Nicky's back and you stare up at the ceiling. You actually come, surprisingly, and it is not that long after you come that the pain in your pussy stops.

You know that you and Nicky are going to have to look each other in the eye and talk about it. But that's exactly it: because it is Nicky you hold in your arms – and only because it *is* Nicky, and no one else – you know that it can't be just another screw either of you just blow off. Just another screw for you, you mean, you don't know if Nicky actually has slept with anyone before. You've never seen her with a boyfriend.

And at this precise moment, Nicky gives you a wide, beautiful smile, and that's how you know Nicky is the one. The do-till-you-die, heart of your heart one. And you are going to be hers, too, only she doesn't know it yet. You know right then that you don't have to wait for a knight on a white charger to sweep you away, to defend and to protect you. Because Nicky will do all that. You don't care if she is a girl. In fact it might be even better: the two of you can maybe understand each other better than if she were a boy. And plus, she can make you come. She doesn't know that yet, either. She has to ask you afterwards, on the bed, while you lie petting and talking and stroking each other's bodies. It irritates you when people have to ask you. Mark always asked, and it got on your nerves. Especially since it usually meant you had to lie.

You talk about Seattle that night, and Oregon and the whole Lower 48 and what you are going to do with your lives and where you are going to go, but all you really remember later is the dream-like wonder of having Nicky in bed beside you, actually *Nicky*, with her hair so sharply cut and hanging in her eyes and pretty, and you with that little voice in your head saying, now I have someone I can be sexy for, now I have someone I can be slutty for, now I have someone for whom I can try out my whole bag of tricks and it actually *means* something. It feels totally different from Mark. It feels totally different. You feel vulnerable, like the wind coming from the still-open window is rushing through each one of the unguarded gaps between your bones.

That night the two of you make the inside and the outside of your sex hurt again. It becomes raw. The colour over Nicky's cheeks is deep red – not the scarlet colour that often hurts your eyes, but instead the tone that soothes your eyes and makes your stomach feel hollow. You are slow... you wonder if your own mouth is as swollen as hers, soon it is, she kisses your lips so they swell puffed up, she kisses away the last traces of lipstick, then she kisses you, then she kisses you... When you wake up you are both in love. She doesn't say it yet, though. You know you aren't the first two young lovers in the world, but it feels like it. You know it's stupid to say you feel like you're going to be together for ever after, but it feels like that, too.

The window still stands open in the morning. You have lain there all night kissing and pushing everything further, and you have the taste of Nicky smeared all over your mouth. You detach yourself from her hold and stretch out in the patch of sun on the bed. You can still see the artificial raspberry tint on your nipples and you tease them, the left breast, then the right, until Nicky takes notice again and buries her mouth over them in the same order, the left breast, then the right. While her apple mouth works away on your right nipple you take in a breath; it is like you notice the curve of your breast for the first time and the nipple, the nipple is made up of dozens of globe-like tiny segments, like many tiny salmon-eggs. It is disgusting.

It may sound stupid to say you have never really looked at your breasts before. But it is true. And now you don't want to look too closely; the fear is you will become sickened. Especially as you do not know what else you will find when you look too closely. You don't know where to look or what to do.

Everything feels totally different.

When Nicky's head next comes up to your own – you think she is intending to kiss you – you dodge her and quickly adjust your body to a sitting position. People always like you more if you withhold something from them. "I'm hungry," you say, "aren't you hungry?" She's ravenous. "Let's go find one of those cute little cafés down the road we saw when we were walking up," you suggest. Nicky first gives you an intense look – and your heart beats rapidly when you meet her eyes, just as it's done for years when one of you catches the other looking. Now you realise that the excitement you have always felt is something different than what you supposed it to be. You have never allowed yourself to identify this feeling. This was a mistake.

Then Nicky nods. "Getting something to eat might be a good idea." Her tone is calm but belies, you feel, the obvious electricity between the two of you. This nonchalant act means she hasn't even realised yet how in love with you she is. She's kidding herself, of course.

3. Ellen

When I first met Carol and Nicky properly, I was already an old lady of twenty-four.

I could tell something was brewing – in a pre-destinal sense – already earlier that day when I did the laundry. Susan had begun by whispering to me: *it's today, you know, it's today. Something will happen today.* I knew what she meant immediately: Susan had been whispering in my head for years that the day would come when things would finally start to click into place. I didn't know the details of her predictions, yet I knew my life was going to alter, to shift, to move. Still, I hadn't heard her voice for months, nor felt my senses soar as they always did when she approached and gripped on my mind. So I suspect I took her re-emergence with some relief, relief that Susan herself had not been lost in the wash. As I loaded in the clothes, my body was already beginning to open up to her again, to respond to her knowing voice. And Susan wrapped up all my immediate world around me in her tones: the dirty laundry, the washing machine, the detergent. Things became alive that weren't before. The washing machine, sensitive to its own steel and to the sharpness of its lines. Its newly organic metalness drew in breaths of molecular composition, drew in the overwhelmingly mind-jarring flood of my brain, drew in the water bursting through my skull. And Susan's words licked at me as seductively as lake waves on a lily-pad. *It's them. It's them.* I didn't know who *they* were, exactly. Yet.

I don't tell stories. Susan is a rush of sense impressions; she derives the essence from just about anything and puts it back into my mind to be pondered over. She feels like LSD's big sister, only permanent and less vulnerable to whim. Susan is not like acid in all ways, however: she is focused and clear and, most significantly, can be momentarily self-adjusted. She's been here for so long, whispering, and I don't remember when she started. But she speaks as if from under water, no matter how clean and vivid her words, and there is always a great weight attached. A mission. But as inconvenient as it is for Susan, I've yet to figure my role out.

I had short, shiny black hair and brown eyes when I first met Nicky and Carol properly, and it wasn't likely to change. I was one-half Italian extraction, one-quarter Dutch extraction, three-sixteenths German extraction and one-sixteenth Native American – or Native North American, actually: an Athabaskan tribe from Canada. I was also one-half Japanese, three-fourths Scottish, nineteen-fifteenths Ugandan and two-thirds Finnish. My Samoan ancestors never got mentioned. I was three-eighths Colonial British, one sixty-fourth caterpillar, a smidgen of cold cream and almost entirely French. My iris was surrounded by a cold dark circle, my limbs were sturdy and shapely and my tongue sharp and quick. Short, shiny cheveaux; sturdy, shapely shins; sharp salivary sensor. Ssss... Ssss...

I was vivid. I was not subtle. It always makes me giggle that I once expected pastels from Susan, or mutedness or even numbed softnesses, flow as opposed to pains. If anything, pitches are too high, too cracking, too precise and clear. If anything, the buttons of feel in my hands detect everything, princess-in-pea-like, I am god, I feel all the infinitesimal dusts, even, in doubled and tripled-up layers on the ten digits above and below. Try walking like this – little mermaid steps on knives – and you will pray, I tell you, for all the old days of calluses. There have been no pastels so far, I promise. When I was younger, I'd tune down the reds and blues and oranges until they were pink, sky-coloured, beige; I'd push Susan's influence off my synapses and sensors. But I don't push her back anymore, and this morning her meaning was implicit: *you'll meet them today.* Implicit means total clarity of intention and belief. Because, of course, when one sees clearly another side to an argument, it is difficult to argue. Susan had never been wrong before.

"Ellen!" Another, more socially substantial, voice broke into my thoughts. My brain wetly spooling inside my skull, I drew back from my guard at the spin cycle. "Don't forget to do the dishes."

No. I would not. My roommate Jackie entered the room.

"I'm going down to the Jag later – you want to come?" Jackie was a big, dangerous butch girl with short blue hair and many piercings, and though she might have been my type, there was limited eroticism between us.

"I have to work today. I might catch you there later."

"Whatever." Her non-committal voice was no intentional slur: we had reached the plateau that platonic roommates often do, a dull compromise of civility and tempered nagging. Yet Jackie was the closest I had to a friend. We had been roommates for years, sometimes with others, sometimes just the two of us. We went cruising together and, a long time ago, had even slept with each other a couple times.

But we were roommates because we could exist together in a stale symbiosis, neither of us giving much thought to the movements or lovers of the other. Still, I longed for something more – real loves, real friends; I longed for the clarity and bite that Susan was always promising me. Destiny. But I felt myself growing older in the world I had chosen here in Seattle, the cosy little world of gossip and girls and occasional boys, of scandals which at the time seem very meaningful but lose their sting when year after year the same scandals repeat and only the characters have shifted...

I looked out the kitchen window before I began the dishes. Dew was still drying on the green grass. It was slightly chilly, but I hoped the day would be as hot as yesterday. Seattle sun often burned until the last days of September, and late August still held a lot of promise. I opened the window, the latch sliding cool against my skin, and I thought I could smell rain. But maybe not, maybe it was just a quick whiff of damp, or mulch. This moist, slight odour reminded me suddenly of summers back home, the dark silt of damp forest and the lakes. *The lake.* My head cleared suddenly; I plunged my hands into the welcoming warm froth and scrubbed my dishes clean. Jackie had already left, and I was alone in the house. *Today.*

On the kitchen table was the residue of Jackie's trick from last night: torn packets of lube, clothespins and suspicious stains on the wax tablecloth. I sighed; I might as well clean that up as well. We had once had an agreement about no sex in communal areas, but the forbidden had obviously proved too tempting for Jackie.

I threw away the lube packets, keeping my fingers well away from the gelatinous goo that was oozing out. I am allergic to nonoxynol-9 and I had several small cuts on my fingers. I scrubbed the tabletop clean, until it shone so that Doris Day herself would be proud. I picked up the two clothespins and looked at the little wooden vices lying in my palms. I knew, of course, what Jackie had used them for. I could even see her tightening the makeshift nipple-clamps on the rubied beads of her trick's tits, if I tried. Jackie's sub would be excited, watching Jackie's hands nearing her breasts, and she would be watching Jackie's expression, trying to work out her movements. Well, that was Jackie's cup of tea. To me it just seemed very painful.

I rinsed out the dish-rag. I was different from Jackie and I knew it. Like many others put in the easy category of 'SM dykes' before me, pain didn't turn me on at all. I ran my hands through the lukewarm water of the basin until they started to feel greasy, covered with food residue. I turned the tap back on and moved my hands under its stream.

No, I suppose the reason I had fallen in with Jackie and with the whole crowd of girls I hung out with was because we ostensibly had things in common sexually. Not just the gender we fucked, although that was predictable and occasionally variable. In the small incestuous dyke circles of Seattle, your web of friends grew out of past sexual entanglements: from exes of exes, even currents of exes. Your friends were those with whom you had things in common and hey, guess what – sex was that commonality. Since I had fucked many of my friends, and since many of my tertiary friends were being or had been fucked by my friends, it was no coincidence that my crowd shared some of my sexual tastes.

I turned off the water and hung the dish-rag over the faucet. Yet, I acknowledged to myself as I rubbed my hands on my jeans, I did not fit easily into the usual SM categories of top and bottom. Nor did I really consider myself to be the flexible third alternative, a switch. Perhaps when it came to games of dominance, but not the circular games of pain that Jackie so enjoyed. I didn't like receiving pain and I didn't particularly like dispensing it.

I grabbed my rucksack, turned off the lights, and made sure I locked the door behind me. I often forget to. What I *do* like, and what categorises me with those more concerned with a mix of physical pain and enjoyment, is the inexplicable rush of release from bonds. If one is physically constrained and fettered it can feel safe as much as it can feel dangerous. It doesn't always have to involve sex (although it's an excellent combination) and the loosening is a perpetual triumph. If it is me who has been bound, then I feel as clever and as jubilant as Houdini as I am untied – I have been strong enough to stand it all – and the emotion feels more like good sex than anything else I know.

If I have tied someone else, as I release the bonds I become the hero I know I've always been at heart. I rescue and I release. Sceptics and critics of kinky sex always concentrate their complaints on what is staged and what they perceive as unpleasurable, and never on what is *achieved* – in terms of emotion or in pure metaphysical pleasure. I can have every element of a Greek play in my bedroom, and I suspect that the ultimate catharsis so strived after by the masses is no less for a contemporary setting. People forget this.

Rescue. Rescue them. This time I had no idea what Susan meant, as I raced to catch the bus that ran down 14th Avenue. Normally I'd walk, but I was late again, god help me. I never wear watches. I start watching them all the time and get obsessed. I had one when I was a kid, a stupid Snoopy one with a floating tennis ball, and it drove me crazy.

"You're late," said my boss as I walked in, stating the obvious. I worked there as a token rough (but cute) barista in the coffee-house.

"Sorry." I slipped on my apron and took over one of the cash registers from the grumpy, Gothic-looking boy whose shift preceded mine. "May I help you?" I forced a smile onto my lips, and took the customers' pretentiously complicated orders of caramellos, double macchiatos and biscotti. This aspect of pulling espresso gets to me so much that when I go out to coffee-houses, I end up just ordering filter.

My boss sidled up to me. "Have you washed your hands yet?" she said.

"Before I came," I muttered.

"Come on, Ellen, you know the policy here. Hurry up, I'll cover for you."

I walked to the staff washroom and ran the cold tap over my fingers. *Water.*

"What?" I looked up. No one was in the room with me. Nobody had said anything.

When I returned, my boss gave me a dirty look and stepped away to make room for me. I swallowed. A striking woman and an equally glamorous girlfriend stood there waiting. I hate serving cute people, especially those cuter than me. I get very self-conscious. But still, I was obliged to serve a Jayne Mansfield with big soupy eyes and her hick-Elvis girlfriend complete with sneer. The only thing that let this girl-Elvis down was the fact that she had a terrible haircut: some sort of power-suit bob. She had made matters worse by combing her bangs into a 50s pompadour.

They had to be from out of town.

"Do you want something to eat? Our special today is fettuccine with remoulade sauce..." I rehearsed it from memory; I didn't even have to think.

The blonder of the two picked up the menu in an unsuitably brusque manner. This type of crassness didn't suit at all. I like my femmes to be consistent femmes. I am a traditionalist at heart. But something clicked – a weird surge of sensation in my skull – and I felt

I had to say something.

"Hi, I'm Ellen," I said.

"Hi, Ellen." The blonde girl spoke. "Carol. And this is Nicky." The names seemed familiar but distant, like the blonde was speaking them on a radio full of static.

Nicky nodded at me, her silky thoughts and her Elvis pompadour bobbing down in a slightly delayed reaction to her chin movement. Carol ordered, unimaginatively, the special for both of them and they sat down. It did occur to me to wonder why Nicky didn't speak for herself. But she seemed too detached for that, too cool, she was Jayne/Carol's silver icing, her fellow-come-merry. Venus as a boy. I watched them both for a second longer than I should have until they grew aware of my scrutiny. *Today.* I wasn't sure how to label the tension surrounding the three of us. During the pause in which I tried to figure it out, and before I turned away to serve another customer, steam began rising from the floor, curls of smoke rose to all three pairs of ears *you jayne/carol elvis/nicky* as bright sparks began popping popping off all around through the steam. I would see just steam, and then a *-blue-* like a popcorn kernel would materialise as a light source, dime-sized.

-pink-

-green-

    -yellow-

I ignored the woman waiting at the cash register and walked over to where they were sitting. Truthfully, I couldn't give a shit about the other waiting customers and besides, my boss was helping them now, anyway.

"Nice to make your acquaintance," I said. Was that a faint Southern drawl I suddenly came up with? Sometimes I surprised myself. "Is this your first time here? Are you comfortable where you're sitting?"

"Oh yes, great. It's nice, thanks." Carol spoke for them both again. Nicky tersely smiled an affirmation, another subtle grimace. She ran her fingers through her pompadour and looked away. They were both so dated, like they'd been caught in the Butch/Femme fifties and then deposited – smack! – in my lap. *You'll meet them today.*

I decided to prod. "Are you new here?"

"We're just in town for a couple days," said Carol. Nicky still didn't speak. I could tell Carol was used to being the centre of attention. Come on, Carol, let Elvis growl for herself, I thought. One of Carol's earrings began to grow suddenly, twisting three more inches out towards me before it turned into a steak knife. Maybe she had heard my thoughts.

Elvis made eye-contact. Zoom! "Do you know some places that might be nice to check out?"

Did I ever.

-pink-

-gold-

-silver-

-blue-

"There's the Jag, that's good. And the Rose and sometimes up above the Broadway Market…" It occurred to be for the first time that they might not be dykes. But that was highly unlikely. The dynamics between them, the proximity of their bodies, the shared glances all pointed to a relationship of both a sexual and emotional nature. And if I was wrong, well, maybe some provincial little minds would be opened tonight.

"Ellen! Get back to your station!"

I gave Nicky a wink as I walked away. "Maybe see you guys tonight?"

"Maybe." Nicky stared at me levelly before I walked away to take orders from the impatient line of waiting customers. When I finally caught my breath enough to look over at them twenty minutes later, they had already finished their meal and left. There was no tip on the table. Fuck 'em.

*

I lay in the bathtub, my toes curling over the edge of the old Victorian tub, complete with its own set of toes. Clawfoot tubs were one of those quaint details particular to Seattle, along with heroin and large walk-in closets rented out as rooms to students. I bent my knees to stick my feet back in. The water soothed them; my feet were sore after the hours on them at the coffee-house.

"So what was the big deal, Susan?" I said aloud. "If Nicky and Carol were who you wanted me to meet, then what exactly did you want me to do?"

"What?" hollered Jackie from her bedroom, where I could hear her preparing for her evening at the Jag, snapping bands over her wrists, wrestling on her leather chaps.

"Nothing." I muttered. "*Well?*" I asked Susan again in a much softer tone, the water cooling around me. But Susan was silent.

"You sure you don't want to go?" Jackie called out.

Well, why not. I dragged myself out of the tub and stood dripping on the mat. I had only soaked, not properly scrubbed myself clean. But I was in such a foul mood that I relished my uncleanliness. There would be a certain *schadenfreude* in making those near me uncomfortable with the smell of my coffee-house sweat.

"Hold on a minute, I'm coming after all," I shouted to Jackie. I went to my room and didn't towel off. I pulled my cut-offs over my wet legs and pulled on a T-shirt.

When I came out I noticed Jackie's disappointment with my particularly vanilla choice of clothes. The contrast between us made her look over-accessorised, the SM dyke version of a Joan Collins. I could tell she felt uncomfortable next to my evident lack of need to define my sexual tastes so obviously. Fuck her, too.

4. Nicky

She stopped Carol in their walk back from the café that evening, thinking she was the most lovely person she had ever seen; she stopped to pull Carol around the side of a dimly lit 7-11 store and put her hand up Carol's skirt to feel her. The taste from the morning had stayed on Nicky's musked lips and eyes. Carol slid down on Nicky's hand, eyes closed, and Nicky had no idea what she could be thinking, as she became lost in the easy luxurious kisses Carol gave her, the exquisite heaviness of Carol's tongue. *This is what all those boys back home had, this is what the boyfriend had,* thought Nicky, *he had this woman, but now I have her, I own her;* and Nicky was received into the mouth of the lovely curves of Carol, the wet inside of her cheeks, her smooth enamels.

For an inexplicable moment as they kissed, Nicky remembered again the forest interior near where her uncle had his cabin. The scent of smoke blew in between her lips; her mouth started to water. She remembered the trees and what might happen if she got inside them. She could get lost. She had always been frightened of losing her way; throughout her childhood she had felt urgency as she stepped inside the woods. Further down the hill from where her uncle's cabin had been, there was a creek which fed the lake. She had a memory of having played in the creek. Of the pungent smell of spruce and trickling water. Nicky as a child had been warned, though, of the creek, and she usually shied away from it. The creek led to the lake. The lake was where the accident had happened.

The colour of her memory was deepening to a half-sour green. Nicky withdrew her hand from between Carol's legs, her fingers now moist and warm. But the image in her head remained. She had wet her feet in the musky water of the creek; she had crawled upon the bank and begun to run down the hill to the lake. She was eight years old. Her cousin had drowned two years before, and if her Uncle Joe found Nicky playing near the lake, she surely would be spanked, no matter how nice her uncle was or how sad he'd been since Susan died. *Mush, mush. Faster.* The trees were moving in on her. *Hard. Sharp. Making her cry.* Through the woods she ran, shouting and dashing past the tree branches. *I can make it, I'll make it there,* Nicky thought, though she was losing her way as she kept on plunging through the brush; there had been a ringing in her head then and her breath was quick. *Wake up.*

The memory of this time felt more real than Carol's hand in hers as they walked towards the Seattle bar; Nicky breathed in the crisp night air of the city but she could barely catch her breath.

The room was crowded with bodies, smelled of sweat and was filled with cigarette smoke. She felt odd about entering and uncomfortable with Carol hovering at her side, though she was relieved no one had asked for their IDs. Her neck prickled; she had an irrational fear that she would be recognised by someone from home, although she realised at the same time that it was a two-way process – if someone saw her here, she'd have as much on them as they'd have on her. When she first entered she took in sensations as if she were blind: she was able to hear, thudding, the terrific beat-beat-beat of the electronic bass in the music, pulsing up round and full through her body; she was able to smell the ashy scent of nicotine and tar, of sweaty salt, but as far as her sight was concerned it was if it were veiled and muffled. Her feelings regarding the situation were so intense that she had entered some kind of emotional overload. At this point she attempted to see through the darkness which pressed uncomfortably on her, but the sensation remained that of attempting to open your eyes in a pitch-black room.

Gradually, however, both her eyesight and full self-awareness returned to her, this time with a clarity of detail which was as disturbing as the visual block had been. Carol was on her left and through the fluorescent filter Nicky saw hundreds of tiny bits of lint and dust on Carol's hitherto relatively clean black dress. It made her stomach turn, slightly, but then she remembered acutely both the night before and the walk from the café, and remembering she started to notice again the creamy colour of Carol's soft skin, and deep in her stomach something tightened which made her feel good, not nauseous.

There was a couple kissing further on ahead to her right, and both of the girls seemed to feel Nicky's glance as she stared at them because they drew apart, and one of the two even smiled at her. Nicky had never seen two people of the same sex kissing so openly. She couldn't imagine why they looked so relaxed. And straight ahead, all the way across the room, was Ellen, the waitress from the café. Nicky recalled that it had seemed as if Ellen had been flirting with her, but she wasn't sure. She ran her tongue across her white teeth, but could still detect the familiar residue of smoke. How *could* you be sure in such a situation and how could you risk anything at all by asking?

That day in the woods long ago. Two years after Susan died. Nicky had planned to follow the creek down to the lake. Her jeans were wet from the ankle to the knee, with unease they became her cousin's clothes still damp on her flesh. She was being chased by things other than the trees, she thought, and her fear grew. *I can't run for much longer,* she thought. Then she saw the point where the creek hit the lake, hidden by the vines, and she waded again through the water, rafting herself through the dank liquid until a current seemed to catch her, spinning her and then heading her on a rush of water towards the lake, and she stood whole and dripping on its banks, and she knew that she had beaten whatever it was that followed her; she had outrun it; it was far behind her.

And of course Carol had been there at the café that afternoon, too, right behind her. Carol had looked just beautiful, her round blue eyes watching Nicky's every move, her voice practically a coo. And she was so soft, she had been so soft and lovely and pretty, just as Nicky had expected she would be *fluid soft applesoft lush* She was still beautiful even now in the club, but she didn't fit in – most of the other girls had short hair, like Nicky's own (though hers was not clipped close like a boy's, which seemed to be the fashion here), and very few wore makeup. Certainly none wore it as thick as Carol did.

She shifted so that Carol would not notice her embarrassment over the fact that Carol looked all wrong. Her long blonde sculptured curls looked very silly here in this dark, fashionable, smooth club with its fast throbbing music, music that made Nicky think of cities, of hardness, of slick sex, of adrenalin. She wanted *that* kind of of eroticism, the opposite of the dreamy wet lushness that had been last night with Carol. Immediately she felt guilty and disloyal for thinking such things, particularly with Carol literally right there on Nicky's arm, her eyes shining in excitement, the whites visible in the dark room.

It had been dark, too, in the woods that time, and to the side of the creek the olive colour of the spruce needles spread its scent through the cracking of tiny needles, each needle separately emitting the scent of the greened fresh wilderness. The scent's sound pierced her ears and heart. She had been right on the edge of the lake. The feeling had stabbed her like a pain, like a dagger of freshness. The sky huddled over, open yet growing dark, and when she had looked up through the branches, the sky went wide on all sides all the way up, but the earth only went down to the earth. Though the sky was held open above her, her awareness had only focused on the ground near the lake, on tiny green tendrils growing up through the soil, on the moistness and rotting and the life-process, the organicness of the woods, and the way the soil itself had breathed and repeated itself, giving off a gamey odour. *Wake up.*

The girl called Ellen did fit in, Nicky realised uncomfortably, and at a loss of where to look next, her attention focused on Ellen's haircut. Her short cropped hair was exactly what it should be for this place, as were her manner and movements – casual yet fluid and snakish at the same time. Nicky suspected that Ellen was unstable, but Ellen was definitely hip – she knew what happened in this place, her ease meant she had been here many times before. Maybe Nicky ought to have her hair cut equally close, instead of the short angled bob

Carol had insisted on right before they left home, which Nicky rebelled against with a slight pompadour curved by hair mousse and patience. Certainly Carol herself needed to reassess how she looked. Ellen had a kind of look which Nicky wasn't sure she liked – she might even prefer Carol's look of mysterious old-style femininity, of secret artifice – but Ellen's look certainly worked here; combined with Ellen's slender, compact body, the look achieved was one of tensed nonchalance. You didn't know where you stood with her. That kind of thing usually terrified Nicky. Like if an infant was about to jump out of a baby carriage and take you by the throat. It was unlikely, so you shouldn't be frightened, but you were anyway. It was the same with Ellen. Maybe Nicky ought to affect it herself.

Nicky knew she was staring across the room, but she couldn't help it and besides, Carol hadn't noticed. She guessed Ellen was a couple years older than she and Carol – probably over twenty-one. She lowered her eyes. Ellen was dressed in ripped cut-off jeans with a bright white T-shirt over her small breasts; her nipples were distinctly visible through the stretched sheer cotton. Nicky looked up again and was mortified to notice that Ellen had caught her gaze. Ellen nodded at Nicky and then, seeming to recognise them more precisely, broke off her conversation with the girl next to her, picked up her beer and came towards them.

Carol saw Ellen just before she reached them. "Oh, look who it is," she said. Carol sounded excited.

"Hey, you guys," said Ellen, drawing level with the two of them. "So – you did go out on the town after all. What do you think?" Nicky didn't know what to say.

"It's just really nice," said Carol, finally. She beamed at Ellen, who ignored her and directed her attention at Nicky.

"You having a good time?" Ellen asked.

"Sure," said Nicky, "yeah, we are." Nicky lightly touched Carol's waist and kept her hand there, to show Ellen that they were ones, too, and hadn't just stumbled in the place unaware.

"Do you hang out here a lot?" said Carol. Nicky cringed at the clumsy rephrased cliché, but it seemed to finally do the trick as Ellen turned away from Nicky and now directed her full attention on Carol.

"Yeah, I usually come here after work. I worked here as a bartender for a while..." Her voice, which had certainly begun with a clear strong direction, somehow lost its route during the second sentence as Ellen seemed to fade out, her eyes growing distant and her manner disjointed. She appeared confused, but as Carol and Nicky exchanged glances she seemed to catch herself and her focus returned. "Well," Ellen said, taking a drag on her cigarette, "What now? Are you staying here for a while?"

"No, I think we're heading down to Oregon," said Carol, before Nicky could answer.

"Oh." said Ellen. "That's just really nice." Nicky noticed that she slightly mimicked Carol's previous assessment of the club. She wasn't sure if Ellen did it on purpose. "Hey, I should come down and visit you guys some time," continued Ellen, seemingly struck with fresh inspiration.

"*Mmm.*" Carol made a non-committal noise, but flashed Ellen a smile before excusing herself and picking her way through the mass of people to the bathroom. Nicky and Ellen stood alone together; Nicky supported herself with her hands behind her, leaning on the table in back of her.

"*Mmm,* indeed." Ellen said. She winked at Nicky and scooted herself in closer to her. They were both, Nicky saw, holding their breath. Ellen took a step so that she was mere inches away. She was speaking to Nicky. This time Nicky was aware that their breasts were brushing together and the warmth that she felt down in her cunt affirmed what she had always been afraid of, what she had dreaded: that she lusted for and desired women. That she wanted to fuck women. Not just Carol, for that was something different altogether. That was a childhood sweetheart, a life-long crush kind of thing. She could accept that. But now this, another woman, not Carol, was making her feel horny, too.

She tried to listen to Ellen and to understand the words she was saying, but all she could concentrate on was the imagined slickness of Ellen's pussy, of her own spot which was wet, wet and then Ellen kissed her and she could feel her body responding, Ellen's lips soft on hers and yet impudent, her tongue jarring between Nicky's teeth. So that first Nicky revelled in the kiss and then in the midst of sucking on and in Ellen's tongue, Nicky pulled away, overcome and frightened.

Ellen grabbed Nicky by the collar of her shirt. "No tip? What the fuck were you playing at, Elvis?" she said. In her surprise, Nicky did not trust herself to move; what was she talking about? She just hung there, swaying at the end of Ellen's raised fingertips. *eyes closed claws of a dread man ripping flesh* She watched Ellen's face change back to its hip, flat appeal. Ellen then let Nicky go, but she murmured a word which to Nicky sounded like "water". Oh, god, of course, the girl was on drugs. She was dehydrated. She needed water. That explained a lot. Nicky could feel herself shaking. "See ya around," said Ellen with a wink and sauntered off. Nicky placed both hands on the table to steady herself.

This feeling had curled up in the muggy air; the earth was like a swamp of dark, timorous organs. And Nicky had stepped into the lake and begun to float, spinning away on her back, the dark muskiness and the sound of the clear water enveloped her as she drifted on without really thinking. The water was cold, but no colder than the creek had been. She was a good swimmer for an eight-year-old. She had passed both the Polliwog and the Minnow swim tests. She floated out to the middle of the lake. Lidding this body of water were the spruce trees and their thousand separate brownish-green needles. Nicky had gotten a feeling of being on the edge of discovering a very, very great thing. The wildness was gaining on her; the smell of the wood itself was like a fresh dose of smelling salts – it woke her up to what was really there. There was a fire burning somewhere near the banks of the lake, it was not something that she could see, but she was aware that it was there on the edge of her consciousness. The smoke scent was there. She had been here many times before. She had forgotten the lake, but now she found she remembered it again. She'd keep floating back and no matter what else changed in her, she couldn't leave the lake or woods behind. She was fully awake.

She could see Ellen's back disappearing into the crowd. She took a breath and then reached for her beer, longing for the liquid against her throat, carbonated and alcoholic, begging her attention away from what had just taken place. As she drank it down and wiped her mouth dry, she could see Carol returning from the bathroom. Carol's eyes were popping out everywhere as her head turn from side to side to observe the sights. She looked, thought Nicky, unfortunately like the hick she was. Carol reached Nicky's side.

"Why are you shaking?" she said, running a quick finger up Nicky's arm.

"Let's go," said Nicky, "I want to get out of here."

5. Carol

With your cannery earnings, you and Nicky rent a two-storey house down in Oregon, the cheapest on the block. Your new digs are in a small suburban area just outside Eugene, where any given lawn is perfectly mowed to a height that is evenly matched by each neighboring household. Inside the furnished house there are hints that it is not so clinical and pristine: it smells as ripe as a greenhouse. In terms of structure, the house is set up strangely, with many different levels and many twists and turns as you walk through it, looking for more flaws, things which will make it more individual, less mass-produced.

And you do find small nicks in its suburban perfection: it has dingy paint that once was white and now is fading off the concrete walls, peeling off in mottled waves to expose crude cement beneath. The colour that has remained on the walls is the yellow of old nicotined wallpaper. Too many smokers have lived here before. You hold onto these small faults as fodder: not everything in this Norman Rockwell town is perfect; you might not be the only freaks in town.

Still, if the landlady knows or cares that you are more than friends she doesn't let on. It isn't like she could be all that picky; the house used to be a second-rate warehouse before it was 'converted' and is unlikely to pass any housing test. After you pay out every cannery cent in advance for a year's rent, your money still looks good, with last year's Alaska Permanent Funds (a thousand bucks per resident per year; can't argue with that) in your mutual pocket, plus Nicky's student loan because Nicky's been accepted at the university in Eugene. You're set for quite a while.

This move to a stable place can only be a good thing. Nicky looks happy. She looks good smiling because it magnifies the rest of her looks. Her eyes are the colour of pale lemons and there are dark rings that frame her irises. Her eyelashes are also dark.

After you have lived here for a few years or so, after Nicky graduates, the two of you are going to move to Portland and maybe have a baby. You haven't told Nicky about the baby, but you can't wait; you really love babies. Even when you go in a mall you like to hold and cuddle them. Nicky would have a beautiful baby. Like her eyes, her skin is yellow. It is beautifully bronze. And like her eyelashes, her hair is dark and thick. And then her muscles. They move well together. Even the muscles on her face, they tighten and run over the bones. But now you worry a little that people may think you're a pervert or a child molester or something. If you have a baby. But they can't tell if you are gay, can they? It's not something that shows.

You're going to do a couple courses too, after she starts at college. She'll be using your car to get there, but that's okay. Meanwhile you're going to cook and clean and fuss over Nicky and you really, really can't wait to get started. It's like this: when you aren't directly with Nicky, you can't stop thinking about her and wondering if she is thinking about you. It feels good being together. It started feeling really good the day you went in that place in Seattle where the crazy girl worked. It was weird that she was gay, too. Because before you never noticed whether girls were gay or not – except maybe when you wondered about Nicky and you. But you can tell now. It means stuff like short hair, small hoop earrings, a little swagger. Some women even cut their hair short, bleach it and wear lots of makeup. That's the option you'd prefer. The makeup bit. But it does seem to rest on whether you have short hair. That's what counts. If you want to be gay.

You don't have short hair, though Nicky does and she seems to be much more popular with those kind of girls than you. The day after you got down to Oregon, she went to a barber and had her bob chopped off. Now it's as short as a boy's. She always points out girls with short hair but she won't let you cut yours. She says she likes it the way it is. You see a good deal of this type of girl when you travel into Eugene but still, you never speak with them. Why should you have to talk to them? *You're a couple, not a triple or a quadruple,* you joke together. You love it when you laugh together like this. You love silly, private jokes between the two of you. You don't want Nicky to look or talk to girls, but if she talk and flirts with boys it doesn't bother you. That's an easy one, since Nicky never looks at boys. It bothers Nicky when you do. She thinks you'd run away from her. But you would never do that. You are in love with each other, doesn't she understand? A couple. You feel warm deep inside when you think of the word. A couple. Nicky is all yours.

As you lie there together in bed she catches her breath and takes your hand; she turns your face towards hers. "You're beautiful," she says. You flush. Maybe you do not know how to respond. Her skin is tawny yellow. "You are," she says, "your lips, hair, your tongue, your eyes, your body – oh, your lovely breasts…" She grips and shakes you until you become frightened. You don't like being held too tightly. And maybe slowly she takes her hand away and looks you in the eyes. "Because I love you," she says. And then maybe she puts her arms around you and strokes your hair and you let her and she does not let you go.

Nicky has funny ideas about what is sexy. She likes that whole wrapped-in-plastic, meet-him-at-the-door stuff that even *Cosmo* doesn't suggest anymore. Like not wearing any underwear. Okay, you've done that for her sometimes because you like how it feels with only a short skirt on and alright, it gets you a little wet. You don't care too much that you, what's the word, subordinate yourself. It should be completely different with a girl. And the first few times you act out this type of old-fashioned sex kitten role, it doesn't bother you. You've done it for years with boys, after all, these are skills you know well. But then it sort of starts to get to you. Something's different about the way Nicky looks at you these days. It's like she's – judging you. Like she's not entirely satisfied. You're going to have to start to look like the other girls so Nicky will look at you the way she used to. The way she looked at you in the woods that time. The way the forest looked that bright autumn day resonates in your ears and mouth when you are awake and in the rich soiled musk scent you run over in the slur of your dreams; the forest is musk. You have your photographs to remember that day by. But you do not always remember your dreams.

You kiss bare-torsoed in the warm light of the tower, your nipples against her nipples, your back feeling the weight of your unbound hair. You twist your hair and bind it up. The wet is dripping out of you, between your legs, through your undergarments and stockings. She holds you tight so you won't shiver. Her mouth is smiling and her cheeks are flushed. She kisses you first quickly, like a joke, and then the two of you kiss slowly.

Nicky's kissing you slowly and her cheeks are flushed. She brings her hand up to the small of your back, but your hair no longer touches her fingers as it has before. Because now you've gone and gotten your hair cut short. Not too short, just above your shoulders – but before it was so long that you could sit on it, could feel the weight of it unbound on your back.

You and Nicky are going to get married, or do some kind of marriage thing. You think maybe you could get married in San Francisco, but you will have to save up for it.

"That's a long way off, sweetheart," says Nicky. She touches your hair. "I liked your hair when it was longer," she says.

You've done the wrong thing by cutting it. Though you thought it was the right thing. Now you must grow your hair long again for Nicky. And bleach it, too; she likes it blonde. Sometimes it's a pain, bleaching and then conditioning the over-processed hair. Is it worth it? Sure it is.

After a month your hair is longer. Does Nicky look at you more often now that it's grown out a bit? Sure she does. Does she stroke your hair more frequently? Sure she does. And that's what you wanted, wasn't it, for Nicky to look at you. You're growing your hair for her again.

You begin to grow your hair. She still wails for you. It pains you that you can't speak clearly, only see each other from a distance. Every day you brush

*your hair out, soon it will be long curls that fall nearly to the ground. Long,
yellow curls. Yellow is your favourite colour.*

It's her birthday. You are cooking dinner in your freshly painted
yellow kitchen. *I hope my hair is getting longer, I hope my hair is getting
longer.* You're thinking in circles, words looping like a merry-go-round:
again, then again. A kitchen *should* be yellow, shouldn't it? It's your
favourite colour. You like it that way, humming to yourself in your
bright, sparkly kitchen, cooking dinner for your sweetheart. A creamy
blue-cheese and beef dish; your mouth is watering in anticipation.
The meat is browning nicely in the pan. "Nicky," you say, "could you
give me a hand?"

"Sure," she says. "What do you want me to do?" She runs her fingers through your shoulder-length blonde hair.

Hurry up and *grow*, you think. "Hand me that bowl, please."

Nicky hands over the blue plastic bowl full of meat pieces you have
so skilfully tenderised and chopped in big succulent pieces, but her
fingers falter and the contents fall all over the floor.

"God. I'm so sorry, Carol. I'm such a klutz. That's why you're such
a better cook." You consider that maybe you're a better cook because
you do it more often, but you don't say anything. It's her nineteenth
birthday, after all.

As she bends over to pick up the bloodied pieces off the floor with
her bare hands, on her knees there she reminds you of how shy and
apologetic she used to be. That's because you have a brief flash of that
time when you guys were kids and practically the same thing happened. The two of you were helping your mom cook. Bloody cubes of
meat, ruined on your mom's clean floor. ("I always said it was so clean
you could eat off it, but let's not risk it," your mom had said, smiling.)

Nicky had run immediately for the vacuum cleaner; she was so
embarrassed and besides she knew where it was kept. Though she was
laughing, Mom practically had to wrestle the vacuum cleaner from
Nicky. Nicky had a tight grip and had managed nonetheless to suck up

some of the pieces of raw meat into the machine. Brett had to take the whole thing apart the next day so the stuff wouldn't rot inside it. Rotten, festering meat.

The rotten moist mask of the woods tempts you from the window, but you cannot leave the tower. "Let down your hair," she calls, and somehow this time you can hear her. And maybe this time it will reach. Your hair has a fruity smell; sometimes you bundle your hair up in your hands and put your face in it, breathe in the curls. You unfurl the long curls; they have grown so that they almost reach the ground again.

The weight of her body is incredibly painful. Every foot she nears closer to you is a terrible pain to the roots of your hair. When finally she reaches you, you are on the floor sobbing in pain. How can you get out of this? You've got to get out of here. But how?

The next week Nicky spends a lot of time away from home because classes have started. The first day she's gone you're going stir-crazy; you've got to get out here, out of this house. Back home, they call it cabin fever. You're just about ready to leave for a short walk when you hear something out on the lawn. You go outside to see a middle-aged man and woman walking quickly away, and there on the lawn is a big sign scrawled in black permanent marker. The words spell GET OUT DYKES. But the letters are half-covered by dripping shit, so you have to squint for a second. The dog they got it from must have had diarrhoea or something. You shout at them, but they are long gone. You go back inside, take the sign to the kitchen and sit down in a chair to wait until Nicky gets home. No, you were wrong. You *are* the only freaks in the neighbourhood, after all. You've been singled out. You wait at least three or four hours; the kitchen is beginning to really smell, but you can't bear to look right now at the stainless steel sink where you put the whole mess or else you'll throw up.

"What is this shit?" says Nicky when she comes in. Nicky doesn't get the irony, she just grimly walks back out and throws it all out in the garbage can, comes back and takes a shower. She's furious.

Afterwards you get a little weird about leaving the house. Not that phobia disease really or anything, but just a little skittish. You think that those people who did it know *nothing* about you. You have aunts and uncles their age. Would they do something like that if they knew that you were gay? You don't think so. Older people like that always like young cute girls like yourself. If they don't think you are too cheap. Well, older men always like you, anyway. And you've always been pretty popular with your parents' friends, male *and* female; you don't understand why these neighbours would do something so hateful. You aren't the *type* of person they should do that kind of thing to. Maybe Nicky is. It's not fair to think this way, but maybe that's the way it is.

But what you'll do is, you'll stay at home a lot more, to make sure it doesn't happen again. At night you whisper your decision to Nicky and shake her slightly while she sleeps, but she doesn't wake up.

Nearing dawn you shake her awake. "We'll have to hurry," you say. She looks at you.

"I can't take you." she says. "I'll fall to my death on the ladder of hair. And you would, too. If the ladder were to carry two, the cumulative weight on the hair would strain it." You look at her.

"Can you bring me a piece of rope each time you come," you ask, "so I can weave the strands together and escape myself? There wouldn't be a danger. They take the loose hairs with them after they comb my hair, so I can't fashion ropes from my own locks." This is not the first time this idea has come to you. You wait for her reaction.

"I'll try," she says, "of course I'll try." And so she goes but not you. And as she goes even her descent is a terrible pain to your scalp.

I'll try, you think, I'll try. You're in bed with Nicky. She's got her Walkman on and she's trying to read: *The World According to Garp.* She keeps chuckling. You wonder what she's listening to – Circle Jerks, Black Flag? She likes hard, harsh music. She doesn't like what she calls soft music, like Johnny Hates Jazz or even Oingo Boingo, which is one of your favourite groups. They're not soft, either, they're just not all guitar, with beats sped up so fast you can't think. You wonder how Nicky can read at all, with that clamour in her ears. How can she concentrate?

You stroke her stomach, her legs, her arms and she shrugs you off. She likes to be in control even when she's not in control. This kind of ploy you're doing right now will never work on her. It never has before; she has to want you first. But it would work on you, if she were to stroke you and kiss you. You would get turned on. But she is not you. And still you persist with the kissing, the touching, the caressing, knowing full well she will not let you in, but still you want to show her. This is how you show love, but she doesn't know it. This is sex to her, and this type of sex is not the way she wants it at the moment. Christ, why doesn't she just unfreeze herself, join you in the deep kiss that would feel so wonderful and honest right now? But she won't. Because she's not the type.

It's the same long fight when you and Nicky begin to fight, with only bitty pauses in between. You hate this godforsaken state. Oregon is just small town after small town. Whereas Alaska at least had the forest and the mountains. And it's too hot here. Maybe Nicky is tired of hearing you bitch; she said this last week when you were filling out your own application forms for the University of Oregon for next term, just for fun. Don't bother, she said, but you think she was joking. Then she said: Well, it keeps you busy, so at least you'll stop bitching about the weather.

What's another sexy technique you can try out on her? Hmmm. It can't be too honest, like last night. It has to be masked. There is a seduction ruse you know. But it works best with someone the first time that you meet. It involves a lighter and two smoking participants. You light up their cigarette and then wait until the other person's eyes meet yours over the flame. Just for a second, understand, you shouldn't overdo it, you should be subtle. Isn't that right? Then you can sneak a second look, that second look after the first flame is often the most devastating. That bit about eye contact is the most important thing, actually, when it comes to the art of seduction. You hold the glance until the last possible moment. But of course everyone knows that one.

A dream you have had. "This time I had hung myself on my hair..."

Your lover looks at you as if she were concentrating, her eyes holding yours until the last possible moment before speech: "You must be very, very careful that you don't become entangled in your hair and that hangings don't accidentally occur. And don't lean out the window," she says, "if you were to fall, your hair could choke you."

"I know," you said to her, "I must be very careful. You always take care of me."

Your hair keeps growing.

Nicky has bought you a new dress. She likes to do this sometimes: buy you new dresses, underwear, shoes. "Thank you." You give her a kiss. "You always take care of me." You wonder how much it cost. Not too much, you hope. The money is ticking away.

There's the idea that men – and women too, you have to assume – are not by nature monogamous, and thus they constantly crave that they are with a variety of women. But of course you can fool Mother Nature, can't you? And always dress yourself in new, exciting clothes and fashions and hairstyles and thus the man – or woman – subconsciously believes that they are with someone entirely new. Perfect, isn't it? Will it work? Yes, there's the rub. As one of your English teachers used to say.

You don't get into college. Well, she always was the smart one. Even when you were in elementary school together you'd cheat off of her and she'd let you. You can't cheat off someone forever, can you? When they reject you at the University of Oregon counselling office, they tell you that maybe you should try to get some community college under your belt to raise your grades. Nicky doesn't seem to think it is a good idea; you think she is a little ashamed of you for being dumb. But you surprise yourself and drive over to the community college anyway. You sign up for three courses: one in psychology, one in beginning photography and one in home economics. You can do all these courses by correspondence, too, so you don't even have to leave the house. If nothing else, then you might learn some new recipes; Nicky and you are both getting pretty sick of your limited dinners. You are almost at the point of insisting that she cook more often herself. But then what you dread most might happen: you guys might start to fight. You spent all that time fighting with Mark, and this time you want it to be different. Your parents never fought at all.

You stand by the door at dawn, plaiting your hair. You can distinctly hear the creaking of the footsteps. Are they what you dread most, or what you love most? They tread through water; they step through bushes. Your lover comes up behind you and runs her hand over your buttocks. "Stop," you hiss, "you must climb down."

"Certainly," Nicky says, and walks away. You resume plaiting your hair, and listen carefully. Someone has circled the first round of the tower now, walking slowly. Nicky has come up behind you again. "Come on," she whispers your name in your ear again and digs her hands in your skirts between your thighs the way she knows you like her to. She grips you there and holds the grip and waits for you to respond.

"Stop," you whisper at Nicky again, but you know she can tell you are aroused; she has already sensed it by the pace of your breathing. Your head bends back to hers. "You have to stop."

"Say that you like it," Nicky says to you as she rubs your thighs. You are so frozen with anxiety, frightened that you will be heard and investigated, that you do not answer.

"Stop," you finally manage to mumble. People will be able to hear you, even locked in here. They will be able to find out.

"No," says Nicky, with her lips on your ear.

"Yes," you insist. "Please stop." Now she is behind you and playing with you until you become sticky. You are frightened of being overheard. Her fingers move in and out inside you, very wet.

"Say you want to," she says, "because I won't do it if you don't say I can." Something's drawing closer, the final spirals of the tower twist towards you and you are very tired and aroused, so you say that she may do what she wants, and she enters you standing there behind you, lifting you up slightly to better position you. When she thrusts, each time you feel a mixture of three parts: excitement, anger and fear. When soon she is finished and you are doubled over, you realise no one's coming after all. No one will burst your bubble. No one will intrude. There is something that you meant to say to her, but you have forgotten.

Nicky's eyes are blank and trusting. You falter, knowing you do not know the right words or phrases. It is only when she embraces you after, pleased that you enjoyed yourself, that you again attempt to explain. But you stop explaining, she loves you and she would get angry if you brought it up. But what exactly it is you would bring up, you are not sure.

Here's another one. You have to touch your lips as often as possible, and draw attention to them in a number of ways: pout them, wear lipstick – always deep red, never pink. Desmond Morris wasn't the first to say it, but it's true: red lips make people think of lusty, thrusting sex. *Wine* lipstick is good. Put things in them to suck (fingers are good, pencils are just okay). 'Subconsciously' run your tongue over your lips from time to time. Make a habit of it. Learn to laugh with your mouth wide open; it looks high-spirited and sexy. Keep your mouth open when listening to people and nodding. It makes you look accessible, not just dumb. Try making a habit of this, too.

When it rains. When it rains, water splashes over your eyes. It wets her eyes, too, after she climbs up; is it possibly tears? You slowly open your mouth, accessible only for her. You breathe in the kiss she gives you and, kissing her, you notice a new scent that does not seem to come from anywhere specific. It could be described as a wood smell, similar to spruce and cedar. It could be some kind of conifer, perhaps an extinct type which can no longer be found. One whose vestiges of scent capsules are left in other, hybrid evergreens.

The most important thing about a conifer is that when the cones are thrown into flames, they spark out in explosions and bring new colours to the flames themselves. Where the cones go the fire is touched with red hues, or bits of blue-flamed spark, even fires whose flames are close to green. Even within a treeless tower, even in a shell of water, you can remember this type of thing. And sometimes this feels so good that you don't much care that you are where you are.

You don't like it where you are, hanging outside the student union waiting for Nicky's class to end. She comes towards you, flushed with knowledge and you bite back the terrible envy you feel. You're like a mutant praying mantis, except you want to prey, not pray: on her, and all she's learned today. You want the knowledge, too. She pays for both of your coffees and the two of you sit back down in the breeze.

There is a woman in line getting a coffee. She must be a gay, her hair is so short, in a crew cut and, besides, she's bleached it blonde-orange. Her face is sexy, you realise, if androgynous. She's wearing a short, kilt-like A-line skirt and she has a tan, narrow body with high breasts. Her shortened child's T doesn't cover the bottom of her breasts; the rush of heat between your legs embarrasses you. Even if Nicky hasn't seen her yet, you are going to point her out.

"There's one for you, that's your type, there," you say to Nicky.

"Not really," Nicky says, "but she's pretty cute."

"How cute do you think she is," you say, "cuter than me?"

"What?" says Nicky.

You say: "The girl. You want to fuck her."

"I don't know what you're talking about," says Nicky. "I give up." And you are fighting again, in a flow so predictable and linear that there is only your crippling jealousy holding you up, your envy as ballast, as your pride, your pride.

Sometimes her skin will feel right in the way skin occasionally will, next to yours. Your heart will cease beating for an instant; your pores thump instead. Your flesh takes breaths as you are pressed against her.

At this moment, when your heart is not beating and your lungs stop their flexing, the sweat-pores of your body continue inhaling and beating against her skin; the same openings on the skin of her body respond. An instant, skin: one breath, one beat. In sync. Then in your body you are breathing and thumping again.

If you often glance at your own breasts, other people will look at them, too. If they're not looking already. Touch is important. Try to touch the other person as much as you decently and within excuse can, but much more importantly: touch yourself. Touch yourself, in front of them: all the places they can't but would like to touch. Your breasts as if by accident, your lips, face, arms purposefully. Stroke your legs. Stretch your body out on the chair in front of them, imitate the habits of a cat. Tell me stories, Nicky will whisper in your ear in moments like these. You curl and fit your bodies closer together and tell her incidents that you remember. Your lips move against her throat, nuzzling a pulse. Perhaps she can cipher, without hearing, the words you speak from the movement and shapings of your lips against her throat.

You've gotten some mail. *Dirty faggots, you'll rot in the justice of hell.* What idiots; obviously you're women, not boys. Only boys are faggots. You won't tell Nicky about this, just this once. She gets upset so easily these days. Her studies are getting to her: the freshman year of university takes a lot of concentration. Whereas your own classes are easy, as Nicky is quick to point out. You spend most of your time snapping pictures in the backyard, reading Freud, testing out new dishes. Nicky's having a harder time of it; she really doesn't need to know about this new development. And maybe you will get stronger if you keep it to yourself.

You begin to want to keep your hair to yourself. But she comes nightly now, shouting for you to throw it down, and even though each time you do what she asks, the pain never seems to go away entirely. You grow resentfully used to it. You are getting stronger. She brings you small treats, although she says she will not risk bringing you anything too heavy, such as an entire rope by itself, for fear of weakening your hair. You have been waiting to ask her this again, but you have waited until this opening she has offered you herself. "Have you brought several rope strands, then, several pieces of rope for me?"

"I forgot them," she says, slightly irritated. "But I'll remember them the next time that I come." And the next time you receive more trinkets, but no rope section. She does not speak of the rope, and you do not ask again, better to have something concrete, such as her visits, better than nothing at all. She comes, in your dreams, every night.

Nicky cries in her dreams every night. Her classes are difficult. She's worried that she's stupid. She's obsessed with the idea that the other students think she's poor white trash.

Soon, baby, soon, just relax, soon, just relax, soon all will be better, we've just got to relax and settle in. We're just homesick, we've just gotta get used to it.

Soon, baby, soon.

She is like a baby.

She cries every night.

The cloistered night itself cuts off all your length of curls and then you're crying, too. When she comes on the night that follows, you can show her nothing through the window but your shorn head. Again, you cannot hear her as she calls to you, though you are aware that she continues to come every night and at intervals during the day, when no one can see her approach. But an idea is growing in you. Your stomach grows bigger and marks develop on it and on your thighs. Your breasts grow heavy. There must be an answer, but there are no responses to your riddle. When you deliver this thought, it looks like you with soft curls like your own and you have almost prepared yourself to read and code it through when it is taken from you. Your thought has been stolen. You've fought for it; a war of wills has won it from you. Not even the sight of your lover below can warm your mind, unfreeze your skin.

*

After two months of living down in Oregon, you get a phone call. You like to talk, so you rush to answer. Your parents? Nicky's college? You playfully fight Nicky for the phone, and she wins the war for the receiver. The person on the other end is still speaking when, glassy-eyed, Nicky lets the receiver drop from her palm. You pick it up and listen to the murmuring voice for a second. *Dykes. Beasts. Rape kids, you molest them, ought to be shot. We're going to kill you...* You hang up the phone.

Nicky has her thumb between her lips. She is using your 'self-touching' technique, you see. Of course, in the circumstances you are not at all seduced. She has a distant, frozen look to her eyes that you have come to associate with people losing it. Nicky's mom had it when she'd been drinking – so she nearly always had it – and Mark had it too sometimes.

"I don't touch kids," Nicky says slowly, "I don't get it."

You look her straight in the eye. "I do, Nicky: lesbian, therefore pervert, therefore paedophile." You got the connection, alright. You saw what they were getting at. And Nicky was supposed to be so smart. When she bursts into tears and quickly stomps upstairs, presumably to sleep, you think: *No.* You are getting tired of it. Something is snapping in you, but it hasn't quite been severed. You are beginning to think that Nicky is weak. Whatever *she* had in her seemed to have been severed miles back along the road and long, too long, ago.

6. Carol

When you turn on the bedside light, you can see that Nicky's eyes are terrified. But she doesn't say anything and reaches for your embrace, the flesh on her arms warmer and more tender than a heated pillow, not dotted with sticky sweat as you supposed. You hold her for long minutes in the orange electric light until her eyes close and, lying so near, you can detect the dreaming movements beneath her lids as she falls asleep, flickering as erratically as her mind when she is conscious. And eventually you fall asleep, too, and though the room seems dry and safe and soft and cosy, there is fear lodged within it, and you know this. You know this.

You awake the next morning before Nicky, and are surprised to discover that you are still holding her in your arms, because normally one of you would have pushed the other far away by now. You look down at your bodies for a moment, lumped snugly under the covers. Your hair has grown out from the previous cutting in straight, shimmering lengths. You have brushed it regularly, remembering the rank, woody breath of it, remembering the perfumed stench of your previous hair. Now your hair is an inch or two past shoulder-length, in your eyes and splayed over the comforter, looking like the dry heat of straw. And since you had gone back to sleep with the lamp on, artificial light combines with the greyish glow of morning through the curtains to make the whole room look pretty depressing.

You slip out of bed and in your pyjamas you pad your way into the kitchen to get the paper and some hot chocolate. The tiles are cool on your feet and it is as if you can feel each tiny grain of sand separately. You can hear Nicky stirring upstairs and know that she will be down soon.

But when eventually she trails herself into the kitchen, clutching your bathrobe around her, you are stunned by her expression. Nicky's face is drawn and almost haggard. You don't feel like conversation either, so you mumble good morning, take hold of the newspaper and take a sip of your hot chocolate. You look down into the sweet mug of instant cocoa and you see the cool white teeth of marshmallows; you pluck from the syrup several melters. You feel rather cold towards her. "So what's the matter?" you say. You know that with the weird mood she's in, whatever she says to you is going to end up in an argument. She is going to be dogmatic. You know it. She always is.

But Nicky sways towards the chair, still clutching the purple robe around her. She covers her face with her hands; you notice that her knuckles are white. "Look, Carol. Do you remember the day my cousin died?"

"Vaguely," you say. You really don't want to discuss *this* again. She's always going on about her *feelings* regarding that particular day. She's never said it directly, but sometimes you get a creepy feeling that in a roundabout way, she may be blaming you. Something to do with the fact that Nicky was supposed at your house that day, though you have no idea what that has to do with her cousin drowning, and Nicky's never been too explicit about what actually did happen.

"Well, that day –" she says, then pauses.

"Yeah?" you say.

Now she starts speaking again. "You remember those camping trips we used to go on, you know, when your mom would invite me."

Of course you remember; your mom always felt kind of sorry for Nicky, so she'd ask her to come along, too. Nicky's parents never went camping or anything like that. Her mom was passed out lots of the time. Her dad worked on the Slope and only came back every two months or so. So you say, "Yeah, I remember."

"Did we always sleep in the same tent together, just you and me?"

"Come on, Nicky, you know the answer to that as well as I do." She did, too. The two of you always slept in the pup tent. But you never messed around or anything like that, really, if that's what she's getting at. You would giggle and tell each other ghost stories the whole night until your mom and dad would tell you to 'pipe down' and Brett would yell at you from the tent nearby. That always made you guys laugh even more. It was lots of fun.

Nicky reaches over, takes your mug off the table and takes a sip. You don't say anything about this theft because you don't want Nicky to get mad at you. You notice that her hand is shaking, but her eyes are looking mean.

"Nicky, I –"

She interrupts you, glaring, almost splitting in two with an anger you can't source: "The stuff with your brother, come on, you know…" Nicky breaks off her speech. "You know what I mean," she snaps. "You know exactly what I mean."

"No, I don't." You say it kind of rough, but genuinely, you're perplexed. Nicky tries to stare you down, but after several moments retreats into herself, pulls the robe tighter and walks back upstairs. She is a confusing girl. More interestingly, you didn't know you were capable of staring Nicky down. Where does she get off, anyway? You take your second sip of hot chocolate. Little white mallows popped up from dehydrated states; you can feel them all separately, tiny white columns perched on your tongue. Nicky was forever going on about your family just because hers was so fucked up, and right now you simply don't have the energy to work out exactly what she means.

Into wetness your tongue twist-flops again, plop-plop, you drain it all, wipe your mouth and secretly think

that she doesn't come by as often as before, but when she does she stares up at you – but not in her familiar wistful manner. Instead she stares levelly up at you as if she were trying to work all of this out, work out exactly why you are up there and she is on the ground. You do not bother to return her gaze, but you grow sadder and more bitter with every day that goes. Why didn't they lock her up as well, you think. Bubble-wrap her up as well. She is as much to blame as you. You won't feel sorry for her, you won't. She was always bad, in a way, even as a child she was malicious and would scratch, pinch.

Because like your mom, you've also always felt kind of sorry for Nicky, left all by herself in a house where her parents were never home. But now you're not sure. Nicky brings a lot of stuff on herself; it's like she manipulates it so it's the worst possible situation for her. Of course you still love her. Of course you do. It's just that now that you're stuck at home all the time, you're piddling minutes and then hours away until Nicky comes home from college. Still, you've completed your three community college courses by correspondence and you got 'A's on every one. You were quite proud, in particular, of your photographs of things around the house. Apparently, they showed 'originality'. You haven't told Nicky your grades, because if you're afraid of anything in relation to Nicky, it's her laughter. She thinks it's dumb that you're at the house so much; dumb that you're only doing correspondence courses and not real university classes. Still, you have a plan: next year you're taking out a loan and going to college, too.

Most of all you hate the waiting, resenting her. She can go anywhere she wants. You think. She is not bound here nor anywhere else, like you. If you were free, you would walk all the way home to the woods where first she kissed you. You are bound to her, and yes, you hold this against her. This is not a true relationship, you think, because I have no choice. It would be a true love if only you could choose from many. Out in the world. But here you are only caged. You are caged, like a monkey or a bird or a criminal or a freak exhibit or a student on a spring day or a slave or a businessman or a typist or a nun or a POW or a factory worker or a dutiful wife

or a princess in a castle, your hair again is falling down. London Bridge, London Bridge. Take the key and lock her up, lock her up. By the words she uses when she calls for you, you understand you are to let your hair rain through the window like water. You do and it reaches all but a man's height from the ground. You could count her visits in months now. If you wanted to. Swing, swing. She leaps and catches your hair, swaying. This, too, is painful. You are crying as she climbs through the window, though you come together in an embrace and your tears stop. For months she will come calling your name, and you will let your hair down as she comes. You won't not let it down. As she comes. When she comes. Whenever she comes.

You won't let Nicky down. You become the perfect girlfriend. While you've been studying modestly by correspondence all this time and are supportive in all your outward actions, Nicky has finished her first semester at university. You guys don't go home for Christmas. Instead you have a quiet meal. You cook turkey, green peas and Jello salad. The sign people don't bother you any more. All is calm. All is bright. No nightmares, few arguments. *And lock her up.* You leave your house about twice a week in January, usually for shopping. Because of this Nicky seems worried; she tries to get you out more. You can tell she blames herself, but you just turn off, turn off; let your mind go blank, your eyes go glassy; she can't get at you, no one can. You have entered the land called Haze. And you really like it there. No one can touch you; few dare to poke their fingers into numb.

One day you capture an insect together. Neither of you know what kind of insect it is but you decide to let the bug leave the room. You put the bug on your fingertip and let it crawl on the wall outside the tower window. That night you and Nicky sleep, deeply, deeply in each other's arms. Just like before. Just like before, everything is alright. Nicky's chin is heavy on your right breast. And you dream. Around four a.m. you wake up and speak sleepily to her. You tell her what you dreamt, that you saw her looking for a place, looking for the lake in the woods.

"What lake?" says Nicky, startled.

"The lake where your cousin died."

"Oh," says Nicky, "I thought you had forgotten about that. I have." Her face welds shut on the subject.

Awakening further, you feel relieved that you are safely locked in the house and not the woods. Though beautiful, the woods are unsafe, as Nicky tells you. Uncontrolled. Unknown. And when you wake up in the morning, you are both on separate sides of the bed; not even your toes are touching. Nicky's eyes are trembling beneath her lids as she clutches most of the comforter around her. You take your pillow and hold it over her head, so that a squared shadow darkens her face and neck. You lower the pillow, slowly, slowly, until it remains two or three inches above her nostrils and mouth. How easy would it be? Probably not very. Instead you cosy one foot up closer to her, stroke her toes and then kick her sharply, quickly in the shin.

"Hey!" says Nicky, waking up. She knows you've woken her suddenly, but she doesn't know you've kicked her to do it.

"I'm so sick of this," you say, "I can't go anywhere. There isn't anywhere to go."

"Oh, come on, please. Quit complaining," she says, "You're making *me* feel guilty. It's not my fault that you've locked yourself up in the house."

"But it's your fault that you don't do anything to help me."

"So quit harassing me," says Nicky. "If I stay here with you all the time, I'm locked up, too. It's not like I don't appreciate you." You give her a look. "I don't *have* to be with you. Think about it. You're lucky, girl, and you know it."

"Oh, I am," you say, absolutely as sarcastically as you can, you're a thousand scorpions gliding through syrup, "I'm very lucky." Neither of you speak for a while. You sigh. She seems to be waiting for you to say something, but you don't speak.

Here at this point she trails her fingers across your body. "You know," she says softly, "sometimes I like to see you confined. The sun doesn't reach you much. The pallor suits you. Your skin is such a pretty colour." Here she lowers her mouth to your upper legs. "Sometimes I like the idea of having you all to myself. My beautiful princess all alone in her tower." You know she is trying to be romantic, but despite your growing arousal, you feel sick.

The bug has crept back in. On the windowsill, right near your face. Because of a sudden wave of hatred you stab at the insect with your finger and leave it there on the sill while you lie with your lover.

"What you're saying reminds me of something," you whisper as you lie there with your lover and as she continues to move on you. "It reminds me of that time long ago in the woods." She stops her movements.

"No, go on," you say.

"We were in love then."

"Aren't we now?" you ask.

"Of course," she says, as her head flicks down before she goes down on you again. "But it's not the same. And anyway, you know that I don't own you; you know you're free to go right now if you want to."

For you have a choice whether or not to release your hair and accept her. Deeply and mossily your pubic hair is breathed in. She blows hot air through the miniature, tight curls.

"Do I really?" you say later, after you have succumbed to her hands and tongue. "Do I really have a choice?" If you chose not to have her come to you, you could refuse to throw down your hair. But then to have no company. No one at all; a big empty house. Just like Nicky had when she was growing up. No, thank you. You will take whatever human companionship you are offered, and this is why you are, in a sense, chained to her company. Chained and trapped. You say this aloud, but Nicky can't hear you. She's locked you up; she's locked you up.

Nicky wakes you up the next night by whimpering next to you. It is rather disgusting: the sheets are damp with sweat and you dare not sniff them for fear that it will be the pungent sort of sweat, as well. Oh god, not again, you think, but you turn on the bedside light and roll closer to her.

"What is it, sweetheart?" A little tenderness. A little tenderness is needed for this.

"A dream. A bad dream."

You try to stroke her shoulder, but she flinches and moves away from you. She doesn't want to be touched. You feel hurt, but you are not terribly surprised. It's really not personal; Nicky just gets like this sometimes. Once, she told you that the worst thing you can do is touch her after a bad dream. You feel tempted to french-kiss her to test this reaction out but, with effort, you restrain yourself. "What kind of bad dream?"

"About your brother."

"What do you mean, my brother? That's weird."

Nicky sniffs and stops crying. "You don't fucking get it, do you, Carol?"

"Nope."

"Well, fuck you." Suddenly Nicky flings herself out of bed and the blankets over you. "Fuck *you*, Carol." She grabs some clothes and is out of the bedroom, slamming the door behind her. And you once again are alone, you're chained, you're bruised, you're fully awake.

And what is she thinking, now? *A princess all alone in a tower. All alone in a tower.* It is true that she wishes other lovers, has wished them, in fact, for several months. You know about this. *But she is still lured back by you: enjoying your beauty; finding your red lips and your long, long hair exotic.* That's got to be it. Perhaps it is even your helplessness, the knowledge that without her you are diminished; you fade away. Take the key and lock her up. How would she be thinking about this? With pleasure? With exhilaration? What would be running fluid through her mind? *Perhaps her pulse and loins, quickening now at the thought of you: you are entirely hers. Only hers. And your beauty is only for her, for no one else can touch you.*

You can hear the front door slam shut as she exits. She will be thinking about what you said about being all locked up. You know how her mind works; what she will be thinking of

pictures of the slaves she has seen, with their shackles and bound feet. She is thinking: how would you look bound? And she is sick and perverse, to be thinking this. You are aware of this. Thinking of your flesh, so soft against an ankle band, how the binding might chafe at your ankles, and she's growing excited. My fair lady. My fair lady.

She does come back for lunch; she's got no classes for the rest of the day. She sits sullenly at the table, thinking only of lunch. You are aware of this. Waiting for you to serve her, which you do with ill grace. This is conceivable: that she would be thinking joyously, *and now I own you. I possess you.* And would she really be thinking something that obvious, that raw? *All alone in a tower.* She could be. Some knight in shining armour, huh? The thought of you being there, all alone, entirely in her power. *Why, you are completely mine, she would think, you are completely at my mercy and in my power. She would think of your entrapment and it would titillate her. She would grow stiff and wet against the coarse white hairs of her horse; the animal feeling this and reacting as if it is whipped, faster, faster, breaking, snapping –*

Everything you say she answers with a snap, so eventually you give up attempts at conversation and sit smouldering at the other end of the table, chewing on a piece of cheese sandwich. She will not make you cry. No, she won't. But she's trying to; she's trying to make you break. Your fucking white knight. *On the horse and whipped on speed, a fleeting remembrance might pass into her mind of when she used to stand waiting for you; of a time when it was you who had the power. You've tied her down with wiles and complaints.* She's thinking that kind of stuff. She's making you feel bad, bad, bad.

Suddenly you can't take it a second longer. You slam your fist down on the glass table, rush to Nicky and grab her face in both of your hands.

"What's going on?" You are almost pleading. "Come on, Nicky, what's the matter?" Nicky's eyes are rolling around in her head. You don't like it when it looks like people are scared of you, it makes you nervous, but this is what Nicky looks like until she pushes you away and runs to the bathroom to throw up.

She comes back, her jaw set in determination. She sits down and compliments you on your tomato soup. You are hesitant to say anything; you're going to treat this drastic mood swing gingerly, you decide. You attempt a faint smile. She flashes a weak grin back, and then her face darkens and she starts speaking very quickly about 'homophobia' and the 'harassment' of the neighbours – oddly, since it was months ago – her body leaning over the table towards you passionately, it becomes words and more words to you, *sign confronting breeders and the why don't shitty thing to do* Yes, you agree, it was a shitty thing to do.

"I really love you, Carol, you know that," says Nicky. "I'm sorry I've been weird lately, there's something weird in my head, something I'm going through –"

You break her off. Yep, it's transference, alright. Textbook case direct from your correspondence course. Transference of what, though, you have no clue. "That's okay, Nicky." It has to be okay. Nicky needs you. That's clear.

She doesn't need you. But she does return, and the next night again, and the next night again, and despite yourself, you beam from her renewed interest.

She returns that night and the next night again. Maybe I don't have the right to attack her for being free, you think. It's not her fault that you're here, but still a thought persists in the back of your mind: if only she could bring a rope with her. But she still forgets the strands, and still insists that an entire rope would be too heavy, and that your hair would break with both her and the extra weight of fibres, plummeting her to her death. Would you want that?

Would you want that? So you acquiesce. But she does not mention the rope, and you, afraid for some reason to broach the subject, are quiet. Last time you mentioned it to Nicky, she looked at you like you were crazy. What on earth are you talking about? Her face had even looked brightly curious. But you had let it lie, and had waited for more time to pass.

Some time passes. *Now maybe she is thinking constantly of the picture in her head of the shackles binding your feet; you bet she is aroused to the point of breaking, almost.* Her resentment of you grows: how can you exert this control over her? Yes, indeed, how can you? But you are still locked, plumped on top of yourself like one Russian doll inside another inside another inside another…

In a way she is as bound as you. More so, even. Your looks now beginning to repulse her, yes, you imagine that in fact she finds you dull, though probably no one else would think so. That's what she would be thinking. Yet you hold her. You have always demanded too much, wanted too much power. It must be like a spell, yes, you ask too much of her. *chafing bending pinning*

"Let's play a game," says Nicky, your lover, after she has climbed up. *The whole way up the tower on your hair. How her arms must ache.*

"That's a good idea," you say and hell, you want to say it, because sex has grown tiresome – no, boring – as of late.

"I've brought you a present," she says, and takes out a pair of iron cuffs.

"Aren't they heavy?" you say.

"No, not at all," she says. "But you could try them. Can you put them on for me?" You shrug, then clasp them around your ankles, left ankle first. She stares at you. You think: she is not staring at my legs, nor even my ankles. She is staring at the cuffs themselves.

"You look really lovely," she says. She sounds insane; you think that what she says sounds a bit off the beat; it really does not apply to you at all, as if there's a different concoction of you in her head than what you really are, something she is making up instead of looking at you for yourself.

Her hand tightens on your waist. She moves it on you slowly, with her thumb sinking into your flesh. And you both sink to the floor, sitting. You notice uncomfortably that she has one hand on her crotch, and the other on the cuffs and she is caressing the metal in much the same way as she recently caressed your waist. She keeps her eyes straight ahead. She is not seeing me, you think.

With a graceful movement she pushes her hand into her pants and what is more, up inside herself, touching what you imagine – for you are certainly familiar with these parts of her – is the beginning of the curved bowl of flesh inside her, touching the ridges which you always imagine are dark red or plum coloured – though of course you've never quite seen this deeper interior of Nicky. She begins masturbating quickly until her body cramps and the droplets of ejaculate fling towards the window, sparkling but also slightly viscous, like water touched with a thumbprint from a shell's interior. She takes her hand from her trousers with an equally graceful movement.

There is a pause. "You going to do something for me, too?" you say. "Are you going to touch me like that? And not just bind me up?"

"Of course," she might say, but looking displeased.

The calculation of bondage has become the final straw; you can't take it living with perversities like that, who could? And what has become of Nicky, your Nicky? And if you have been locked up, well, you are going to unlock yourself, starting now. You pack a sports bag full of clothes and toiletries and a couple of other small things and you step outside the house. It is a cool day in an Oregon winter – which feels like Alaskan summer. Nicky is at college, not due back for a while. Across the road and further down the street, you suddenly recognise the old couple who had put the sign on your front lawn. You are neighbours. You still wonder why they stopped giving you and Nicky a hard time. Well, you'll never have the chance to become close friends, because now you're skipping town. Such a shame.

You are shaking all over; it has been three weeks since you last left the house. For the last few weeks, you've had groceries delivered, though you've told Nicky that you've been going out for them.

You feel like you will faint from the heat. But the weather's not so hot: it's you. You place one foot on the asphalt of the driveway – Nicky has had sole use of your car lately and she's got it today, too, damn her – and try to raise it again, but it feels sticky, although eventually you follow it with another step. This continues until you stand on the sidewalk.

You look behind yourself. It has taken you ten minutes to get from the door down the driveway. You look down to the end of the street to where you have to walk and keep your vision focused on passing the evil couple's house.

Funnily, it all gets easier and quicker, and when eventually you turn the corner on the next street, your steps are energetic – jaunty, even. You find yourself able to breathe more freely and by this time you can even look back to your own street with clarity and feel not even a tug. A couple cars beep their horns at you, but you do not pay attention to these people. You do not wiggle your ass; you do not step one foot directly in front of the other.

You don't need a car. You've got money in your pocket. So you walk directly to the bus station and get on a Greyhound for Seattle. That's what you do.

7. Ellen

Susan didn't tell stories. But she did tell fibs. She lied to me. She said that my orders were bacon, eggs and two toasts, when actually it was one bagel, plain, and two double-tall lattes. She got me fired from jobs; she made my relationships break down. You could say it was because I was irritable, that I was manipulative, that I twisted and turned my way into the stomach linings of my boyfriends and girl-friends until they didn't know how to cut themselves clear of the hooked, clinging viper that was me – and that would be true. But it was also true that while Susan was the poet, the seer, the sibyl, the ora-cle of the first degree, I was the one who did the cutting away: I peeled away layers, I washed away films of dirt and dust until everything reached perfect clarity. Perfect, perfect, perfect clarity.

But what clarity needs is the story behind it, the anecdote com-plete with concluding moral. The epic szyzhet sweep, the credits at the end, the Gordion knot undone with one clear cut and no fibres dan-gling limply, no spare ends or loose vines – just the pure, beautiful lust of a razor-sharp blade. A hand clap in the middle of the mind to wake it up. More immediate than a fire's burn or even ice-water thrown quickly over flesh. So let me continue with this story of Nicky and Carol, and I'll see how far it gets me. I'll see how far it gets Susan. Which is me. Which is her till she cracks, and me until I get back to the story, back to the beautiful sensation of – I don't know what. I don't know what.

Nearly six months had passed since the two occasions on which I chanced to meet Carol and Nicky: first at the coffee-house, and later the same night at the Jag. These months had followed the usual old patterns, and within me Susan had remained quiet. I dated a guy for a while but that finished after Christmas. The sex was okay, he was nice enough, but I kept on with him a lot longer than I normally would have mainly because I knew it got on Jackie's nerves to have a guy in the house. But she couldn't say anything, either, after all her proselytising on the future of a new queer nation, where every bisexual genderfuck known would be acceptable. I liked to test Jackie's politics – it's not the nicest of games to play on your roommate, but it kept me from being bored. And still there was no word from Susan. I felt that I had done something wrong the day I had seen Nicky and Carol, had somehow missed my chance, but there was no way of knowing that for sure.

I had lost my coffee-house job and now worked in a pizza parlour, where I sometimes went flying to islands, to planets and clouds through the flexy-bendy fluorescent straws through which customers sucked their milkshakes. I didn't keep my jobs for long. I didn't keep my relationships for long, either, which was not due to a bisexual promiscuity, but rather to the fact that sometimes my sweethearts just go floating and flying away, they etherise and I can't hold on to them no matter how I grasp, they're ghosts. *Forget about them,* I was always waiting for Susan to say, but she was silent.

Working today, I balanced two Canadian Bacons with Pineapple and delivered them safely to the appropriate table. Why had these girls stuck in my mind? Was it Susan's suggestions, or had they actually looked familiar? I had never even found out where they were from. At the Jag, I had slunk over to them for the second time that day to strike up a conversation. I wasn't going to, but Susan was urging me, *do it, do it,* so I did. Then she told me to leave them alone, so I did what she suggested then, too. I don't always take on her suggestions in my head. Only when I feel like it. Only when I want to. Only when it feels right.

"Table of one in Section B," I was told.

"Okay." My hands were blistered from the hot flat serving pans. And it was then that I saw my serendipity. When coincidences are so perfect, they cease to be coincidental; it could only be fate that caused the jaynegirl Carol to be sitting here, right now, today in my particular

Kathleen Kiirik Bryson

section. *Say hello to her.* And Carol's return marked the return of Susan, as well. *Go on over there,* said Susan. *Come on, do it.*

"Hi," I said. I gave her a sweet smile. "Happy New Year." Okay. That was pushing it, maybe – we were already well into the second week of 1989. "Can I take your order? Our special today is three slices with a large Coke and extra garlic bread for $5.95, or two extra toppings if you buy a Super-Size Personal Pizza." I was well aware of my boss listening with one ear from the cash register; she had already had some complaints about me and I wanted to make sure I got my spiel right. Carol would understand the code with perfect clarity. Honed. Clear. She would understand my meaning purely, even past silvery and fluent slipping... she would understand my secrets like caffeine shot straight to her hot brain, breaking through ice. Whoosh.

Carol was squinting at me like she was trying to recognise who I was. I thought that was clever, and proof that not only did she know the code, but also that she knew my boss was watching me and wanted to be careful. I respected her for that. She was that clever. She was clever enough.

I felt myself noticing things I hadn't before noticed on our previous meetings. Her eyes were a crystal-blue Technicolor but, I noted, all-in-all numb until they became animated with specific thought, such as when she ordered the two-topping special. A rucksack lay beside her feet and I knew this would irritate my boss, who disliked vagrants. I smiled at her; I was happy that she had come back to me and I knew it was right. Her left eyebrow had a bit of a twitch when she returned my smile. I felt myself adding up in desperation all the details I could glean at the moment. When I brought her extra garlic and black olives Personal Pizza, I slipped down into the chair beside her, and felt like I was poised just before that swoop of burn or freeze would hit me, a moment Susan would approve of, the superdrug between my right and left ears.

I was poised just before I sat down next to Carol and took off like a sled down the hill to the lake; I could feel my face burning as I

– 120 –

prepared myself. Poised. The imagery was from Susan: that was the kind of sequence she liked to place so skilfully in my head. I thought the memories were my own and real, but they could have been forged by Susan in a cunning moment. The pictures came rushing at me: a sled ridden on dark ice down the hill with dark ice to the lake with dark ice. I had always been the champion who pushed the sled back up again, cheeks on fire. *Be a hero. Come on.* The small grey twinkle of silvered snow, the top white crust of fresher snow, I remembered that. And I always remembered the speed down on the black ice; runners screeching on dark icestones. To the left was the forest marked by old shadows, snow-dipped to surfeit and now with the new bruise of shadows again. Between the husk of whispering was jettish sky, to the right the frozen of the lake. In all matters it was a stately oblong, solely a potential, but for all practical purposes it was only a frozen flat and no more than that. No more than that. And I was at the top, the pinnacle once more. Where had Susan taken me?

I had to be here in the present; I had to push Susan back; I had to concentrate on what Carol was saying. She was speaking almost as soon as I slipped down next to her. "I hope you'll forgive me for asking, but aren't you called Ellen?" I smiled at her but didn't say anything. I didn't need to. Her eyes had darkened; they were ashy-blue, almost a bruised colour, like lupines. There are trees whose blue branches hold an even darker tinge. There are trees which even at this time are distant, half-forgotten through the hiss of spruce.

She was talking again, but the words swam over me. I was too busy noticing certain things about her, the scarlet marks of her lipstick on her corduroy jacket, the dangerous earrings she wore. She would think I was a friend this time, and it would be true. Last time I wasn't a friend to her, not a good friend. I had lost the two of them too quickly. For her, I smiled widely: my face cracking, my teeth chipping down on sensate enamel, silver holes burning out in my fillings, rotting organic decay nudging on either side of my mouth, as the embryo cavities were not yet fully formed. I was beginning the fall down again. I continued with the falling-down. Straight into the arms of the ice. Down the road glacé with stonings frozen under *frozen under*, tiny rocks peeping up through their windows in the hill. A sheet-glass/thin-slats glaze. And then I stopped. I was... Silent.

She was very beautiful. I couldn't remember precisely how Nicky looked, other than a perfect butch fifties prototype. Carol referred to her with a snarl drooping off her face and eventually I realised that Nicky had not been nice to her. But still I said nothing, because I knew instinctively that my smile would cheer Carol as much as any comforting words might do. She was opening her heart to me, I was able to come into warmth, into the warm yellow kitchen of her pizza-parlour soul.

Going-in, the warmth, the warmth of this sheltered room in which we sat. I distanced myself from what Susan ached to show me. The result was all forest trees united, covered, the branches clad like frosting postcards – a retreat from frigid itching towards yellow, red and warmth. I picked up a laminated menu and ran my hands over it, a simple grounding device. I breathed into my palms, grazing them lightly against my open mouth. Always, as I touched it, my skin felt cool to my fingertips and to the end of my tongue. These were the only points of heat that I could move. Or wiggle. I watched her earrings slowly move. From out the window radiating I could see the restaurant's yellow squares, warmths, panes. Which did happen to be cold lights: the winter chilling did not change to heat even in a bath of illumination. To get that feeling, it was necessary to step out on the thick of it, so eventually it was time, I stepped, *Silent. Don't move.*

I stopped myself just before I walked out on the lake. I could feel Susan's retreat. I was in yellow. Carol's smile glowed as her mouth took in the black olives, extra garlic, oregano- and basil-laced smoothed tomatoes, crunchy yeasty chewy crust. I brushed the snow off me now, laughing; kissed her on the cheek. The cheek was flushed, like mine. Enter in the kitchen, packed with cushions, fire-warmed. A bright puddle of flame added garnish to the process. I was in fire now, not freeze.

She was quoting Nicky: "So, she said, 'Carol...'" It suddenly clicked that I had them in my grasp again. And what did Susan want me to do? *Susan?* But she was silent. So how far did I want to jump into the lake? How deep did I want to go? Deep. Very far. A cold *burn*, that's how deep I wanted it.

I was still sitting down at Carol's table and smiling at her, feeling beatific peace glowing all throughout me, shining out through my pores like a flashlight in a tin can studded with holes. I felt so good that she felt so good in her taste of deliciousness, the Coca-Cola swarming in her mouth, the plumped black olives heading towards her gut. Carol's words hummed into my head, *Do you* there were a couple words there, *know* another one, *of a place where I can stay.* Suddenly I realised she had asked me a question. No longer poised on the brink, I was sinking down, back down to the restaurant table on which I saw again her nestled question curled up, its tiny heart pumping fast and furiously away through the sheen of its fur. That's more power to me, I could sink cuddling into the padding pillows of the restaurant chairs while my toes did their warming-up. How quickly I would drink the steaming, spicy cola I would be served. Snap the pizza crust with my sharp teeth, snap. It was always beautiful and sensual after a fall.

"Shh..." I told Carol. "Of course, you come to stay with me." A light, a brilliant light, peaked in me at that exact moment and I felt a tremendous joy and all of Susan's vast approval. I had said exactly the right thing. Everything was exactly right. I felt the swoop then, felt my gathered senses break in half, exposing their difficult essence under the brittle sheath which covered and protected them from air. Someone would touch their meat soon, someone would touch their softness which opened up raw and fresh. In the meantime, though, my senses thus exposed, soared. What ecstasy. What a scale with which to begin an ascent!

And finally, I let Susan back inside: I felt the snow crystals in a thaw throughout my hair, running down my face now as water as I looked out through the window that still spilled lights on the snow.

And it was winter, see a blackness of the sky with astral stones across it, the glittered stars like flakes themselves except spread thick across the black, and spread further than the meshed stars layering the grey of ground. I remembered that. The vision from the pizza parlour spiralled out to this; to iced heavens, then it spiralled back absolutely into me in the sweating room. Into me. In to me. Warmth/Red/Cold/dagger of icicle/red-blood rush and warmth. *All drunk in by me, In to, Into sucked in the bones of eye, me, I'm warm. I'm spinning. I'm cold. I'm watching.*

> *I'm silent breathing twitching.*
> *breath*

We walked down the less genteel side of Capitol Hill to my place. I was conscious of Carol's presence there beside me. Her long, bright hair and her curious blends of vanilla and other perfumed scents. Her dark red lipstick cherrying her mouth. I observed her slowly lick her bottom lip – I was sure it was unintentional, but a jolt of sex slivered at my cunt, nonetheless. The girl was lust, personified.

I couldn't now remember why it was that her girlfriend had impressed me so much more than her before. I had obviously missed such important details as the cool softness of pale flesh, the frosty sprinkling of freckles on her nose, her smoky lupine eyes, the scent of sex that rose up from her. I had probably thought at the time that Nicky had been a much more obvious and accessible fuck. Through my sheer greediness for an easy lay I had probably messed up all of Susan's plans. I had been neither subtle nor thoughtful. It irritated me that I should be so superficially transparent. I would not be this time. I'd keep my senses tuned for undercoats, grace notes, overtones, back-flavours, partialities, blends, subtext. I'd take it slow. I'd wait.

I was silent to Carol, but Susan was chattering away in my head. *That's right. It's going well. Now you must remember and react.* Remember what? React how? I had no idea.

We passed through Seattle's Easter-egg collection of freshly painted Victorian houses, to looming tenements and then finally to houses once more, unpainted and drab sisters of the yuppie-owned buildings further up the hill. This was my neighbourhood: a predominantly black community, with slumming white artist-kids or broke white queers. I suppose I fit the latter categories. I was mostly white, and mostly queer.

I had had an affair once with a rich white girl who lived in the sky-scrapers up on 13th, and from the top of the hill you could see all the way to Bellevue. Seattle was purportedly built like Rome on seven hills, and from the skyscraper view that time I could see not only Queen Anne hill, but also an extended Elliott bay, both lakes and all the way past my own house in the Central District. I could see how green Seattle was, and I appreciated this in a city – there were few places, I had discovered, that offered both a sense of nature and the city anonymity that I so often wanted. In Seattle, too, I could smell the salt and rising rain on the Puget Sound water, scents I had known since childhood in Alaska and still craved. It wasn't raining yet, but it was going to, sure as sin. I considered sharing these thoughts of home with Carol as we walked but hesitated, knowing the context would be lost.

As we came to the block on which I live, I turned to Carol and smiled. "Where are you from, then?"

"A little town in Alaska. You wouldn't have heard of it."

"Really?" I stopped walking and looked closely at Carol. A hell of a coincidence. Maybe there was more to Susan's wild visions than I thought. "What's the name of it?"

"Little Novgorod." Her tone was clipped and short. Carol didn't seem to want to reveal much about her origins.

"Wow." I was stunned.

"Have you heard of it, then? That's pretty unusual in itself."

"Well," I hesitated, searching for my key as we approached the sec-tioned house in which I lived. "No, the weird thing is, I lived for quite a while not so far outside Little Novgorod. In a... community out in the woods. Outside of town. I guess you could say I spent my school-days there."

"McAlester's Children's Home," Carol stated baldly, as I unlocked the front door. The light was on in the kitchen.

"Yeah, but the orphan side of things, not the reformatory," I assured her.

"Hmm," was all she said, as I led her through the cluttered hallway to my room. "You're right. That *is* weird." I could hear her breath quickening as she spoke, and I wondered if this was due to nervous-ness or arousal. How far would this girl go? What kind of games would she let me play? *Remember.*

As we passed the kitchen I paused to step in and turn off the light, which was when I saw Jackie sitting there reading. "Oh," I said, "sorry. I didn't realise you were in."

Jackie raised one eyebrow and smiled, closing her book. I looked at the title: *Bright Lights, Big City*. It was *my* book, off the bookshelf in *my* bedroom. I would talk to her about that later. I watched Jackie's quick appraisal of Carol, and Carol's reaction to her. Oh, so Carol liked them butch. I was beginning to feel some misgivings about tonight. *Wait,* Susan told me.

"Have fun," Jackie commented and, with my book, withdrew more slowly than was necessary to her bedroom, not breaking her gaze from Carol's. Jackie irked me; it wasn't cool to try to pick up your roommate's tricks, especially when nothing yet had happened. Jackie had obviously struck out earlier tonight and was testily taking it out on me.

After Jackie closed her bedroom door, I leaned over Carol. I took her hair in my hand and lifted it slightly. I was just slightly taller than her and I leant down to touch my tongue to the fine hairs on her neck. Carol turned around, her chest trembling with too-swift breaths.

My hand was still in her hair as Carol swivelled to look at me just before she moved to me and laid her stained lips of tropical red on mine. My mouth opened for her. I felt my hand release from her hair and we kissed and then kissed longer in the hallway until I eventually slid away.

"Wait," I said. I took a step backwards from Carol. "Just wait." I led her to my bedroom and closed the door behind us. We both sat down, shyly on the bed. *Wait,* Susan reminded me.

Carol took my face in her hands and started kissing me again, and I felt tears begin to roll in fragile spheres down my face. I did not anticipate this particular detail. I didn't want to wait, but I felt a wave of intense sadness rise within me. For some reason, I was being laid wide open by this woman, and I wasn't sure I liked it. I had instead envisioned semi-kinky games of minor bondage with scarves or something mild. I had been looking forward to Carol's tentative expression when I would first suggest this, followed by coy daring and finally unexpected excitement. I had planned on savouring all the predictable nuances of a vanilla virgin. But now I found myself sobbing instead and it was I who was as vulnerable as a child, with Carol's arms around me.

"Ssh..." she whispered to me. "What's wrong?" I looked up for a moment and was startled to see a look of resentment cross her face momentarily before it disappeared in a genuine sympathy. Perhaps she had played this particular role before. Maybe she was the oldest child, or maybe she had alcoholic parents. I didn't care.

"Susan," I sobbed, grabbing onto all the flesh she held before me: her encased breasts, her soft arms. I rocked myself into her.

"Shh..." she said, holding me and soothing me. "Who's Susan?"

But I didn't answer and instead I let myself slip into her embrace. I liked this feeling of being mothered and comforted; I wailed out and it felt more cathartic than all the games I'd ever played in bed. I didn't even care what Jackie would say if she heard my cries.

"Shh –" said Carol. "There, there." She stroked her fingers through my short straight hair and then her motions changed. It was not what I expected, because she was not maternal; she twisted her mouth onto mine and I felt the viciousness of sex bite at me once again. I sat up straight and kissed her back, kissed her so hard that it was I who plundered her. I would have the upper hand. She would not get away so easily this time. I shoved her on the bed and she writhed beneath me. I put my hands under her shirt and up against her mountainous breasts. She had fabulous tits and I tore at her bra; I wanted to feel flesh and only flesh and I wanted her nipples poking stiff into my palms.

Carol groaned, and I rubbed peremptorily at her sex before I thrust three fingers up her wet cunt and then, much more slowly and with her encouragement, my hand curved into a fist. She rocked herself on me, and I made myself deliberate and careful with her – fisting is not dangerous but it does take skill. My own crotch was soaking and I thought, well, if I still want the scarves later then I could wait – we had all night. I said it aloud: "We've got all night, don't we?" *slow twitch-drunk and spinning cold and watching wait – breaths –*

Carol looked up at me. "I don't know." *Wait –*

8. Nicky

Ever since Carol had left, the weather had been wonderful. It didn't suit Nicky's mood, but there you were. She felt fragile most of the time, as if she were just waiting for someone to say the wrong word, the black magic word that would turn her crazy, the word that would make her absolutely lose it. She didn't know what that one word would be, but she suspected it might be 'Carol'.

Nicky sat on the porch steps, her fingers alternately running over the smooth tin of a soft-drink can and then turning it with rigid digits, twisting and crushing it. And then feeling the smoothness again, straightening the tin. Can aside, it was awful to think there was something she could not fix. But there had been nothing she could do about Carol's agoraphobia. She had the opposite affliction: when Carol had been here, Nicky felt trapped, needing to get out. But even then she had retained a tenderness towards Carol, suspected that at some level she was still in love with the thick bleached hair, the false eyelashes, the soft voice. The spell of Carol's soft arms holding her, holding her deep down when she had bad dreams and couldn't sleep.

Nicky realised she was close to cutting herself on the tin. Too sharp. She put it to the side and laid it down on the porch. Without warning, her eyes began to water; she had to blink rapidly. Down the road, someone was burning trash and grass – maybe the assholes who had placed that sign right smack in the front yard. She ran her palm over the wooden step she sat on. Next to her was a little pile of rocks she had collected absent-mindedly, picking them up from the ground near her. They now made up a little pyramid. She didn't know why she had done this – it was an old nervous habit of hers and she hadn't done it for years.

It had been a week yesterday since Carol had left. And yesterday Carol's mom had called and Nicky hadn't known what to tell her. *Your daughter's gone missing, Mrs. Flanagan.* No. Of course not. Anyway, the phone call meant that Carol hadn't gone straight back to Alaska. Nicky had said that Carol was asleep in their room, but that didn't seem like a good thing to say, since Carol's parents were sure to try again today. Nicky stared glumly out from the porch. In fact, it had been a damn stupid thing to say, because the next thing Carol's mother asked was if they shared a bedroom, wasn't that kind of cramped? She told Carol's mom she had meant Carol's room. *Don't worry, because we have plenty of space.*

Plenty of space. Space. Carol was afraid of it; Nicky had thought she wanted it and now she wasn't sure. Carol's arms tight round her as she slept. Tight. Safe. Space. Nicky felt a salty tear slip into her mouth before she admitted she was weeping. Wet. Soft. Safe. She buried her head in her hands. She had ruined everything. Nicky's shoulders shook as her sobs took over her body, echoing deep in her head, deep in her head, deep in her head; she couldn't stand it.

She was crying with abandon, her head still buried when she felt a hand on her shoulder *slash ash scratch-pinch-rip* She had always thought she would scream when this moment came, but all she saw now was bleached, heady terror; she kept her arms around her face, *white terror couldn't see* Smoke curled quickly in between her teeth; it was happening so fast, faster than she heard the voice connected to the hand, now she was scrambling to get away from the hand, half-crawling, fast, but the voice which came with the hand was soft, it was Carol's voice saying *Nicky, are you okay, Nicky, Nicky* – and though Nicky was still shaking herself safe of the sticky hand, she stumbled, fell on the porch and found herself looking up into the worried face of Carol.

"Nicky, are you okay?" Carol said again, her hand on Nicky's shoulder again, and this time Nicky didn't flinch and Carol's arms went around her and held her tight. Safe.

Nicky was safe in Carol's perfumed softness. She looked up with her tear-stained face to meet Carol's gaze full on this time, as an adult looks at another adult. "You came back." Carol nodded slightly. "I'm glad you did." Nicky kissed Carol the way she knew Carol liked: deep and rough. The way Carol didn't usually kiss back. But now Carol was kissing roughly, too, all the way upstairs to the bedroom.

After sex Nicky drifted in Carol's arms, happy but still not knowing exactly why Carol had left; she also couldn't remember why she had ever wished that Carol would. If they both shared this selective amnesia, perhaps there was still a chance of pleasure, of things not getting too fucked up. Her earlier panic had released all her fears; Nicky now drifted fearlessly towards sleep on Carol's breast, no longer afraid of anything: serial killers, fires, vampires, worse. No longer afraid. She had all she wanted: the taste of Carol on her fingers, caught in her hands.

Carol was talking. Nicky floated on in the bed to the background of Carol's murmuring, no longer sure what she was babbling about, not listening to Carol's talk of revelations and her trip – she had gone up to Seattle by Greyhound, that much Nicky gathered. But she just let herself flow in Carol's arms now; she was happy. She was happy, wasn't she; and when was the last time Nicky had been happy and not worried? She wasn't sure. The scent of Carol was vanilla and warm yeast. Nicky felt love-sweet-love and all the mush that goes with it. Although she wasn't listening to Carol's explanations for her departure, she felt sure that she would be able to accept them whatever they were. For all made sense, here she lay with Carol again, so now all could be right in their world.

Later that day they drove the car out to the shopping district. It was air-conditioned inside the mall of department stores and small boutiques and Nicky felt the sweat cooling on her body. Carol headed for the cosmetics department as soon as they had passed through the doors. Typical, thought Nicky, but this week she was determined to think it with affection. She caught up later as Carol was admiring the glistening wares of a shoe shop. "Nice," offered Nicky, envisioning

Carol stomping about in a pair of the shiny shoes. They were like the boots and high-heeled shoes the more dangerous girls of Portland wore. She watched Carol's lips move with her speech. Nicky thought, I've seen shoes like that before in magazines. I like them.

Carol's lips continued their journey, but Nicky didn't understand what she was talking about. Still standing outside, she looked inside the shoe store and a square of light from glass ceilings of the mall hit the back wall of the hollowed-out space, where there was a rack of clothes and shoes. She went closer to the window. Jewellery and post-cards, perfumes and feathers. *A pair of black high heels, glorious.* She had always wished Carol would wear some shoes like those. They were so vampy and old-fashioned. So falsely feminine. *Stop.* Not this store. *No.* She'd drown.

"Come on, let's go in." Nicky dragged Carol into the boutique. Carol looked surprised: probably because Nicky was not the greatest fan of shopping. Nicky was hoping Carol would buy that pair of shoes in the window, but Carol was looking at other boots and shoes – shiny patent-leather pumps with three-inch stiletto heels, a red-trimmed pair that were as dark and as detailed as if they were lingerie or corsets for the feet. In the shop as well were necklaces and shiny pieces of glass mood-rings. I feel like I've been here before, thought Nicky. It reminds me of something. Things which shift and change...

She had to stop looking. There were greeting cards, too – vaude-ville, made of shellacked postcards and yellowed sheet music. On the cards were old photos from the turn of the century, women with chilly, staring eyes. Vintage. Judging from their expressions, they could be dying or already dead. Of course they were dead. If they were twenty then, they'd be well over a hundred and ten by now, in 1989. They were as distant and receding as raindrops in a lake, their influ-ence growing fainter with every moment that passed...

Nicky turned away from their eyes and looked at the rack of jew-ellery instead; she would soon be slipping. But her eyes drew her back to these old representations of women with their wiles and all the other things she hated. She peered at one of the greeting cards. The costume on the woman must have been worth a lot, complete with delicate eyelets, the proper whalebone stays at the proper time – if someone used this they would have the perfect figure. But it was false. All lingerie, all sexy shoes were false. A sham. *Now you're slipping. You better wake up. You better wake up.*

All the shoes in the store squiggled and blurred before Nicky's eyes; she rubbed at her lids to wake herself up out of the fog. *wake up wake up wake up* The trees couldn't speak, so it couldn't be the whispering trees; she was in treeless, dry suburbia. But she couldn't rub the sleep out of her eyes, instead she found herself here in this boutique with Carol, her hand on a shoe with a heel like a pickaxe, a sheen like a beetle. A woman's heeled shoe which was the most perfect, terrible evil object she had ever seen and which hurt her eyes.

"Are you okay?" asked Carol, "Are you too hot?"

"No, I'm fine," said Nicky. "I'm just fine. Look at these shoes here, Carol. They're perfect, so trendy – they'd look great on you."

"Think so?" Carol was doubtful.

Slipping. Slipping.

perfect for Carol or even perfect for you, these little sharp shoes, and these costumes and feathers and pearls and rings and the cold staring eyes of the women... You take as many as you can – look, you've got to get the shoes at least, for you not for Carol, for you this time, for you the poison beneath them is gorgeous for you

"I think they're fucking beautiful, Carol. I'll buy them for you if you're not sure." They were nearing the last of their Permanent Funds and Nicky's student loan. But she had cash in her jacket pocket, the monthly shopping money she had forgotten to hand over to Carol this morning. They had a lot of food stocked up. Cans, boxes, frozen meals. Carol had to find a job eventually, anyway. Nicky would get the money back sooner or later.

The Shoes. Black and perfect and shiny. Nicky wanted to get them in a room all by themselves, take them under the covers with her and stroke them, feel them, own them. They were her shoes. But what she would say, to get them close to her, was that these shoes were intended for Carol.

"Well, alright. I've just never seen you get so excited about clothes, that's all."

But she never asked. Nicky was slipping now and annoyed, forgetting her relationship resolutions now, but she didn't care. Slipping into falseness, slipping into moist femininity, *you know what happens if you stay down too long, don't you   Not the trees – bubbled-drowned wet flesh*

"So what's the hurry then?" Carol asked, as if she somehow knew the importance of the Shoes.

"No hurry, I just think they'd look good on you." But it was urgent, wasn't it? It was most important that Nicky bought the beautiful, evil, feminine shoes. Most important. But how could she express it? Carol didn't know how close they both were to drowning, how close...

look at this postcard, these lovely shoes and the corset on this woman – they tell a story, too   do you know this story   do you know how this story goes? it goes like this: beneath beauty there is poison, but if you can immerse yourself in it, then you'll be released from pressure – you'll be soft, you won't be forced to think – the stiff shoes have ossified the softness, pinned it down inside a beetle-shell of patent leather, but in the leather pocket is still softness, and softness is so easy and so tempting do you know how this story goes

"I just want," Nicky carefully explained, "to get you something special. To make up for everything. To celebrate a new start." She felt relieved. It sounded genuine and it was, in a sense.

and you'll start slipping soon,   they're perfect, look at the heels, four inches if they're one, black leather   so perfect – and look, they're just your size   lovely witchy ones with the points showing   glass-heart necklaces flashing jewellery lovely smooth scalloped patent leather ones

I know, I know, you're coming towards them, you're picking them up   you're coming

The mall grew hotter. At home, of course, it would have been freezing on a January day like today, but even in summer it would have made up for it by being sharp. The trees would have held her. The trees were all sharp. They would have woken her up from the gloss she was being clogged down in. But you make your own choices and she had made a choice to leave. Carol was her only real link to home, so sometimes she'd grab Carol's chin and look hard into her eyes. But she'd never find an answer at these times, only another person, an alien staring back at her. Carol was looking at her now, actually, but as always, Carol's timing was badly wrong. Nicky was going down in pure coagulation. She was going to bury herself in all the superficiality, until her very flesh became plastic and dulled, with nothing sharp in it. *Wake up. Wake* – Perfumes, lotions, shoes. She could learn quite a bit from Carol on that front. Nicky was a quick study.

She looked Carol in the eyes. "So, will you let me buy you those shoes?"

Carol seemed happy at this request, obviously she had not expected that Nicky actually would buy them. "Oh, thanks, that's so sweet." She gave Nicky's shoulder a squeeze, very reluctant still to show any real affection in public places.

"That's okay, you owe me." And Nicky winked at Carol, pinching her bottom quickly and slyly. She pressed her up behind the counter, out of the sight of the sales assistant, whose commission-gleaming eyes were fixed on the cash register. The four-inch, gloss-licked shoes were expensive.

"Ouch!" squealed Carol, coyly, and the sales assistant looked up momentarily. Nicky looked up at the counter, too, and saw again the spit-clear glass necklaces and the glass mood-ring baubles, full of tiny imperfections and bubble-flaws which did not at all detract from their glisten. The sales attendant was still looking at her cash register totals.

"That will be $350," she cooed with an over-courteous smile. "Would you like anything else?" Something flashed then in Nicky's mind, but she answered *no*.

The sales lady put the shoes in a crepe-lined box and then deposited it in a plastic bag with a large, satisfying *thump!* Carol squeezed Nicky's arm again, quite excitedly. She might have wanted the shoes anyway, thought Nicky, even without encouragement.

"Cash or charge?" lipsticked the sales attendant. Nicky fondled the outside of the plastic bag. *soon*

"Cash." She handed the bills over to the attendant. Carol looked worried, for a moment. "It's okay," Nicky reassured her. "We can afford it. I checked. Besides, this is a little bit I put aside. It's my money, and my treat." Well, that was the end of this year's student loan money and probably the end of groceries for the rest of the month too, but what the hell, she couldn't remember the last time she had had such a strong compulsion. Except for maybe a minute ago.

The sales lady deposited the plastic bag in Carol's hands, wondering, no doubt, what kind of sugar mamma Carol had landed herself with. *It takes all kinds, Judy,* Nicky could hear her saying to her friend from accounting that night over after-work drinks, *it takes all kinds.* Nicky felt again the atmosphere of artificially cooled air circling in on her in the room. She and Carol headed for the door.

A security guard stepped in front of them. Nicky's heart jolted. "I'm afraid I'm going to have to ask to see your bags, ladies," he said in a friendly tone.

"What?" Carol was outraged. "What kind of shit is this? Nicky, what the fuck!" But Nicky, frozen, couldn't move to defend either of them. The security guard slid a hand down deep into the olive-green plastic bag which held the shoes Nicky had just purchased, his hand coming up dripping with several glass mood-rings, the 1970s type that had a resurgence of popularity perhaps five years previous, and now seemed to be fashionable once again. "What the hell... there must be some mistake –" Carol whirled around, upset, looking for support from Nicky. But Nicky still couldn't speak. A small crowd had gathered and Carol's cheeks were growing redder and redder.

"I'm going to have to ask you ladies to come with me to the back office, now," said the security guard, politely. Numbly, they both followed him through the onlooking and unfriendly, curious faces to the back of the store and through a door that the security guard had to first unlock. They were ushered inside, followed by the guard and an immaculately accessoried and kempt middle-aged woman, tan-weathered and pretty, whom Nicky assumed must be the manager. The door clicked behind the woman, audibly.

The manager's voice was chilly.

"I don't think," she said, "as the cash purchase was considerable and the three rings only sale items of ninety-nine cents each, that we will have to involve the police. But," she leaned forward, her perfectly bleached and coiffed head dipping down to look straight at Nicky and Carol, and said icily, "I would like to make it absolutely clear that neither of these two girls are welcome in this store again." Carol didn't say a word this time, probably struck dumb, Nicky figured, by the ageing and besuited spectacle of what she would look like herself when she was fifty-five.

And Nicky had nothing to say at all.

They were both quiet at first as Nicky drove the car home, Carol's fingers tightly clutching the olive-coloured bag. She seemed distracted. It's been four minutes, thought Nicky, I'll give her another two before she bursts out with something.

The silence lasted only one more minute.

"But Nicky!" Carol's voice was miserable, half-pleading. "You didn't really take those rings, did you?"

"No, of course not," Nicky soothed Carol, comfortingly. "They must have slipped off the counter, or the sales lady maybe knocked them off into the bag." Nicky's heart was beating steadily now, a healthy slow beat. She manoeuvred the next right-hand turn carefully at the red light.

She was very conscious of the green bag Carol still clasped as they unlocked the front door of their house once they made it home. But

Carol appeared to have forgotten the importance of its contents, as she dumped it unceremoniously by the telephone table and rubbed her forehead.

"I've got a headache," she said. "I have to go lie down for a while." She didn't look Nicky in the eye as she tripped her way upstairs, closing the door behind her. Nicky heard with relief the click for which she was forever listening where doors were concerned.

She picked up the green bag and walked softly to the living room. She set it next to her college book-bag and sat down on the couch. From her book-bag she withdrew a magazine and placed it next to her on the couch, and then she stuck her hand into the green plastic bag and slowly drew out the box, which she put next to the magazine.

Nicky listened carefully. The upstairs bedroom door hadn't opened; Carol was probably asleep. When she opened the magazine she first noticed the large, somewhat glistening pink breasts, bulbous ornaments hanging off the torsos, breasts should be smaller and flatter, she felt, judging from the body sizes. The tits were obviously false and added on, like bulky refrigerator magnets. Added on. She felt a dart of fear that Carol would come in to the room, right now. What would she say? Nicky's hand moved on and then into the box, removing the high-heeled shoe. She touched herself until she was wet, her free hand alternating between the spiralled, almost regal, twist of the black pin-up girl shoes and the magazine pin-ups themselves, shaven and bald. Smooth. Dull. No hard edges. She listened for the opening click of the door upstairs. She was living art, not life. And if she drowned herself enough in the wet, the soft, the fluid, the artificial, the disconnected, the whole fucking charade, then she might never have to wake up again.

She dragged one finger along the sheen of the shoe, leaving the wet smear several inches along it before she wrapped it up in its crepe camouflages again. Carol would find that green bag just the way she left it. Then she put the magazine back in her book-bag. Now she was drowning for sure.

9. Nicky

After she came home from college one night the following week, Nicky managed to ignore the petulant flash of the answering machine for a full fifteen minutes before she grew irritated enough to press the PLAY button.

Hi, you guys. Long pause. The voice began again. *Hi, Carol and Nicky. It's Ellen here. Carol, it was good to see you up here last week. I just wanted to ask* – Pause again. – *Well, I was coming down to Oregon anyway, to see some friends in Salem… or was it Portland… and I thought well, maybe, if it's okay with the two of you, then maybe I could come and crash with you guys for two or three nights or so, if it's not too much trouble. I'll give you guys a call in a couple of days when I get down there.* There was a click and a beep as the answering machine turned itself off.

That same Ellen girl from the club. Nicky felt immediately nervous at the thought of seeing her again and slightly aroused. This was the first she'd heard about Carol running into her up in Seattle and she briefly wondered why Carol hadn't mentioned the fact. But maybe she had and Nicky hadn't been listening. Yes, of course, Ellen must have gotten the number off Carol. Odd that the two had made contact; Nicky had always thought Carol had been jealous the last time they met up – oh, it had to have been over a half-year ago now. So now the two of them had made friends. That was good. She replayed the message to listen to Ellen's low, cherry-smooth voice again. There was a certain quality to the voice – it sounded buttered, over-polished.

Nicky was pretty convinced that Ellen had a screw loose somewhere.

Her visit would mean a change, anyway, and someone else to talk to. Lately even sex was predictable. Carol would keep coming up with stupid scripted little ploys like a frustrated housewife. It was like she needed a cliché as an excuse. Even in other areas of life, she seemed to summon up Mary Tyler Moore as some kind of chirpy role model. Femme was femme, and that was fine, but give me a break. Whereas Ellen, as Nicky recalled from that bar in Seattle, was far more direct than Carol. Ellen hadn't given the impression that she had to resort to either ploys or subterfuge. There was something there that was very different from Carol, something sharper. Even if Ellen drifted off in mid-sentence – even if Ellen never seemed to be able to follow a thought through to a conclusion – the manipulation, diversion and artifice were just not present. This could not be said of Carol, who drenched herself in falseness. Nicky reckoned this was because of Carol's worry about her own innate emptiness. It was fucking exhausting. The constant attention that was required to coddle Carol's fragile ego was draining. No, Ellen wasn't like Carol at all. She hoped.

She walked over to the cassette player she'd lugged down from Alaska and put on the D.A.F. tape the girl from her Oceanography 101 class had lent her last week. It was German music, really sharp and grinding. She liked it. It made her think of fucking. Of fucking someone like Ellen.

Ever since their trip to the shopping mall, Nicky had felt Carol's beauty losing its potency like watered-down perfume; Carol was getting stale. It was just a headache altogether, the whole kit and caboodle. She was anything but sharp, but even in her smoothness Carol managed to make simple things difficult and most things a pain. Most things an effort. They were beginning to snipe at each other again, but Nicky refrained from saying anything too cutting for fear that Carol would take off a second time. Sometimes, though, she wondered how it would be with other girls. The girl from her Oceanography class, Jeanine, had slipped her phone number into the plastic cassette sleeve as well, but so far Nicky hadn't done anything about it.

The drumbeat was bursting out of the boombox like a giant's footsteps: FE – FI – FO – FUM. And Nicky still remembered the incisiveness of Ellen's kiss in the bar that night. Nothing soft about her. Who cared if she was crazy, she really was luscious. Though a little twisted.

She had a feeling Carol wouldn't much like the idea of Ellen crashing at their place. She hadn't told Carol about the kiss, so she was unsure why she sensed that she'd be jealous. Probably it was guilt on her own part. Yeah, so sue me, Nicky thought, it was interesting to kiss a girl other than you. Nicky was remembering how it felt now: Ellen's curved, experienced smile against her lips. She was so very fucking tired of being good all the time; she wanted to pinch; she wanted to scratch through. If she was honest, what happened in the bar that night with Ellen had been extremely flattering. It was easy to develop a crush on a person. Had she wanted that particular alchemy to occur that long-ago evening? Did she want it to happen again?

She walked over and turned the volume up, even louder.

Carol seemed pleased but preoccupied when Nicky detailed the message in bed that night. While she'd been shopping the week before, Carol had been handed two free tickets to a film preview, one of those screenings where the audience write down their comments on a questionnaire, ticking off which bits they loved or hated. Nicky hated shit like that, and she'd had the night class anyway. So Carol had gone to see the movie – apparently about a high-school clique where all the girls had the same name – all on her own, had loved the film and had been in a good mood ever since she returned.

When Carol didn't say anything about Ellen, Nicky added: "What's so great about a 'high school' film, anyway? I hated *Pretty in Pink*."

"Oh, but this wasn't like that at all," Carol murmured, still absorbed in her book, "this one was really clever." It was an old hard-back they'd purchased at a garage sale for a quarter last month, only because the title (*The American Way of Death*) was so weird. It turned out to be a strangely compelling exposé of the funeral business, by someone named Jessica Mitford. Nicky had already read it; it had made her feel queasy: everything was a lie and scam, according to the book, even death.

"You probably only like those kind of films because you had such a perfect adolescence." She was prodding Carol, trying to get some kind of reaction, and didn't know why.

"What are you talking about? Is your memory that bad? Of course I didn't." Carol didn't immediately put down the book, but eventually she turned to Nicky. "You know she's from Alaska, too."

"How about that?" Though by now, Nicky was distracted by the odd-looking insect squashed on their windowsill. "I wonder what *that* was." They were still burning trash outside, down the street; she could smell the smoke. She'd have to close the window.

"Don't know," said Carol. "But get this – she lived at McAlester's Children's Home." Carol caught Nicky's attention this time.

"That's weird. They all went to our school, too. Though I guess she would have graduated years before we did. I sure don't remember meeting her – or anyone named Ellen, for the matter." It was a long speech.

"Yeah, it's kind of an old-fashioned name, more for women over fifty or so. But then I guess 'Carol' is, too," Carol admitted.

"Mmm." Nicky grew disinterested again. She was thinking, guiltily, of her magazine. And the Shoes. And, in some deeper knot of thought in her brain, of Ellen's mouth as it had been that Seattle night.

It was three weeks before Ellen finally showed up. She hadn't rung first, and turned up during the day when Nicky was at college. Nicky came home to find Carol chattering happily to Ellen on the futon sofa in the living room. They were drinking from a pitcher of iced vodka and lemonade and neither was surprised by Nicky's entrance. Ellen merely smiled brightly at her, once, before returning her focus to Carol. But the smile was more than enough. Nicky's abdomen began to feel warm. Ellen still liked her, liked her enough to fake a certain casualness. Nicky did it often enough herself, so she recognised the signs of quiet flirtation.

She got herself a pop from the fridge and joined them. "I prefer watercolours for fireweed," she heard Ellen say. From what Nicky could gather, Ellen had studied Painting for a couple years at UW, before dropping out. Maybe she should have studied elocution: she was trying with difficulty to spell out something about fireweed compared to lupines. Nicky felt nostalgic as she listened to them speak. These type of flowers had grown on the outskirts of the forest near where she had lived, and by high summer had encircled the lake by her uncle's cabin as well. But she had always found flowers annoying, and preferred the tall trees. *Do you remember, Nicky? Do you remember us as well?* Perhaps this had kept her from other types of loveliness; had blocked her off. But oddly, she remembered the wildflowers now in great detail. Maybe flowers weren't so bad after all. Fireweed: the tall, pink- and, later in the summer, violet-lilied plants that animals loved to eat. Even children loved breaking open the green stems to suck out the sticky cotton shafts inside. They had always been sweet, Nicky remembered from childhood. Fireweed didn't grow down here. And wild lupines she remembered too, flowers which were somehow more rounded and domestic. Their colour was more artificial than that of fireweed, like lavender paint. She hadn't seen any down here yet either. *You better wake up.*

Now she remembered that Ellen was from Alaska, too. She watched Ellen pause, and waited patiently for the next delayed thought to spill from her lips. My god, the woman was inarticulate. It didn't look as if it were bothering Carol, though. Nicky felt a surge of irritation. She had gotten flack from Carol her whole life over her reluctance to speak fluently and often; Carol had taken it personally as a sign of tight-lipped withdrawal; had complained that – as she put it – Nicky had an admirable vocabulary, it was just that she never put it to any good use. What the fuck do you call going to college then, Nicky thought. She looked at Carol's face carefully, waiting for it to flash into impatience with Ellen. But it didn't: Carol remained bright and attentive to Ellen's halting speech. Switching her gaze to Ellen, Nicky made the discovery that Ellen was older than she had originally thought – maybe in her late twenties or early thirties. Nicky slouched back against the hard-backed chair and ingested a long, cool swallow of Dr. Pepper. She started to listen to what they were saying, hoping to attach herself eventually to the discussion.

But the comparison of the flowers' qualities, although important to Nicky, was not further dwelt upon by Ellen and Carol. Nicky would have liked to join in with her observations on the subject of Alaskan flora, but as usual the conversation had shifted and moved on by the time she decided to join it. Nicky felt a wave of homesickness for the wildflowers, but it passed and left her merely listening. Ellen was saying, rather rapidly now that she had hit whatever stride she had been pushing towards, "I see what you mean. But there's not a thing to do there. And it's so fucking repressed. There's not a single person I'd call sex-positive. Not one."

Carol looked nervously at Nicky, and then finding no answer turned back to Ellen. "This might sound kind of dumb, but what's 'sex-positive'? Do you mean HIV?" She was hesitant.

Ellen made a rather artful shift from incredulousness to patronising helpfulness. "Well, Carol," she said, smoothly and with no trace of her former faltering, "It means to be positive about sex. Remember?" Carol glanced quickly at Nicky and then away. What was that about? Ellen continued: 'You know – with no hang-ups about jealousy or exposure or possessiveness. Sex without a blush," Ellen finished triumphantly. Carol appeared impressed and embarrassed, simultaneously.

It sounded alright to Nicky. But she rather liked the whole fact that she hid her porno magazine, that she had cleverly disguised her fondness for the Shoes even on the few occasions when she'd convinced Carol to wear them. It was deception itself that was getting her off; she guessed she was not sex-positive. Christ. It hit her. That meant she was deceitful, too. She was as synthetic as the rest.

At that moment Ellen spilled the pitcher of chilled drink onto the futon, soaking through the mattress. "Shit," she said, biting her lip and looking at Carol. This expression, too, looked contrived. "There goes my bed for the night."

Carol put a hand on Ellen's shoulder. "It'll be okay, Ellen, don't worry. You can crash in our room."

The three of them slept the first few hours at least, but when Nicky woke up around three a.m., she was convinced that the other two were also awake and equally uneasy. It was the warmest February she had ever experienced – and so the window had been left open – and they were all in their underwear. Nicky noted with irritation that Carol had still not removed that insect from the sill. And although Nicky lay on the right side of the bed with a bit more space, with Carol's back to her and Ellen's back to Carol, it felt like a line of sweaty sardines. As they lay there stiffly, Nicky felt that she had to rapidly make an excuse and get out of there for at least ten minutes, then wondered why she had even mentioned this out loud. Only Carol mumbled an 'okay'. As soon as Nicky left, she questioned why she was doing it, *why was she leaving them alone,* what was the dumb reason which led her to test the two of them like this? But that was a ludicrous thought, wasn't it? They were both attracted to Nicky, weren't they, and were jealous of, rather than drawn to, each other? So why was she testing them? Why did she feel she already knew the outcome of this particular test?

Fifteen or twenty minutes had to have passed while Nicky stood there in the bathroom, looking at herself in the mirror. Finding finally no new revelations, she splashed water on her face and dried it roughly with a towel. When she returned and crawled in close to the sleeping figures in the bed, she could see Carol's arm draped over Ellen's body. They both appeared to be sleeping peacefully and deeply, but Nicky's adrenalin poured into her veins. *You better wake up.* Yet the stream of anger was clogged by the possibility of being cool and accepting, maybe just joining them in sleep, joining them in their not ill-intentioned cuddling. Perhaps even in the morning all would unite in a lush non-monogamous orgy, the proof of how cool and sex-positive they all three could be. Now she knew why Ellen had taken the trouble to define the word.

Nicky knew she had a choice, and that she could ride it through this way if she wanted to. A familiar taste rose in her mouth; the burn of the trees and all their flavours. If she was calm, then maybe the sick feeling in her ribcage would never emerge, or else turn into lust and she could get out of the whole thing without a loss of face. Only, that is to say, if she decided to be cool about it and pretend that it meant no betrayal to her. This was one lie she could choose to follow, but it also seemed a risk-filled path.

Direct anger was something she knew better. She'd better be sharp. *You'd better be sharp.* She'd never been in a situation like this before, yet the sick jealous anger she was feeling was very familiar. It was this sentiment that was going to carry her through. How dare they lie there, with Carol's arm casually thrown over Ellen in sleep, as if it were all perfectly natural, as if it were all perfectly okay? What had they been doing to make them feel it was alright to fall asleep this way? *Wake up.*

Nicky poised before the rim, ready to dive in, but *choking you'll choke* An unbidden image of spruce trees flashed in her head and she hesitated. This was the way people drowned. She had to have it clear in her head; she didn't want her ears filled with water, she didn't want her head filled with water. How dare they try to drown her? She had to make herself go sharp and mean, and very quickly. Else she would drown in their syrupy sweet, and fall prey to their ploys of suffocation. She would not drown. She would not drown. She thought of the elongated, prickly stilettos of the Shoes. She had been mistaken: even they were hard, not soft. *Make yourself go sharp, Nicky, hurt and stiffen and you'll survive*

Nicky eased herself onto the bed and in amongst the pale cream sheets which partially covered the other two girls. The white expanse of Carol's broad back was facing her. Nicky knew how easy it would be to accept and put her arm around Carol and cuddle into the two of them and all would be okay, to some degree. She could still choose a gentle route; she hadn't fallen off yet. *You better wake up.* But as Nicky lay there staring at Carol's white back, her fingers came out and, like she was twisting the face of a watch or a doorknob, she pinched a circle of Carol's skin with all five fingernails and twisted sharply in a clockwise fashion.

Carol's body jerked up before she woke up and she was muddled and half-asleep, "Ow!" Then she woke up a bit more. "Hi, honey," she murmured, "what is it?"

"What is it? What is it? What do you call this shit?" Nicky's voice was already rising; she was violently ripping the sheets off Carol and the now not-sleeping Ellen. "What the fuck do you call this?"

"Oh, I'm not going to lie to you," said Carol.

"No, I should think you're fucking not going to."

Ellen was looking uncomfortable. She said, typically, "Look – I'm going to leave and let you guys –"

"You fucking hold on a second, Crazy Ellen," Nicky said, "You wait." Nicky was half-straddling both of them in the bed and she knew this was, without any doubt at all, what was known as a 'bad scene'. "What happened?" When she saw Ellen and Carol exchange a look, her heart sank.

"We were just lying next to each other, it was nice," Carol said, "and I started touching her because it felt so nice and then we started cuddling."

It was awful, Nicky couldn't believe how clearly she could picture this in her mind, or how true it seemed for Carol to be saying precisely these words, unapologetically. It was like the worst of dreams, only it was far too real. Her stomach was crushing together jealously, in pain. Ellen looked frightened; this was far too heavy a scene for her, Nicky figured. She was used to cool, callous – perhaps sterile – polyamorous trysts, nothing like this. Nicky wondered how long it had been since Ellen had cut herself off from proximity to this type of disastrous emotion. Carol was still talking, attempting to placate. But Carol had done exactly what she had wanted to. And Nicky was still aware that as little as three minutes ago she had had the choice to make all of this a good thing, and that there was now no way it was going to be anything but terrible, and there was even the possibility that it could turn out to be murderous.

"I asked her to put her fingers up my cunt," Carol was saying, "and she did, Nicky, and it felt good. Sometimes you do things because it feels good and right, not because you're hurting someone. What feels good can never be wrong. It wasn't like we really fucked, Nicky."

Nicky turned on Ellen, but didn't touch her. "How long did you stay up there?" She was purposefully crude; her face was bitter and fixed. "Did you keep your hand up Carol's cunt for quite a while, Ellen? Did you feel your fingers go all wrinkly from Carol's cunt, her cunt, her CUNT?" She screamed the last word.

Ellen stared down Nicky, then eventually turned her head away and looked down at the sheets without comment.

Oh, even at this late moment Nicky could choose to be cavalier about it, she could accept Carol's and Ellen's human nature, but maybe you never can, when something like this chews so hard on your heart. Maybe with all the anger rising to your mouth, you never have a chance, really. Maybe the reaction is all programmed in. Maybe just as naturally Nicky would have done exactly as Carol had with Ellen in the lightly drugged horniness of demi-sleep and the tension between the three of them in bed. But Nicky was astounded not only by the fact that she had been virtuous and had in effect missed her chance with Ellen back in Seattle, but also by the fact that she'd had all of it thrown straight back at her, *smack!* She was close to grabbing Ellen's fingers and smelling them as proof, but she didn't act on this. Something ticked slightly and thankfully in her brain because of this decision; she was obviously still in control.

Ellen, a coward again, was saying, "I'm just... going to let you guys... work it out and –"

"The fuck you don't," Nicky said. She grabbed Ellen like a thing and not a person, with cold blood she grabbed her by the crotch and she said to Ellen, "You mean she got to fuck you when I'm the one who said no, do you mean she's the one who ended up fucking you –" Nicky held Ellen with one finger gripping her ass and one halfway in her cunt. Then she released her. Ellen wrapped herself in the sheet and went out to the balcony where Nicky assumed she sat down against the cold wall.

Nicky and Carol were left on the bed in ugly morning twilight, that colour of hangovers and violent arguments with lovers. They sat facing each other, entangled in the remaining bed clothes. "Don't you love me anymore?" Nicky said.

Carol looked at Nicky. Carol's face was truthful. "No, not really," she said. It was the opposite of what Nicky had expected her to say.

A grey breakfast. Ellen at last made an appearance again at the table, where Carol and Nicky were sitting silently, thoughtfully chewing their toast. Ellen sat down in the chair next to Carol, a judged distance from Nicky, and began what sounded like a carefully rehearsed speech: "Look, I'm taking off, I've got a couple days left before I have to be back and I know some people in Portland, like I said." Her bottom lip trembled effectively. "Thanks for having me, you guys," she continued, "it's been really fun."

And to make matter worse, to drive home the point that it had been the most terrible of visits, Ellen was the kind of person who felt like she had to lie to be polite. Nicky would have preferred an old-fashioned curse, perhaps a challenge to a duel. A thrown punch. Just not hypocrisy. She couldn't stomach it. No concessions please, Ellen. No neurotic balm. Just say what you have to say, and leave. Ellen could barely speak an honest sentence straight through; she wasn't direct, after all. In Nicky's brain the trees whispered: *You better wake up.* She was as deceptive, as artificial, as secretive as Carol was. As the Shoes were. As Nicky herself could be if she hadn't avoided that trap.

"Oh, no, you can stay; please stay, won't you, Ellen?" It was typical that Carol would say that. Nicky cast her a dirty look.

"No, I've got to be going." Was that smugness on Ellen's face? *The bitch.*

"I'll give you a ride to the bus station," Nicky said. She wanted her away as quickly as possible. Somehow, maybe, she and Carol could work this shit out.

"I'll come too," Carol said quickly. Because she wanted to catch one last glimpse of Ellen, no doubt. Christ.

"Okay," Ellen said. "I've got all my stuff packed, so I'll wait outside until you two finish breakfast. I think you probably want to talk." Nicky felt – no, she *knew* – that this little scene had been manipulated to the precision of Ellen's wishes, just as surely as she knew that Ellen didn't want to walk all the way to the bus station, and had been angling for a lift.

She pounced on Carol as soon as the porch door slammed and Ellen went outside to wait: "Why did you do that? Why did you ask her to stay?" Carol didn't look up and meet Nicky's eyes.

"Look," she mumbled, "it's not always just about you. Sometimes I get tired of being in a relationship, too."

"Now there's a surprise. And there I was thinking that you went up to Seattle because you wanted a little vacation."

"Nicky –"

"Shut up." This conversation was nearly unbelievable. Nicky blurted out what she wanted most not to say: "You don't love me anymore. You said it yourself last night."

Carol looked at her from across the table. Nicky felt spluttering and graceless; she could sense her face turning red. "No, I do," she said. Her voice was cool and controlled. "Maybe I put it wrong last night. I'm just tired sometimes. That's maybe why I left; I haven't been feeling like I'm in love lately. But I think I do love you, Nicky, I really do think that. And I care for you."

I care for you. Kind but ultimately chilling words, or words to mark genuine affection, even hope? Nicky looked over at Carol, her cleavage still tempting enough for a thousand sailors. She was lovely even with no makeup, certain fatigue and with her hair standing up. Nicky's own body ached from the lack of sleep and the endless, circular, tearful weave of their discussion after the incident last night. After Ellen had retreated to the soggy futon couch downstairs, Nicky and Carol had begun to argue and then to scream. As Nicky thought for several minutes about what happened, unaware that she was still staring at Carol and that time was passing, the corners of Carol's mouth opened and she stuck her tongue out at Nicky. But this was it. This was the revelation: the new thing Nicky had been searching for earlier in the mirror. Why *not* make fun of it all? Why not? Nicky suppressed an urge to burst out in laughter.

"Stop that." She made her face stern. "Be serious, Carol."

"Why?" Carol stuck her tongue out at Nicky again. "Why do we have to be serious all the time?"

"Because –" Nicky looked at Carol. *She's being deceitful; you better wake up. She'll pull you down.* "Because –" Carol put her thumbs in her ears and waggled her fingers at Nicky. "Because –" *the little games they play to get you exposed, before they suck you down in the –* "Because – oh hell, I don't know. Come here." Nicky kissed Carol in exasperation.

"See?" Carol raised her head.

"See what?"

"It's going to be okay." Carol smiled gently.

"Maybe." They stood in an embrace, Nicky feeling the pound of Carol's heart pulsing up through both their bodies.

Someone cleared her throat. "Can I come in for a sec?" Ellen came back into the kitchen, carrying her suitcase. She sat down on one of the kitchen chairs before them.

"Look, I'm sorry," she began. "I didn't want to start any of that, and I apologise."

Nicky stared at her, uncertain what to say. Uncertain what her own feelings towards Ellen were. She noticed Carol bestowing on Ellen the same tender smile she had just received.

"It's just that," Ellen got up slowly and approached them both;

Carol and Nicky still hung frozen in their embrace. Ellen reached out a hand and stroked Nicky's jawline, the jaw Carol had always described as clean and boyish, and then a curl of Carol's hair. "It's just that I think I like both of you, and there's an important reason why, but I can't remember it right now. But shouldn't this – the liking – be enough?" She put her lips on Nicky's mouth and kissed slowly, and despite herself Nicky felt her body respond. "Or this?" Ellen whispered something in Carol's ear, and Carol smiled again. Nicky waited for herself to feel rage, but she felt nothing. "So here I am," Ellen took a step back and looked at them both, "here we are."

Ellen shut her eyes, put her arms to her sides, and waited. The moments ticked by. With her eyes closed she looked vulnerable, Nicky thought, and scared. She wondered if she had ever looked so scared before herself. *A wet stump in a clearing; the dry crack of carved tubes.* She shook her thoughts away.

Carol had her fingers out, gently smoothing Ellen's dark hair.

Nicky thought: I will leap across this chasm of fear into the unknown, and I will be rewarded. She leapt. Carol stepped forward at the same time as Nicky did, and Nicky folded her body into the flesh of the other two women, her hand on Carol's waist; her lips on Ellen's lips, moving into a kiss which was somehow both soft and coarse.

It was a delicious thing to kiss and fuck and be held by another woman than Carol without guilt or remorse, only pleasure. It was no bad thing. It was no bad thing at all. Oddly, Carol herself had never looked more beautiful or desirable than in the moment right before Nicky realised Ellen was going to kiss her, too. Nicky didn't feel angry. Or jealous. She felt fucking good.

Now, dozing later in the afternoon, Nicky was relishing the delicious languor that comes after having spent a morning doing sluttish and nasty things. She hadn't felt it since the early days with Carol. The bliss of having two lush bodies in bed beside her, the luxury of having her face in one cunt and her hands fucking another, while all the while someone had been alternately licking and fucking her. All this at the same time. The pulsating, swollen wetness she knew was waiting, right there at that moment. Priceless. No wonder lesbian orgies were the top-selling porno videos ever. Watching it was one thing, but Nicky was living it, and no dirty old man could ever experience it *that* close up. Priceless, that's right.

What a beautiful day! She stretched herself out against the two of them in the bed. When she tasted Ellen, she was reminded of fireweed. The sharp, slightly sweet taste. She moved on up and ran her tongue across Carol's mouth. It was an obvious comparison, after the earlier conversation, but still – Ellen was the coin's other side to Carol's lupine qualities and her salty, domestic sexuality. Yes, flowers had their charms, thought Nicky, at least in terms of metaphor. Candied purple-blue lupine or bright hectic fireweed. Or both. Why not both. Nicky grinned. The word *lupine* was rounded and safe and curved and sweet. The word was originally Latin; it meant 'wolf' or something like it. Something sharp buried under soft, *you should never trust anything, never trust*

Fear rose in Nicky and she jerked away from Carol's mouth for an instant, took her fingers from between Ellen's legs. However, her senses overrode her judgement and her fear and she began to sink down into it all again, drowning. As she kissed and touched the other girls, she grew regretfully convinced that she would always be taking the soft before the sharp, the easy before the difficult. She craved cold and metal and she was ending up instead with the warmth of blurred edges, softness, vagueness.

She was thawing, feeling her senses opening up; she was becoming warm, but in the process her head had become only half-baked, and foggy. She had lost control – no matter how sensitised her body had become to warmth. So possibly she had not truly yet thawed, not really. But these thoughts, concurrent with her limbs and flavours sinking into flesh, were the last things she should be thinking now. *Sleep. You're going to give up; go to sleep.*

No.

Her lips caught Ellen's; for the hundredth time that day, she returned the long-owed kiss.

Later that evening, Carol pressured Nicky to let Ellen stay on for a couple of weeks or so, if it was okay with her job, only if it was totally cool with Nicky, and this time Nicky agreed. But if Ellen stayed longer than just a token few nights, she also wondered how she would react to her own not-infrequent nightmares, for really it was only Carol who truly knew how to keep Nicky safe, lupine-safe from pricking sharp – safe, soft and removed from whatever made Nicky think or truly feel.

10. Carol

It's been weird since Seattle. You're not sure about this. There was a point once when you wouldn't have been able to imagine touching anyone but Nicky, but now Ellen is here too. In theory you should feel freed up with the doors open wide. You should be feeling freshness rushing towards you like a bomb exploding. But it doesn't feel like that; it feels like the bomb is messing stuff up rather than cleansing, and that what is flashing towards you right now is the dirty, putrefying, poisoned threat of a nuclear winter. You've got your hands shielding your face, but you can still see it coming. You're still trapped here and no free-love experience is going to untangle your bonds. It's the other way around; the ropes grow tighter.

So now you climb out of bed over the remaining slumberers, drag on your favourite purple bathrobe and plod your way downstairs.

"Shut the door," Nicky calls out.

And so you sigh and tramp upstairs again, pulling the door completely closed, the way that Nicky likes it. You pause outside the door, waiting for someone to thank you. All you hear is giggling. The sun shines through the window at the top of the hall. Spring is still too hot. Too hot for you. You go downstairs. You are all prepared to make a cup of Mr. Coffee when you remember that you can't afford filter anymore. Shit, you have to make instant and there's just a spoonful left in the jar. If only Nicky hadn't bought those fucking shoes. When you tried returning them, the same manager was there and she laughed in your face, saying that they were 'damaged', although she didn't specify how, and that you had better leave immediately since you weren't supposed to be there and she was going to call the security guard if you didn't leave *right now*. People were listening. You were incredibly embarrassed, your cheeks turning feverish, red. She looked familiar, too, the horrible manager, and you hoped that you didn't know her from home, that she wouldn't call your parents and tell them she had seen you with a girl. Nicky had pinched your ass then, too. You hope that the manager hadn't seen her do that. Basically there was no chance of returning the shoes and now you guys – the three of you, if you count Ellen – are *completely broke*.

You bet you could have returned the shoes if Nicky hadn't ripped off those rings. She was so stupid. It makes you sick. And you had barely worn the stupid shoes that had caused so much trouble, only once or twice when Nicky whined and convinced you to wear them to restaurants or the movies. They were too difficult to walk in, so they're as good as brand new. So you don't get why the lady said they were damaged.

You slump at the table to drink your disgusting instant coffee. Your parents always had fresh ground beans and a French press. You hate living like this. You've got to figure out how to get some money. You twist your hair. But how *can* you get some money? If you get a job, then who will look after the house? You hear Nicky and Ellen kissing and messing around upstairs, and for a moment you're tempted to join them, but you know it's more important to get your thoughts straight on all this stuff. Otherwise you can feel the trap tightening, its ropes constricting and scratching on your skin. You'll have to get a job. You pull on your hair. Tug, tug. Knock, knock. Who's there? But then you remember that you've decided not to ask riddles of yourself, not anymore. Tug, tug.

You could always leave Nicky – leave Nicky and Ellen, you mean – and go back up to your parents. But panic hits you at this thought.

You know what would happen then. Ellen would have Nicky all to herself; you don't know how you're liking that idea. And back up there no one would understand you. They would not understand how you have changed, the slavering boys who treat you like they think you're really easy. They always think you're easy, even though you're really quite selective. Little Novgorod would be fun maybe for a while; you always like attention; you would be the new girl all over again.

But that would be a trap too. This time there would be no way out: just pregnancy, maybe a marriage. Then your life would become involved with your children's lives, and it wouldn't be your life anymore. It would be the next generation's and you would grow haggard before your time. Divorce would come, a couple sleazy affairs, maybe a romantic one – with a milkman or mayor – set to break your heart. A part-time job and then grandchildren, another thing to shift your concentration and attention away from yourself. That would be the biggest trap of all.

Sitting here drinking the shitty coffee and listening to the noises above you, you finally conclude that you can't go back, but you can't stay here with no money. You don't want to get a job. But you will have to. You *are* trapped, you are, truly trapped. You are immobile. There's not a fucking thing you can do. You start crying and then the tears dry up and then you slam your fist down on the pale blue Formica tabletop. The cooing and fumbling upstairs stops for a few seconds and then resumes. The sounds arouse you. If you can't beat them, join them, as long as it's not too... harsh. You raise yourself, drink the dregs of your coffee, run your hands over your body to feel your smooth, excited skin beneath your clothes. You'll think about this later.

Later becomes the afternoon of the same day. It is an unusual moment when you, Nicky and Ellen relax on the cheap lawnchairs in the back yard in the sun. You have not really been with both of them at the same time, at least not when you three are not having sex or working up to it. You are beginning to worry about coalitions; you still remember how bitchy girls got in junior high when you'd hang out in groups of three or more. You were top of the totem pole then, but you softly remind yourself to be wary: *someone always gets left out, Carol. Remember that.* But no, it doesn't feel like that at the moment, out here in the sunlight. It feels safe, and good. And unusual, like you said. You don't need to worry. But at some level you're aware that nothing's changed, you're still trapped. You'll have to get a job. And quickly; within the next two weeks.

Nicky sits in the lawnchair closest to you, her hair glinting in the sun. The glint comes not from the white absence of colour, like your own blonde hair, but from the fact that it is wet; she has just stepped out of the shower. Where she's been giggling under the spray. With Ellen. And Ellen wears Nicky's tartan robe, her naked body drying against its square weaves. Ellen runs her hands slowly through Nicky's wet hair. It's pretty weird, alright. Though you don't feel jealous. You guess you are getting used to the situation, unconventional though it is. And it's too late to untangle yourself even if you weren't, you remind yourself.

Ellen is another kettle of fish. You'll never tell her this, but you could barely remember her from when you and Nicky first met her in Seattle. But then when you recognised her and re-introduced yourself, she seemed so excited and happy that it ended up rubbing off on you. She cheered you up. She is not really someone you'd normally pick out as potential romance material, but once you realised she wasn't stuck up and a know-it-all like you thought she was, you had to admit she could be pretty charming. She is a very confident girl and she is just a bit vacant, too. Like a child, but one who knows its own mind. In fact, her vague confidence sort of reminds you of Nicky's bravado, before Nicky started going a little weird on you down here in Oregon. Maybe it's the appeal of insecurity just as it's emerging into self-assurance, like a chrysalis only partly split. But since you've left Alaska, Nicky's gotten so strange. But that's right, you're not supposed to talk or think about that kind of thing anymore. You and Nicky have 'drawn a line' and you guys are going to 'try again'. That kind of shit was talked about the first day you got back. And so far it seems to be going okay. Ellen does not know anything about the drawn lines. She does not know the real reason you were up in Seattle. She does not know you were trapped. The freaky thing is, you haven't felt a trace of your old fears about leaving the house since you returned. Not a trace.

Things are just so weird at the moment. It's so crazy, because a year or so ago if someone had told you that you would be having sex with a girl you would have laughed right in their face. But now you know it's like anything else, just as sex with boys got easier after you went past the first three or so, so did the concept of sleeping with another girl, as well. And so this whole threesome thing has come to mean nothing more than just a barrier you've passed by. Taboos do tend to get easier once you've gotten past that first time. There are still rigidities and blocks, though. You're not so sure you could go out and have casual sex with a girl who was a stranger. You'd have to have a build-up, wouldn't you? You think so. You're not sure.

For right now, you think you're doing pretty okay by even touching someone who is not supposed to be your one-and-only, your love of your life. You still feel tentative. Like now, for example, when you reach out to touch Ellen's dry brown hand. Yes, you definitely feel conscious that your heart can leap for someone other than Nicky. Like sometimes when you receive a caress from Ellen when Nicky is not in the room or not looking. Fondness meant only for you. But Nicky just seems pleased when you and Ellen show affection for each other. Except for the first night, obviously. Nicky doesn't know about Seattle, of course. That was different.

But, like you said, it takes time, and as far as breaking any rules goes, it seems to be going alright. You haven't had a freak-out yet about dating two people at the same time or anything. The only thing that pisses you off sometimes is Nicky pretending to be so nice in front of Ellen, as if the two of you had never ever had a fight and it's all been just peachy and harmonic even before Ellen came along. This is where it starts to worry you a bit. Because if Nicky can lie and fake about stuff like that, she might be able to do it about other stuff, too. *Ask me no riddles, I'll tell you no lies.* But you'll have to give her the benefit of the doubt. Your thoughts turn back to the money problems. If only she hadn't bought those shoes. You really could use the bucks.

The three of you sit in the sun. Not saying much and trying to pretend that you are all basking in the sunlight glitter. You know it's a pretence because when you try to sneak a look at the other two from underneath your half-closed eyelids, you catch Ellen peeking, too. But she quickly squeezes her eyes shut; she maybe knows or doesn't know you caught her. Confusing, alright. Ellen begins to quietly hum – it sounds like the French National Anthem – and Nicky looks as if she is asleep, although you are a little unsure whether this is true or not. When you were kids at slumber parties and camping and stuff, Nicky used to fake that she was asleep a lot of the time, just so she could eavesdrop and listen to what other people were saying. That's why people didn't like her very much. When you were older, she'd do the same thing at kegger parties, but she switched her method from faking sleep to faking that she passed out in alcoholic stupors. You can guess where she learned that one.

But you're supposed to love Nicky and her little foibles unconditionally, aren't you? That's why you came back to Oregon. Or maybe it was because you were confused and you didn't know what else to do. You tell yourself: I shouldn't think like that. You shouldn't. It's time to clear your head from confusion, it's time to make everything feel less bewildering and less ambivalent. Ambivalent. Bewildering. Confusion. It should be as easy as A-B-C. You'll have to get a job.

God knows *someone* here has to. Ellen hasn't mentioned money since she decided to 'hang out' here for a while and forgo her return to Seattle but Christ, she must have lost her job by now, and it kind of seems that she's not going to be heading back up any time soon. Which is okay, but you want to know where everything stands and you figure the life savings of a waitress – especially a bad waitress like Ellen was – can't amount to much. And Nicky's much worse than her when it comes to financial planning. Your parents may have had a bit more than Nicky's parents had when you were growing up, but at least you knew how to save it and not spend it on any stupid high-heeled shoes and too much pre-packaged food. You want to be able to have treats from time to time – like filtered, instead of instant – but you're definitely not extravagant.

The way you figure it, the three of you have two more weeks on what's left of Nicky's and your Alaska State Permanent Funds combined. A grand total of no more than eighty-five dollars. The Student Loan money ran out about three months ago, at least that's what Nicky's saying. Which is news to you, because you'd budgeted for groceries for at least a few more months. Very soon you can't pay rent, you can't buy food and you sure as fuck can't go buying shoes of any type.

You say, softly, "Nicky." Nicky ignores you, stretches out on the plastic of the fold-out lawnchair and turns her head away from you. You watch her look appraisingly at Ellen.

"You need a haircut," Nicky says to Ellen. "At least your bangs. You can hardly see through them, can you?"

"Hardly see through..." Ellen repeats, stumbling through the words. She must have been asleep after all.

You interrupt. "You guys, we have to discuss our financial situation. If we –"

"Hey." Nicky cuts you off. "Don't you think Ellen needs her bangs trimmed?"

"Maybe," you say, "but we have to talk about this first, we have to –"

"Just a second." Nicky jumps off the lawnchair. "I'm going to go get a pair of scissors." And she leaves you there.

When Nicky speaks again, she says: "I've brought something else." She takes out a pair of blades, its edges sharper than its gleam. It's not a girl's toy. It is the kind with which men trim off their beards.

Nicky returns and cuts.

"Do you want me to trim your bangs, too?" Nicky says, after she has taken the scissors to a fringe which, you have to admit, was beginning to curtain Ellen's face.

"I don't want you to cut my hair," you say, suddenly stricken that this is the case. "You can't climb down; you won't be able to climb down. If you cannot take me with you, then it makes no sense for you to be imprisoned, too."

"Oh, no, really, the cutting's not for that," says your lover, Nicky, smiling. You relax, but are flooded with shame to acknowledge the hope you felt alongside the concern. Hope that you would have company. You would not be alone. But now you have Ellen, after all. You are not entirely on your own. "At least not for the hair on top of your head," continues your lover.

"What hair, then?" you ask. You have hair of course in many places: on and underneath your arms, between and underneath your legs. You even have down upon your face, although it doesn't show unless you look closely. You laugh. "Surely the hair on my face isn't enough to shave like a man's," you say, teasing, "see, little feathery stuff... feel it, most women have it..." You take her hand and place it against your cheek. "Feel how smooth it is," you murmur.

"No, I don't want to have my hair cut," you say. "I want to talk about how we're going to pay the rent next month. And you know damn well that's what I want to be doing right now, not having a haircut."

Ellen stirs from her sun-worship. "Chill out, Carol." She yawns. "We'll figure something out. Nicky and I were just talking about that yesterday, weren't we, honey? That's very funny. Very funny –" Ellen breaks off, laughing "– money." She adds the last word in a whisper.

But Nicky is ignoring Ellen and is looking at you. She has a weird look in her eye.

You take a breath.

Nicky slaps you, and then hits you full across the face. You are crumpled on the lawn, smelling the damp grass and looking up at her, but you are not crying.

"Why would you do something like that?" you ask her. "Why the fuck would you want to hit me?" She is staring down at you and the red mark on your face, feeling her jaw trembling.

"Oh, sweetheart," she says, "Carol," she drops to her knees, level with you. She takes your hand and kisses it, tears rolling down her own shadow of down on her chin. "I am so sorry." She takes you in her arms. She nuzzles your neck, weeping herself.

You feel her soft kisses on your lips.

She buries her face in your breasts.

"You know I would never want to hurt you, not on purpose," she whispers, "I don't know what's happening to me." You find yourself patting her neck as she sobs, consoling her but confusing yourself. But when she raises her teary eyes to your own – something does not fit. Although wet, her eyes are cold, seeing through you; you cannot reach her.

"You forgive me, don't you?" says one of your lovers, with both hands on your shoulders. Your first real lover who matters, your child-hood friend. It seems important to her that you forgive. You look closely at her. How can you not? You know her eyes can be warmer.

"Of course," you whisper, but a chill goes over you, as if you have done something wrong. Your lover lets out your name in one breath as she takes your hair in her hands and rubs it against your face. Then she darts towards you and sticks her tongue in your mouth. All of it, all that can fit deep in your mouth.

The lust that you feel is so heavy that your body reacts before your mind. Your mouth is sucking in her fattened tongue and pushing your own tongue out under hers before you are aware of it; your body has thrust her crotch against yours, your hands have taken hers and pushed her hand under your robe, pushing her hand up inside you, where it is wet, drenched so quickly, from the moment her thick tongue pushed in between your lips. You wish Nicky's tongue were where her hand is, though at the same time you do not want her tongue taken away from its wet swollen probing in your mouth. *Stop, hold on,* you think, as her tongue traces circles in your mouth, painful circles you can feel all the way down in your groin. Where is Ellen, where is she, another person is needed in this act, really, another person to stick their tongue deep inside you while you're being kissed, but that is impossible, you realise, impossible, Ellen is nowhere to be found, you are all alone, as you feel your lover pushing your skirt up even higher, over your hips.

You are all alone. Outside your skull, you are all alone.

The scent of the grass grows stronger. You are losing. Ellen's lawn-chair is empty; she has gone inside. You do not know where the sun has gone.

As you break the embrace, Nicky pulls out the sharpened scissors from her pockets again. "Let me cut off your hair." You know what she means. What can it hurt, you think. It is only pubic hair, after all. And you think as well, what would she do with the scissors if I refused?

When you agree, you admit to yourself you find it arousing – the breath of danger, the blades so close to your clitoris. It takes a very long time, this erotic and dangerous process, a very long time, for she cuts every hair off at its root. But when she finishes, your lover turns towards you, sweaty, and her fingers examine your nude genitals. Wait, she says, probing, I've missed some. And the sharpened edge is out again. One moment, she says, on her knees between your legs with a studied and serious expression on her face. There, she says. And you feel a slight nick on your inner labia. Now it's all gone, says your lover. All gone. Is this the key? All gone. Empty.

Inner labia are as bald as men. There was no hair where she cut you and therefore she has cut for no reason at all. You put a finger between your legs and it comes up a little bloodied, just a spot of blood on your fingertip. The blood barely filling the dips and ridges of your finger whorls, just a dab on the finger-pads. Just a red smear like a tiny men-strual stain, only a tiny sharp cut on the inside fold of your genitals, a tiny nick. You run your fingers on your now smooth pubic mound, and your fingers remember the smooth pubis of a young girl, they are not remembering a woman. You hate it. How you hate her. The sun comes back from behind the clouds; it rains light down on you alone with your bloody finger, your bleeding cunt, for now Nicky has joined Ellen inside the house. Blood on your finger and acres of hair. The key to it all. *Riddle-me-yes and riddle-me-not; give me a riddle, I'll see what you've got.*

You join them inside.

"Hey," says Nicky, scraping with a futile spoon inside the jar of instant, "we're out of coffee. Didn't you remember to pick some up the other day when you were shopping?" You ignore her and go to sit down next to Ellen at the table.

"I don't know if Carol told you, Ellen," Nicky says, throwing the empty jar into the trash. All gone. The scissors lie on the counter, their blades spread-eagled and only marred by crimson stains if you look hard enough. "But Carol used to have a little problem leaving the house. Didn't you, Carol? But she's all better now, of course. Except when she forgets to leave the house to get the things we need, like the fucking coffee." Nicky gives you a quick, bright smile and leaves the room.

"We don't have any money for fucking coffee, Nicky!" you scream at her retreating back. "That's what I'm trying to talk to you guys about, you –" you take a breath "– bitch." But the door has already clicked shut behind her. You are left with Ellen.

Ellen moves her chair closer to yours. You have been staring down at the blue table for several seconds, but now you look up into her eyes. Her brown eyes are not at all cold and you believe you will accept whatever warmth she offers you. You need it. Her lashes close and cut off her gaze. You wonder what she is thinking about. You swear you can smell blood.

Ellen takes hold of your hands; you have learned from experience that she is a very tactile person. Can't she sense the wound below? Open your eyes, Ellen. Your bleeding is ignored: "Carol," she says, and her lids rise, "I know what's bothering you." In your heart you know she doesn't, but why not hear what she has to say? She moves her chair still closer.

"You feel like no one knows you. Am I right?" You are stunned. She might be right. She might be right. You let Ellen begin to stroke your palm as she continues talking. Invisible blood trickles through your fingers. "You're afraid to let me in. But there's a reason why I'm here. You're afraid to let *anyone* in, because you think no one guesses how it really is for you – and if they try, then they don't end up guessing right."

You stare at Ellen. You're being drawn in, hypnotised. You feel mesmerised by her tone, her voice as she strokes your fingers.

"Is that why you're so hard on Nicky? Because she can't guess as quick as me?"

There is just a split-second before you snatch your hand away from her indulgent, caressing fingers. You look at Ellen with a new wariness. She is much more subtle than she appears to be. And if she hadn't added that last comment about Nicky, you might have fallen for the ruse. It is a technique you know well, a tool of seducers and brainwashers. You have never used it yourself, but it has often been used on you before, by 'sensitive' and horny men.

It is the ruse where the seducer makes it known that only he can ever truly understand the victim's true self, the self kept hidden from everyone else. And since everyone has the fantasy of a hidden self, inevitably the victim will be convinced that the seducer can see through her artifices, see what no one else can see. The seducer only has to remember to be general in his assessment of the victim's internal loneliness. It succeeds nearly every time. Certainly, it has previously succeeded with you as the victim.

But it has never been attempted by a woman before, so you were vulnerable and unprepared. Next time you will be more ready. You are going to have to be very careful, even with Ellen, or you will never get free. You feel the ropes tighten. But you are an actress, too.

"What you see is what you get, Ellen." You stare steadily into her eyes. You are without obvious guile.

Ellen shifts uncomfortably. "I just thought maybe you would want to talk about stuff, Carol. I mean, since I'm here as a third party, I can be kind of objective between you and Nicky..."

"I think you've gone a bit past the point of objectivity by now, Ellen, don't you think?" You laugh in genuine astonishment.

"A bit past. A bit passed by –" Ellen has gone vague again. You wonder what it is that sets her off. Confrontation? Any extended conversation at all? She talks so smoothly for a while, and then all her speech breaks up. She adds something, however, just before she leaves the room and closes the kitchen door: "There's a reason why I'm here, Carol. Remember that. I want it to be good with all of us. None of us will lose our friends." Despite the forthright words, she gives you a timid smile before exiting. Maybe she is just trying to be nice. Maybe you *are* fucked up and paranoid, like Nicky says.

You're glad you're able to leave the house these days. Because you want to get out right away before you see either of them, before Nicky comes downstairs or Ellen comes back in. You grab some clothes drying on the kitchen radiator and dress quickly, changing from the bathrobe that you have been wearing nearly all day. It's Ellen's top and Nicky's pants; both articles of damp clothing clamp to your skin with humid, parasitic stubbornness. You take your purse with you as you step out of the kitchen door and towards the front door itself. There is no smile on your face. And then the kitchen door clicks shut behind you for the third time this afternoon, closing itself finally on an empty room. All gone.

That night you lie on the couch in the living room, huddled in extra blankets and a comforter. It is dark, all around you. You listen, but you can hear no sounds at all from Nicky and Ellen upstairs. Maybe they've gone out. Your senses dull, and circle in on you so you hear only your own breathing and your persistent heartbeat. You lie there and listen for many minutes into the dark night until your breaths and heartbeat slow. You feel your limbs enter the consensual paralysis of sleep and at last your mind follows your body, past the freeze, past the ringing, into the hall of mirrors only ghosts know well.

Later you are wakened by a warm hand on your shoulder. It is Ellen who kisses you gently and re-spreads the blankets on the carpet by the couch, beckons you down there. You move down to sleep there, covered by Ellen and the blankets. And as you drift off, Ellen holds you so sweetly and gently that, although you are covered and surrounded, for once you are not trapped.

In the midst of this soothe and your dozing stupor, you hear the front door opening. Nicky. You are not worried. Eventually Nicky also burrows herself into the blankets with you and Ellen and sleeps. Normally you would want to ask questions, like: where have you been? Why are you home so late? But there is something positive about Ellen's presence, you realise, it dulls the jealousy. It makes whatever Nicky does, good or bad, not matter so much. It gives you alternatives.

In the morning you are woken by the sun streaming in; there are no curtains in the living room. Nicky and Ellen still sleep and the rays settle on the three of you lying there, the different colours of your skins, the hair on your exposed arms and legs backlit in relief – as if by floodlights. You let out a sigh from deep within you and feel immensely, giddily happy. At the back of your neck is the beauty of release, release through simply letting things happen. No more riddles. You're going to be an easy girl. You always have been, so why change now?

You lie there thinking. The next one to stir is Ellen. She seems confused, so you hold her until she wakes up fully and comes into herself. Nicky is still sleeping. "Look how beautiful the day is," you say quietly to Ellen. You point out to her the patterns of light on the carpet. "You wouldn't be seeing stuff like this if you hadn't come downstairs to join me." Ellen smiles, you think she understands what you are trying to show her.

"It's very pretty," says Ellen. "Like you." You are never sure if Ellen is trying to flatter you or if she means what she is saying.

"Thank you," you say. You will give her the benefit of the doubt.

Nicky is waking up. It is a school day, after all. She's got to get going. Although you had hugged her while the three of you slept, you turn your back so that you don't have to see her face. You feel the slight twisting sting in the folds of your sex where she cut yesterday.

You are glad you can feel it. If you cannot bring yourself to remember her treachery, at least your body will. Ellen is rubbing her hand across your shoulder blades.

"Look at Carol, Nicky," she says. "Isn't she lovely in the sunlight?" Again, you think you might be hearing a flutter of deceit in her voice. But not all people are as treacherous as Nicky, who merely answers quickly in the affirmative before getting up and leaving the room. And as Ellen coos compliments at you and pets you after Nicky's departure, you almost believe that she means it. The light plays across her skin.

"She doesn't like the nice stuff, Ellen. Don't bother." Nicky's voice breaks in and jars, all the way from the bathroom. "She likes to be treated rough, don't you, Carol? Rough." Nicky enters the room again, clad only in her underpants, bra-less.

She holds a toothbrush in her hands and her small round breasts jiggle as she gives several strokes to her teeth, before walking quickly over and teasingly whacking Ellen on the bottom with the flat end of the damp toothbrush. Ellen is confused, you notice, and looks up at Nicky.

"Treat them mean and keep them keen, Ellen. That's what you have to do." Nicky avoids your eyes, but you're not really looking anyway. You position yourself among Ellen and the blankets so that you do not have to lock gazes with Nicky, even by accident. She flounces down on the sofa above you and Ellen, legs far apart. She gives several more vigorous swipings at her teeth before swallowing the mixture of toothpaste and saliva. You hear the *thunk* as Nicky places the toothbrush down on the side table. She is leaning forward; you are trying to stretch your body as far away from her as possible, but you can feel the tips of her bare breasts touching your lower back as she leans over you and Ellen, searching for something. You know that she is trying to make you feel uncomfortable. You think Ellen has gone back to sleep. Perhaps a case of sudden narcolepsy? How very convenient.

Nicky sits up on the couch again and removes her weight from behind you. You can hear her snapping something with her fingers.

"Wake up, Ellen," Nicky says then. "Carol won't play with me. But look what I've got here – Carol's tights." She leans down and places a gentle hand on Ellen to shake her further awake.

"Tights. Tight," says Ellen, rubbing her eyes and sitting halfway up. You can feel a creeping sensation beginning at the bottom of your spine and working its way up.

"That's right. Tights, pulled tight. Carol won't play these kind of games with me anymore. But you will, won't you, Ellen?"

You sneak a look at Ellen: the expression on her face is vapid and aroused. Ellen likes this kind of thing; she told you so once in Seattle. But you had deferred from participating then, and you're going to do it now again. You feel the sick gathering in the bottom of your stomach. You get up then, naked and gold in the glittering sunlight, and leave. You do not want to see the further progressions of Ellen trussed and tied with your pantyhose, or with anything else for that matter. They can keep your stupid nylons, but you're getting out of this particular scene.

You can hear both Ellen's and Nicky's breaths harden and speed up while you are stepping finally out of the room, after the interminable distance across the carpet without once looking back, and all the while Ellen's sounds turn more rounded and, worse, repulsively, sickeningly sexual and juicy. And a familiar cute, rather throaty noise. The sounds Nicky loves to hear in girls, it seems: Ellen sounds just like you in bed. You retreat upstairs to the unslept-in bed and lie there, aching, the pain in your stomach never fading even while you press your eyes tight into your pillow. You lie in a foetal position willing the sounds downstairs to fade and disappear, the way you did the day Nicky bought the shoes.

You wonder if Ellen believes in escape, and maybe you should help her, but thinking of actually climbing down those stairs again does not fit in well with your present perceptions. You are not even sure if you want to leave the bedroom; you are quite comfortable where you are. She has certainly slowly tied up one of Ellen's wrists by now. Still, you force yourself to get up, to open the door, to leave the room and look over the banister at the top of the staircase at the sexual crawl beneath you. Ellen is in ecstasy, it appears. She loves it. You don't know why you even worried. Nicky looks up at you and then, as Ellen screams in pleasure, she unties the ropes, the pantyhose, the bindings. She throws the rope out the window; you will never get down. You hate her. Now there is no escape. No escape for Ellen. No escape for you.

The spring sun continues to flood in through the windows. It is still a morning. But now of your own accord, you have walked down the stairs. She can make you do things. You owe her, maybe. If what she tries to talk about after she dreams *is* real. Which you don't think it is. But she can still make things happen. Around your own wrists are hair-strands, looped. I can go through with this. I can get by this thing, and then she'll stop. You think this. Concentrate on your thoughts because if you are not thinking, then you will have to concentrate on what Nicky is doing to your body. The way she is feeling it, the impersonal way she looks at it.

"Did you close the door upstairs?" she asks.

"Will you let me go?" you ask.

"Eventually." She makes it so it's no longer your body; it's more correct to say it's hers. If you want to, you can make it no longer your body whatsoever. You can make that happen. Make that happen.

It's a captivity within another one. Nicky with all her closet sadisms, her pinches and traps. It's like an egg, a white thin-shelled chicken's egg. You are the yolk and the transparent strands of your own light hair by which you are bound, the egg's clear fluid. An egg imprisoned by itself. You chuckle inwardly, so that Nicky won't hear you and become angry. And the shell – that's your tower and your house. A double-prison, a brittle shell – you just go ahead and wish that this tower were as fragile, that these bonds were as liquid and as slippery as egg-white. You know that this is difficult, you must understand the thick viscous difference between imagery and life, become more mature, now, do it.

What was that song your mom used to sing? It was a song about riddles.

How can there be a chicken that has no bone?

How can there be a baby with no cryin'?

And now, when Ellen is done, spent, you must wait motionless for Nicky to untie you from your own hair. And wait. "You said that you'd untie me," you say. Complicit, that's what you are. Go ahead, make your voice darker: "That's why I agreed." Take the key and lock her up.

"As if you really had a choice," Nicky says. But you had really thought you had. An implicit understanding. Take the key and lock her up. You played games, the two of you, when you were children in the forest. Though there were no real threats then: no accidental tiny slips, no small cuts. But there was a certain negotiation between the two of you then. And now here there has not been discussion for a very, very long time. The two of you have been entirely separate eggs.

"Untie me," you say. Nicky waits long enough to have you believe she will not, then she does. The end of your hair is flicked towards you by her wrist. A tiny whip, and a small welt rises on your calf. Pretend that you did not see her flick your hair, that you do not feel the stinging caused by the white needle-hair. Pretend you do not notice when she goes. The extension of your own body used against you. Complicit. A chicken in the egg, it has no bone; what's that fucking supposed to mean? A baby when it's sleeping, there's no cryin'. Pretend that the small moon-shaped shiny scars on your scalp that pull when she climbs down your hair are not originally caused by her, and worse, with your partial consent. Your hair will fall off; your face, your nose. You will become a sphinx. Pretend that you are bald, instead.

"Don't you like a little bit of bondage?" Ellen's voice is innocent later that day when you run into each other in the kitchen, after Nicky has left for college.

You've been through car accidents and marathons this morning, so you take your time to gather your thoughts before you answer Ellen. "I don't really. No, not really." Your wrists ache.

"So why not? It's just a game. I think it's sexy." Ellen takes a carton of orange juice out of the fridge and takes a long draught from the cardboard container. Nicky would kill her if she saw her doing that.

"It's because I have a thing about being too wrapped up. I used to be agoraphobic, you know." You get a glass out and pour yourself a drink from the same carton.

"Yeah, I know, Nicky said so yesterday. But I can never get these things straight. Is it spiders or elevators?"

The orange juice stings the small, hidden cuts in your mouth. "It means a fear of open spaces." You do not feel benevolent nor inclined to share yourself with Ellen. "But for me it meant I didn't want to leave the house at all."

"Oh, yeah, I've heard of that. But how come you can leave now? Did something change?"

Yes, something had changed. But you're still not sure what it was yourself. And after today, you're not certain that it hasn't changed right back.

Ellen does not seem to notice that she receives no answer to her question. She grabs the carton again, hoists herself up on the counter and balances, her legs swinging. "You know, Nicky's been saying that she has bad dreams sometimes. And that afterwards, you don't listen to her when she wants to talk. I'm just mentioning the fact. That's all."

"Yeah, well, that's bullshit. I listen all the time." You have half a mind to tell Ellen to get off the counter, as a parent would tell a child. You can feel your eyes narrowing, your jaw tightening, your chest becoming constricted.

Ellen notices your reaction and says quickly, "I don't think she meant anything by it. I didn't get that impression at all."

You remind yourself to be patient; Ellen is in her category all by herself. Your words are slow and precise. "Nicky might like me a little too much. You should watch out for that yourself."

Ellen's eyes are blank at your guarded warning. She tries a smile at you, hops down from the counter and gives you a hug. Your heart aches for her; even if you should ever manage to escape, how could you take her with you? Despite the fact she's six years older, she is easy meat for Nicky's traps and games. And she wants them too badly herself.

That night you lie spoon-fashion with Ellen upstairs in the bed, your fingers feeling the regular tickling of her pulse through her thin, brown skin. For a moment you wish Nicky could be here to wonder at the steady throb as well. What was it, the word that came to you this morning? Oh yes, a sphinx.

Sphinx. You taste the word and you like it. If you're remembering correctly, she was a cold and cruel creature, a powerful female. You need that kind of strength to break out. There has to be something – even a myth – which exists and which is colder, crueller, stronger than Nicky. Something has to be. And if only you have the right key, the right answer or the right cut you will be free. Love is a trap you will never again willingly enter. Sphinx. Sphinx. Links. Bolts. Locks. Damn – you almost had it for a moment, but you've lost it again.

You hear Nicky unlocking the door downstairs. She's sleeping with someone else, you're almost sure of it. She always has her escape hatches worked out in advance, but you – on the other hand – usually don't. You experience a maternal, protective shudder for Ellen. Like you, Ellen has no escapes, but unlike you Ellen does not know everything that you know. Even if she's more experienced in bed, she remains the most vulnerable. Because you are afraid that Ellen believes in the hope of it all – in the 'relationship' – with the fervour of a zealot. If Nicky betrays only one of you, is it still considered a betrayal? Only sex-positive Ellen knows the answer; she knows about ménages, she said, but yet you don't want to hurt her in the asking. She might not know the depths to which Nicky can betray.

*

Your stomach begins to grow slowly and it's bursting with riddles and thoughts. In the moments that Nicky does not come, you sleep with your hands clasped over your belly. But when she comes, she is accompanied by Ellen. And Nicky sneers when she leaves, as she looks down to see you lying there with one hand curled over your abdomen. Ellen, however, returns momentarily and leans in close to you to whisper things:

"Quiet," you say. You turn your head away from her. She takes hold of your hair anyway and pushes it through the window. Ignoring the smarting, you are still lying down while Ellen descends. She is a quick learner, that Ellen. She will not always be a victim.

The television is on when you come back several nights later, after frugal shopping and a fruitless search for a part-time job. This occurrence of TV-watching is unusual; none of you watch it, really, with the exception of the Tracey Ullman show. Both Nicky and Ellen are glued to the set, so after you set the shopping down in the kitchen, you join them before the flickering godbox in the living-room. It's the news. You see a bay with a dark splodge on it. There is a branching spider on the water. It seems to be flexing and extending, but this may be your imagination. The place looks familiar, as does the wide, pale sky and the mountain range in the background. Ellen in particular seems fascinated by the expanse of the water shown; you remember that she once mentioned a preoccupation with drowning. Just like Nicky, you thought at the time.

"Where's that?" you ask them.

"Shh," Nicky says, "I want to listen."

On the television you are seeing terrible things. Seeing the plastered water soaking in its own congestion. Water which is no longer water but a thick evil syrup burping across the ocean. What shows is only part of the spill, the news announcers are saying, it is under the surface of the water as well. Oil is meant to be burnt and you know that fire and water never mix. What your eyes are seeing is a taint, a growing shade on the water but thick, blocked, slick. It is, after all, the same range of volcanoes you are familiar with yourself; the news even shows the long-sleeping Lady Julia.

You close your eyes and rest your hands over the imaginary swell of your stomach. Someone must come soon to take the pollutions away, and to take away the parasite of a notion over which your hands nestle and curl. And then what your eyes are really seeing, finally, is the sight of your stomach growing larger as you sit there on the couch, the thought inside you distending so your hands cannot curl easily over it anymore. What will Nicky say? What will Ellen say?

The contamination has begun. And been aborted. You note – but do not feel in any way – that this time the hair of the pale, see-through riddle you have stillborne is translucent, translucent like your own hair, and curled, coiled. You would have liked to have touched it.

Over the next few days the screen begins to show choking, burn-blackened birds and animals. They are goo-covered and dying. A TV crew's film shows a hopeful attempt at spraying the filth off the barely living, but the creatures are dying of shock and not just from the poisonous oil, but also from the touch of human hands. An announcer says that Exxon plans to wash the beaches clean, but you can't figure out how this will be possible. Inky dredge washes up on the surrounding beaches, clinging to the rocks and dripping from the sand. It is suggested that there will be no fishing when summer comes.

Your hair is turning to jelly and when your fingers run through it, it is dripping, dripping off your hands. Why is this supposed to be what you have been waiting for all your life?

11. Ellen

There was a mess out there. I could see it on the television screen, but I could feel it too. My gums felt the mess; felt the oily juice slipping in. Through my pores, through the holes I have in my body. Eyes, ears, scratches, cunt. It seeped in through the cracks until I felt so full of grease that I had to wash quickly; I had to leave the other two and run, not walk, to the bathtub and wash. Then I was clean. Then it was as close to bliss as it got.

The extent of my love for Carol and Nicky surprised me, even though there had been hints and signs that it would happen. It did much for me by keeping my senses in the past; the two of them reminded me of things I needed to remember: the place we all were from and knew so intimately. I hadn't been there since I was seventeen. The two of them grounded me, but I was not fully protected. But things were getting shaky now, and I wasn't sure I could wing it on my own. And I didn't know if Nicky or Carol could look out for me the way I was used to doing for myself. Their heads were just too full of stuff. Me, I liked to keep my head empty. I cleaned it out from time to time. I washed it out in chilling water. I'd walk out that door into deep early spring *the lilies sing* I believe in everything... I step out onto the lake crack falls of ice in the crackfalls of spring ice it's equinox ice it's do what I want in the springtime of hell *ice* and I step – slowly – One. And a two. And three. What happens on the ice is *ice ice* I step on ice ice all I see is ice ice watch the ice walk the ice see the ice the ice cracks down the ice I stomp down the running ice. *The melting ice ice* Eventually all of Susan's dreams go down on ice. Dead and down and dulled on ice.

No. No ice and no morticians. And all of Susan's dreams for me came round. I was a survivor, but I'll tell more about that later. Another person talked often of survival, and this person was Carol.

She spoke of surviving Nicky, whispered this to me sometimes when Nicky was at college. But Nicky was sweet and attentive to me and to Carol as well. So what was it Carol watched out for to survive? I'd ask Susan in my head but, as always with my urgent questions, she remained incommunicado. So I had to work it out for myself if my observations were representative. Surviving for me meant that if I didn't go down on ice, someone else would, and I didn't want anyone to be hurt; I wanted it decently safe for all concerned. Make it pretty for me and for all the others. Bluewater and pretty. There was a word for it I once read. Mellifluous. It's a lovely word, I often liked to say it to myself to send me off to sleep. The sweetness of water. The transparency of water. The magnification of water. Is there anything at all you can't see closer once it is distorted?

I sat down on the couch when I returned from the bathroom. Nicky was holding my hand, which felt nice. Carol was staring upset at the television, for the television was full of distortions. There were shadows slipping through the water. I understood perfectly well, of course, that this happened up home. But it seemed removed and detached from my heart by now. I was no longer agitated by stuff I didn't want to be upset by. I looked at Nicky, who wasn't upset at all. I had my suspicions that Carol's reaction was more because Nicky came home so late these days. I know Carol worried; sometimes I caught her crying and I tried to give her back the comfort she once had offered me. Somehow I felt inadequate, however, and I'd hold her close to save her. *Remember.* Carol asked me not to tell Nicky that she worried and so far, I had remembered not to tell her. I hated seeing Carol upset. I really did. So I tried not to tell Nicky secrets if Carol really didn't want me to. Secrets. Dirty. Cloudy water.

The dirty water was horrible even though Nicky kept on holding my hand. Maybe Carol was right about it being terrible after all. There was no necessary talk of survivors when water begins with a colour and ends with a clarity. This is why I liked clean water; I liked coloured clear water through which I could see. I liked to dive straight down, when it was more purposeful than merely a fall – I'd be having a ball because when I went... when I went under the water... when I went under the water... when I went under the water the colours went gleaming green, perfect blue, perfect white, the best yellow and me above the water floating and the floating down to me.

"That's fucking awful." The programme was over and Carol offered a comment.

"Yeah," Nicky said, but she didn't say anything else. She gave my hand a squeeze though, before she let go and got up from the couch.

"Are you ready for bed?" Nicky spoke only to me. I felt bad; I could feel through all the holes in my body how this must be hurting Carol. Although we found each other attractive, Carol didn't like sex in some of the ways in which I did. We had both realised this early on without too much awkwardness, way back in Seattle. There were certain ways in which Nicky and I were far the better pair, and one of them was sex. Nicky was a born top, only too happy to dominate in any dark game of excellent bondage I held before her. If I ever brought her back to Seattle I'd have to keep her under wraps – she'd be far too popular. There were even times when Nicky would push the scene further than I wanted it to go. Consensuality became an issue for the first time with me. I didn't think Nicky was bad in any sense – *far from it,* Susan whispered – Nicky always ultimately respected my limits, but she thought too much about the wrong stuff; she dwelled too much on rapid violence, I thought, for her own good. And I could not always understand her garbled tales of childhood fears. Carol would know what Nicky meant, of course, if I went to Carol and asked her, but Carol was withdrawing from both Nicky and me to the privacy of her own thoughts. It seemed now that Carol was thinking as Nicky usually did, mulling and deciphering. Maybe that was good, who knew? In her own blonde way, she was as intellectual as Nicky.

When Carol did share her interior world with us, it was always on the subject of our finances and her determination to find herself a job. She said there was only about a week's worth of money left. Lately she had even taken to declining the offer to join Nicky and me in the bed upstairs, even for a cuddle, and had been sleeping downstairs on the sofa instead. *Go to her.* I listened to Susan and remembered that my purpose here involved the two of them, not just Nicky. I *would* go to her. I didn't want this loneliness for Carol tonight, I didn't want to leave her with the grey television screen reminding her of the defaced pictures it held before. But when I went downstairs to ask, the horrible ugliness on the TV had changed to a calm grey smooth screen.

"Do you want to come up and sleep with us, Carol?" I asked.

"That's okay, Ellen. I'm fine." Carol smiled; the screen held no terrors.

"I mean just sleep."

"I'm fine."

I must have been wrong; Carol was doing okay without us. "Good night." I turned around to go. *But remember* – Was I doing the right thing? Should I leave her? Perhaps things did not always work out the way Susan had predicted. People and circumstances change. Things change from the living, soft vibrant leaves of waterlilies, yellow-green and rich, to drained, white lily leaves. Lilies which vampires have attacked; lilies which mosquitoes have sucked dry.

Carol, Susan whispered, *Don't let Carol be afraid.* But Nicky was upstairs waiting for me and I wasn't sure what I should do. Perhaps I should ignore Susan, just for once. What would happen then? I knew what would happen. The sheen would come in through the cracks in my body, seep up through to the wrinkles in my brain which I knew were active, which I knew existed, which folded over themselves and squinted up there. The sheen would settle in my brain loops until they were saturated and immobile, their psychic power diffused. I tried hard to concentrate my thoughts on all the spirits present the way we had been taught once by a visiting elder at McAlester's. But I am only one-sixteenth Athabaskan and I'm not sure I did it right. My brain did try very hard but I didn't want to be a thinker like Nicky or Carol, I wanted to be, oh fuck, all I wanted to be was clean. *Well,* Susan whispered back up to cracks in the ice and then icings would fall through the crack ice of lake *Well, alright* when I went under the water the colours went... When I went under the water the flowers went white...

I've said I would tell you, so now I will. Released for just a moment from dying oily birds and Susan's tender grip, I will tell you.

I was a survivor from water in the largest sense. I stood on the banks in winter season and watched the ice crack beneath her, crack, crack. I watched as she retreated across the frozen lake; she was seeing things. The birds were flying faster. They were now speeding past her frosted eyelids. She was hearing things. On top of waters. On top of waters. Voices, for example... and all the while, I would hear someone else screaming, too. I thought it was an echo, but it was my own scream. It wasn't just she who grew frosty; I too had to have been feeling a chill of some sort. *I was up against a sheerness. I was breaking off like an icicle.* See. This part of me then this *Then this.* This part of me is breaking off *then this* What was it she would whisper in my ear? *the ice is cracking* I'm cracking up. What was she whispering? Her head cracked on ice. A sharp like a shot up her crack. Susan is dead. Above her the ice cracks and rescue is too late.

Above her the ice cracks. Above her the ice cracks. Above her the ice cracks.

Above her the ice was crackling. Crackling –

She liked to whisper it –

Crackling. She said it didn't matter when you see its cracks, it doesn't mean you'll slip through. You just must avoid it after the rain... when the ice turns soft... when the cracks turn back to water... I was sure she would watch me through the crack. I was afraid she would slash up through the hole, snatch me through the crack. I was afraid I would be skating there in my fur-lined boots with my new muff and she would make a gash and a hole in the frigid ice and slash her fingers through the slit and reach up and snatch me through the crack. *You could have saved me, Ellen. So why didn't you save me?*

It was raining on the ice when I started out on it, which was not promising. I couldn't even guess why I was there, I had always hated the lake. Through the ice I could see something. I could see something. I thought I saw her face. Susan's face frozen below, I had only to scrape the snow with my boot to see her putrid expression. She never floated back to us. I remembered it well. There were loads of dead fish after they boomed the lake for her. Inadequately, I'm afraid. Because she never came up. Oh yeah, they found her *real* body, of course, but not her mind and not her spirit. Those parts of her stayed underneath the water. I tried to help but she fell through anyway. Did I try enough, though? *Come on. Go through the motions.* You, I'm watching all the way from the water below. Cracking up for sure. When I was young, I went out too far in the woods. And there was a lake. And I saw it. I was dry but my hands were wet with blood, you know what I was like. Oh, I'm sick of it, I'm through. Dearest Susan, with your lovely water-bleached bones, the net-lacing of meat still on your lovely shoulders. Throw me in the water and I will never think of the lake in winter. Then the season changed.

Then I watched her flail in spring, drown in spring, ring, ring, I believed in everything. Everything but Susan.

Then I watched her drown in summer, too, down through the pretty water. The water cremated cut off. Till she was fallen the curse and deep in the water. Down beyond the lake and tight. But she won't ask her folks tonight. alright. introduce me one two fright. out-asight. When she went under the water the colours went gleaming green, parfait blue, le parfait white best aqua too and me above the water floating and the floating down to her – and I could taste the lilies. A languorous pouring, but I could still taste that green on my tongue. But I could still taste that wet leaf on my tongue. When she went under the water the colours went... when she went under the water the flowers went white...

I remembered the lake in summer. I could only get this wet, as wet as the lake, when I was expecting something I never got. The anticipation of a mutually agreed captivity. The moment before the cuffs embrace me. On top of waters. Not such a good feeling to be this brittle and prone to breakage, but I didn't know much else. I didn't want the good parts in me anymore, I wanted them *broken off*. She wanted them *broken off*. The passing of time does a lot to cover up the little pains. It's been at least fifteen years, and if you think things over as much as I do, it's just a videotape in your head. Sadly, it all has to go, the good with the bad. But I think it's going to be alright, actually. When fall comes, maybe. When fall comes. Then I'll do it right and she'll be safe.

A season later I again stood on the banks to watch her drown in autumn. I stood in fall, I watched her fall, I had no water. Like before. Mascara made lakes on my cheeks. No more. Check the skull. Là – unceasingly flowing the lake in my mind, mauve purple and red of fish bloodline, but I permitted but few salmon to swim the red. Squiggled them in first be squiggled well out. A lake touching me gets no fish. Near not me close to skull not the flow touched too far the water gets me not alive and no fish

Boom.

I have seen her drowning throughout the year. Those who die young will remain always youthful. And you know one of my secrets.

That night we slept in groups of two and one. The next morning was Saturday; I wanted to go for a walk in the sharp air. I shook Nicky awake. "Hey, how about a walk?" I said. "Do you feel like going out for a bit of a stroll?"

"Go where, sweetheart?" Nicky said, waking up. She stroked her fingers through my hair, just like Carol. It felt nice. I felt like a kid. Like I had a family. I loved it when they made me feel this way. "Alright – answer me now."

"Maybe the park?" I felt excited. I jumped out of bed and dressed myself. It was still early.

"Alright," said Nicky, yawning. "We can have breakfast on the way."

"Well... we don't have any money. Remember?" Last night Carol had said this over and over again. She had sounded like my last foster mother before I left home. And now I sounded like her, too.

"I forgot," said Nicky. "That's okay, we'll make some sandwiches and take them with us." She seemed like she was eager to leave quickly. Then I remembered why.

"Is Carol coming too?"

"No."

We went downstairs and Nicky opened the kitchen door quietly. I knew this was because she didn't want to wake up Carol, who was sleeping in the living-room. She went to the refrigerator and took out the last of the bread, some yoghurt and a hard-boiled egg. She opened a can of tuna fish. I opened the kitchen door again, but stood in its frame watching her.

"It's alright if Carol comes too?"

"I said *no*! What the fuck, don't you fucking understand the word?" Nicky came over to me and grabbed me. I wished I could tell her that I wasn't afraid, but I couldn't speak at all, right then. Carol was immediately by me at the door.

"Did we wake you up?" said Nicky in a slow, measured tone. I looked at Nicky. Her hands were clammy from the egg she'd been peeling and folding into the tuna and yoghurt. Her hands were beautiful. Her hands were frightening.

"It's okay," I said. "She wasn't going to do anything." I was not sure if this is a lie. It was fuzzy in my brain instead of pure. I looked down at my stranger's body encased in clothes, with its adult qualities of breasts and hips and – to a child, anyway – relative height. I had survived to grow this tall. Those who die as children remain stunted but my throat remained crippled and broken even if I had grown up. I gargled through it to repeat what I had said before to Carol, that Nicky wasn't going to do anything that could hurt me. But they were already talking between themselves.

"I've had it, Nicky," said Carol. "Absolutely had it. Where are you off to, some sort of picnic? You know we can't afford that."

"And what do you care?" Nicky raised her voice. "It's not like you listen to anything I've ever tried to tell you, anyway, not anything that matters..."

"Do you mean those stupid dreams of yours that make you wake up all the time in *tears*?"

"Maybe."

"I'm sick of them. I don't know what they mean."

Nicky saw, as I saw, the earnest truthfulness in Carol's face as she spoke, and I watched Nicky's angular face shift into a friend. She was becoming a friend to Carol.

"Look, it's just a little Saturday excursion. I'm making sandwiches, see – I'm not buying anything new, anyway, we're just going for a –"

"Shut up! Your *fucking* stupid dreams! You fucking spendthrift!" Carol was, as they say, spitting mad. Her already long hair began to grow like fire as she screamed, the length festooning in drips of velvet to the floor, the cool paleness of it almost translucent. It was ghost-hair, only I could see its extensions billow out, the locks dropping and folding ever thicker over themselves on the floor. *Look closely.* I made Susan shut up; I had had enough of her. Ghost-hair. If Nicky could have seen it too, she would have grabbed and twisted it in anger; as it was, her fingers went right through it and then stopped before they reached Carol's body.

"Come on, hit me if you're going to," said Carol. Even I sensed the fury in the air. "You want to fucking hit me, let's see you do it."

I stepped in the air which pumped between them; I stepped apologetically on Carol's curled pale forgotten locks still draping down, the pillows of fine hair rising almost to her knees – but Carol didn't seem to notice. I looked at Nicky and behind her, like the back-drop of a stage set, I saw the forest she'd mumble about in her sleep at night and I also saw the terrible, desperate burn in her eyes; I could not offer her the wild spirits she craved. But I thought, I suspected, I hoped I could offer her and offer Carol, too, the peace of survival.

Show them how, whispered Susan. I gave in and obeyed.

"We won't fight," I said. "It's not worth it." I didn't often enter in their arguments, so I shocked them both into a type of silence. Carol broke it.

"Ellen," she said, her tone was blurred and quiet, "I was worried for you." She turned to Nicky, "I was worried. If you try to do to her what –" I pulled then, tight on the ghost-hair, and Carol stopped, paused in thought.

Nicky spoke next, "I'm sorry, Ellen," she sounded ashamed, "I lose my temper a lot. Look, I shouldn't have shaken you, Carol's right." I saw the spirits running away from her eyes, the forest dissolving behind her, quick as water swirling down a sink; I wished I could let her know somehow how important it was not to chase all of the forest away, but how necessary it was to keep certain bits of it, to keep the leaves and needles that were green and sweet and sharp. Not the rotting fear. But this was something all three of us would learn together. It was enough, for the meantime, that the possibility of a wrong direction had been stalled – if not veered.

Carol had her hands to her face and was sobbing in the kitchen door. I felt bright love for both of them. *You must show it,* Susan said. I put one hand on Carol's shoulder in the morning sunlight.

"I think Nicky will lay off on you for a while. And no more pressure on your part either, eh?" I gave Nicky a stern glance. She appeared taken aback but relieved. She nodded in my direction – and then tentatively put her hand on Carol's other shoulder, before she took Carol properly in her arms to comfort her sobs. Tears ran down Nicky's cheeks as well, and mine, and I was brilliantly, joyously happy. "Tell her so," I mouthed to Nicky, but Nicky held Carol for several minutes more until Carol's cries quieted and she trembled less. A shiver began to run up from the bottom of my spine: an important moment was about to occur – one which would change the composition of our relationship.

Nicky's fingers stroked Carol's blonde hair; all was as it should be, the see-through strands below had disappeared into the mist of dust and air from which they once arose. "Sweetheart," she said to Carol, "we're going to get some cash and it's going to be much easier, honey." I smiled at Nicky for saying the right and correct things with the perfect intonation. "We're going back up for a while. My dad got me a job on the spill and he figures I'll net over twenty thousand this summer." I smiled at Nicky. She was not looking at me, but waiting instead for Carol's reaction.

I smiled at Nicky. I kept smiling. Alright. The cracks of the lake bit down hard on a strange feeling and my belfry lakes also kept smiling and squeaking and peeping along in my head. I caught Susan's thought-daggers of pips of cheeps one-bye-one but pain save pain again. I had made her happy. And all the salmon smile-squiggly by her lake. And all my dreams were silver squiggly.

I smiled at Nicky. I kept smiling.

iii. **back inside**

12. Ellen

She sold her car so that the three of us could afford the tickets home. I sometimes thought of it as the last magnanimous gesture Carol made for the triad we comprised – or the first.

Though Nicky was reluctant to speak about the trip up, I understood that we wouldn't be living in Anchorage. Nicky's uncle was letting all of us house-sit for the summer, and free rent plus amenities like a house in the woods with a view couldn't be passed by. The plan was that after Nicky made enough scrubbing beaches, we'd all be heading south again in late summer, maybe to Portland or San Francisco this time. I liked the fact that nothing was distinct and that I could just float along as well as fate allowed for me. I knew when things were right – and this was – so I silently helped Carol and Nicky pack up while they talked excitedly between themselves. I should say, I knew when things were right for Susan. For me, I was still unsure. Carol's mood had lifted once she knew we wouldn't be trapped in small-town Oregon forever, and for the first time in weeks the three of us slept and made love together as a unit, occasionally detaching into momentary couples.

We only had the week in which to get ready. Nicky took her exams early and I helped Carol in her frenetic determination to claim the deposit with a spotless, clean house. It was like Carol wanted to make sure she got some refund on all the experiences she had had there. I tried to let her know how much better it was all going to be once we were back home and just how right everything was going to feel when we were closer to the things which haunted us. And I was persuasive. I had been convinced by Susan's own convictions. But I might have been mistaken with Carol, for sometimes I wondered whether the things which passed over her face when she thought privately were things from the past or the present. It was difficult to tell. For me and for Nicky, too, I suspected, it was the past which was important. Even here in Oregon, once upon a time in the world Outside.

Once upon a time there is a lake in late evening with the sun shining on the water-lilies near the shore. There is a particular concentration of light on the waxy leaves of the lilies, a focusing on some in particular. It means nothing. It is just a zooming-in on something that is not directly related, attention directed to a thing on the side. Focus misses the real thing. The edge of a lake is visible from far away, even from a brightly lit white lily with small bugs on its leaves. A shore assumed. Iceless lake. Alright then.

Alright then. We were almost ready to leave. Nicky was lying stretched out in the bare living room, her entire body basking in the sun shining through the windows. Carol was asleep with her head on Nicky's lap, and in sleep she smiled to herself. *The summer water laps over the lily pads.*

"Come here, Ellen," Nicky whispered, and wagged her fingers to beckon me closer. I went over and sat down by her head. "Do you know what this is, Ellen? Do you?" Nicky made a motion which included the sunny expanse of the room and Carol dozing on her stomach. I didn't know exactly what she meant. I watched Carol's chest rise and fall. "This is pure joy, Ellen. I'm happy right now." Nicky looked down at Carol for a moment, and then looked back at me. *The waxy fruit of the lilies' mouths breathing, sweet jesus it's the lilies singing when they're touched, the lilies opening their little mouths –*

"You know why, Ellen?" I didn't. "It's because we've got everything ahead of us and nothing behind. And it feels new, Ellen," I was convinced I could see Nicky's eyes turn wet, "it feels fresh. I'm going back to it, and I can feel that I am. Deep down where it counts." Her jawline tensed momentarily and then her face relaxed, as if she had told me something which was necessary for her to say. She reached down and absently stroked her fingers through Carol's hair. *sweet jaws and singing one section of white lilies in the lake. All the other lilies were yellow. I didn't feel the need of breath.* I cuddled up to Nicky and lay comforted like Carol, my thoughts turning over what the move the next day would mean. The nervousness was there, but I'd have to start to trust. I would send a postcard to Jackie once we were up there, just to let her know that I was doing fine.

"I know what you're thinking right now," Nicky suddenly said, and I looked up sharply. *through the cracks come your hands* "You're worried about me and Carol getting along. You don't need to worry," she said, stroking my hair now, too, "you're thinking about stuff you don't need to think about." I let my thoughts drift blankly then, to accommodate Nicky, as I lay there soaking up the early summer sun. *through the cracks come your hands summer summer summer*

The plane trip turned out to be turbulent, and several times I felt like I was going to be sick. Carol held my hand until it passed and I felt better, but she finally had to let go when the group of high school boys several seats in front of us kept laughing and making comments. It was a good thing that Nicky was asleep at the window seat. She would probably get too angry, Carol said, and try to confront the teenagers. The last thing we need right now, Carol said.

At that point I looked past Nicky through the thick Plexiglas oval. I could have sworn I saw a volcano puffing away, but I didn't mention it to Carol because sometimes I don't see things exactly right. The captain's voice came over the intercom. *It may interest you to know that we're now flying over Mount Saint Helens.* The PA system was grating but I was happily surprised to realise that what I'd seen had been real. The one occasion I spent time with counsellors at API in Anchorage had convinced both me and the doctors that I didn't see things the same way other people did. Eventually they had to let me go, as I didn't quite fit into the descriptions they had corralled together for patients in Alaska's only psychiatric institute. Some of the consultants hadn't been happy about my release. But yet I wasn't harming anybody or myself. I was self-sufficient and I believe that was the legal definition at the time. Self-sufficient – as if anybody truly is. And I'm still not able to tell the difference between crazy and correct; I've had a problem with distinction for a long time. Sometimes I guess wrong. For example, I thought I should wake Nicky up to see the smoking crest, but Carol stopped me.

"Let her sleep." I did, but later I wondered if Carol wanted to withhold the experience from Nicky so that we could have something apart from her, just for once. A secret – like Seattle. It was a possibility. After a while, Nicky's eyes jerked open and her face went suddenly flushed. And her eyes were glazed. Carol glanced over from my right, said nothing and then took out the in-flight magazine to read. I knew Nicky was having another bad dream, so I held her hand silently for a while under the blanket until she smiled at me and went back to a more peaceful rest. Carol continued leafing through the magazine.

Carol wasn't doing it the right way, but she would learn, we would all of us learn. Carol would learn to understand all meanings, even past silvery or pure fluent slipping… she would understand my secrets like the crack straight through to her brain, breaking through ice. Whoosh. Through the cracks come the hands, summer summer summer. Or take it like this. Once upon a time you go to a lake, swim to the middle. Once you're there you notice all the lovely lily flowers near the edges of the lake. The loons swim slowly from lily patch to lily patch; they dot-the-dot across the clearing water. Where is it they don't swim? Where is it they don't mark with ripples? There, over there, see that group of flowers there, the white ones. Yes, over there. Swim to them. Put your hand among them. We were swooping down now, *please fasten your seatbelts as we are beginning our descent,* Nicky was still asleep; I grabbed Carol's hand and I was terrified, though superficially poised I always remembered what Susan never let me forget: the quick submersion into water, the speed down towards black ice; runners screeching on dark icestones –

I could hear the high school boys snickering again. "Lezzies," one of them said.

"Oh, lay off." I heard another boy. "Everyone white-knuckles it for a take-off or a landing. They're just scared."

"I'm surprised you're not grabbing my hand, you look kind of pale yourself."

"Faggot," the second boy threw back, and I heard them laugh together as the plane descended through the sunny blue to feather-tendrils of wispy white smoke, to plugs of dark clouds and below to the real sky below. The sky I had grown up knowing, the sky which lay under the clouds. It was raining.

My impression after we broke through the cloud layer was one of great space, but as our plane narrowed down on the landing fields, space constricted. The airport fields were huge and ugly and full of dead grass and if this was my homecoming, I thought, then it was as unattractive as possible. Since I hadn't flown out when I left home and since this was my first trip back, I hadn't realised the Anchorage airport was so unsightly. I had set my sights high and was disappointed. It was with resignation then that I disembarked, collected my luggage and checked my ticket for the connecting flight to Little Novgorod. While we waited for the flight, I saw many topical baseball caps being worn defiantly: about half reading FUCK EXXON and the other half reading OIL: THEY ARE US. Carol muttered that she'd overheard that Exxon was distributing the second set for free.

It was a small 11-seater of a plane and one with unpatched holes in the floor, through which you could view the marshes you flew over. The plane was too near the ground to provide parachutes and too far up to survive a crash. The safety card tucked in front of the seats only provided details on using the seat cushions as floatation devices. I rather liked the fact that it seemed grudgingly admitted that no one would survive such an accident; I appreciated the honesty. This was tempered by the prodding reminder that crashes had been quite common in these planes when I was growing up (Alaska Aeronautical Industries: "AAI – The Only Way to Fly" was the motto; we substituted 'die' and it scanned just as well). I hoped the planes had improved since I left home; more importantly, I hoped these were not the exact same planes used when I left home. I hoped they replaced them from time to time.

There was no one to meet us at the municipal airport, but my skin began to crawl with something desperate as soon as we exited the airport to take a cab to the house. The sky was opening up in gallons; I could feel the spin begin to press tight on both sides of my skull; I knew I would soon find it very hard to concentrate. In my head Susan began again, but it occurred to me to wonder why she would broadcast such things to no one who particularly cared to listen. *Then – slowly – dive below, follow their long roots down, down. Yes, the whole of the long flower remains white. The roots go down for many feet below. They look like fingers that keep reaching down, down, so white, so juiceless... Or maybe not. Maybe the roots are pretty, so pretty white they reach all the way down to me, the lady in the lake. Who? The lady in the lake. want to go to the lake with you in late slushy winter early spring how 'bout autumn now it's summer*

"Don't you want to call your family?" A hopeful cab was pulling up to us when Nicky's question surfaced. She hadn't spoken since we boarded the 11-seater in Anchorage, I now realised. The question was directed at Carol.

"I'm going to give them a call later," Carol said. She pulled on the string of her windbreaker. "Once we're settled in."

"Do they even know you're coming home?" Nicky asked, with a measured expectancy.

"No," said Carol briefly.

The cab drove through well-known streets and short-cuts. It gave me an eerie feeling to see the buildings which had risen up since I had left home and the new roads cut into the dirt – some of which were even paved. The town's general atmosphere remained the same, however, and I found this slightly oppressive. I had never liked the town, had never grown up within its limits, and now was glad that we would be staying a good hour away. It was necessary to travel along the dirt road off the main highway for half an hour to get to where we were going. When we at last arrived, the half-submerged redwood A-frame looked disconcertingly familiar but I couldn't place it. A lot of homesteads look alike. I pressed my fingers flat against my forehead.

"Well, this is it!" Nicky looked proud, as if it weren't the loaned house of a relative but her own. The trees whispered and crooned in their shadows over the house. Nicky stopped for a second. "Do you hear that?" she whispered. "Can you hear them?"

"Of course," I said, but she wasn't listening to me.

The nearest neighbours were miles away and I was convinced I could even hear the scab-drip of yellow spruce sap as the three of us stood there with our bags, looking at the house after the cab drove away. It had stopped raining. The trees were vulturing, creeping and swooping over the cabin, but there was a chance they might look pastoral if the sun ever came out. There was the omnipresent scent of mulch and the rotting forest trash of leaves and animal carcasses. My enthusiasm, already dipping from the moment we touched ground in Anchorage despite Susan's many reassurances, began to flag even further. Nicky, I knew, loved the forest whatever its state and no matter how she tried to deny it; Carol was indifferent; but I felt a reaction to the forest as itching and clawing as an allergy. I didn't experience it often, but even I know that it is commonly labelled *fear*. Yet the house smelled pleasantly of wood-smoke as we put our belongings on the floor and flopped down at the table inside.

"Shut the fucking door, Carol," Nicky said. Carol gave her a dirty look, but did as she asked. "So." Nicky sighed with satisfaction. "We're finally here." She wouldn't start her job for two weeks, if her dad managed to engineer the final details. There was no telephone, which irritated Carol, but a note on the large table inside told us Nicky's uncle was dropping by tomorrow to check in on us. *Please don't light the stove or use the plumbing till I get there,* the note added.

"I'm sure it's fine," Nicky said, after we had managed to light the

Franklin stove, heat some water and make ourselves some instant vegetable soups and cocoas. "Let's go down to the lake." *Or maybe a person finally at the end dreams of –*

"What lake?" I said. *Dreams of a set of white water-lilies in a lake –*

"Look at Ellen!" laughed Carol. Nicky's eyes turned to me. It was an assessment. "Nicky, her hands are trembling, you're scaring her. Ellen, you're spilling stuff everywhere. What's the matter?"

A person finally at the end dreams of a set of white water-lilies in a lake, opening their throats in a waxy salute. Of their throats finally opening to start to warble, perhaps she is reasoning that the soft, icy and drained candles have frozen white from the winter and never regained their summer colour. Maybe a person dreams while she is dying that: she has flown through the lake and under the lilies, holding them up while they sing from the roots.

"I mean the lake a little bit down the hill, Ellen." Nicky answered. Her face looked grave suddenly and I had no idea what mine was looking like. "I used to come here as a kid a lot –" She paused. She was looking at me strangely.

"Knock it off," Nicky said. "What the fuck's the matter with you?" Then addressing Carol: "Anyway, there's something I want to do before I leave for Valdez. Maybe I'll tell you guys about it later."

"No, Nicky, tell us now," said Carol. Her voice coaxed. Her fingers curled around the handle of her mug and then the flesh started expanding, webbing out to encase her hand and mug in a cocoon of woven flesh. I couldn't watch it, I looked away. My head, my skull was turning on me. The pressure was growing tighter.

"I said I might tell you *sometime*, so you'll have to stick with that," Nicky said to Carol, rising to rinse out her mug. It was obvious that she was determined to make an effort to get along with Carol. *Now you're going to let us in on a secret.* The wooden floor-beams were vibrating slightly. *Remember.*

"How about you, Ellen?" Nicky said to me, "Do you want to go check out the lake?" But now the Lake is ice. And now the Lake is water. Now the Lake is ice. Now the Lake is ice. Now the Lake is ice, water, ice, water, ice, water so there is nothing clear but the figure of a woman underneath supporting up the lilies, supporting up their lips and necks. *Above her the ice cracks. Above her the ice cracks. Above her the ice cracks.*

"For chrissakes," said Carol, getting up, "Let's all go. Leave the dishes to me, I'll do them when we get back." *Now you're going to let us in on a secret.*

It was all beginning to come back to me as the three of us worked our way down the incline. There were no visible trails and my feet throbbed from the cold wetness that soaked through my tennis shoes, but I was already beginning to remember a similar climb down, long ago. I could make out the outline of the lake below. It had been near hidden by the ragged trees pulling in at us and at first it was difficult to see through the tangle of branches. I noticed one of the trees behind me creeping silently forward on its belly; it stopped its moving whenever I turned around, camouflaged as an old dead stick. The whispering of the other trees had increased in volume to near growls, and I knew they were still attempting to shield us from the lake. Now I was sure I knew this particular lake. I knew it very well.

Secret. I am the lady below the lake. That would be me. Here is where I'm staying, with my eye that looks up on green light in summer. You say you can't think of the lake in summer? Well, I can't think of the lake in winter, either. When I look up, it's the summer kind of water, it's green and fluid and a sheath of movement – it's not ice. But let's not use this word at all – let's just stick with 'water'.

Carol was beginning to whine as we trudged through the muck down the last part of the hill. "Come on, Nicky. We came along, so now you have to tell us what it's about. It's about Susan, isn't it? This is where she went down."

I started to shake, just a little. My legs were shivering as we walked on through the mush.

"I don't want to talk at the moment." Nicky didn't turn around.

We cleared our way through the last bit of brush at the bottom of the hill and found ourselves standing near an old dock of weathered grey wood. The lake spread before us. I had stood on precisely this dock before. Before I had crept to the shoreline to watch. I was trembling. I was trembling all over but couldn't stop it.

"Are you cold, Ellen?" Nicky pulled off one of the two sweatshirts and gave it to me. Yes, I felt cold.

"At least give us a hint," Carol said. "Is it something to do with Susan? You owe us that. My jeans are soaked right through."

"I don't owe you anything." Nicky's face was set. I stepped back so that their backs were silhouetted dark against the lake in contrast to the impending sunset. The sky was dipping to orange and red; several moments passed. I could hear a loon calling from the west side of the lake.

"Yeah, you do." Carol was going to persist; I felt my chest tighten. Nicky turned so I could see her face in profile.

"I fucking don't."

"You do. You've held shit against me for years: the fact that my family had more money. The fact that you had no friends in school. For chrissakes, even the fact that your cousin died because I went over to your house too late that day. I've been avoiding the subject since we got here, but it's impossible *not* to think about it. Everyone in town knows this is where she drowned. And you know what, Nicky? I think you blame me."

"What the fuck do you mean by that? That's crazy."

"Is it? You made me think for years that if I'd only gone over and asked you to come pick berries earlier, then Susan would have come too, and she –"

"– And she never would have died," Nicky finished. "I'm not a kid anymore, Carol. I know that wasn't fair. No, it's something else."

Carol went to the edge of the dock and sat down, skimming her feet over the water.

Nicky stood behind her, clenching and unclenching her fists.

"Do you care about me?" she finally asked Carol.

Carol whirled around. "Do *you* care? Look what you've put me through recently. You must know that you're trying to control me. You've got no heart, no sensitivity –" Her voice went soft.

"Stop." Nicky's voice broke. "Come on, please stop."

"Do you, Nicky?" She took a breath and raised her voice. "Do you have any feelings at all?" Carol was in earnest now. I wasn't sure if I should be witnessing this, but we were all in it together, I guessed.

Nicky's face cracked. She crumpled down next to Carol; it almost looked like she was beseeching her. "I have feelings. I do have feelings. Stuff you don't even know about…"

"Like what? Like what? What do you feel about?"

"I feel about… I feel about us," Nicky collected her breath to speak, "and yes, I feel about my cousin. It would be weird if I didn't – we're at the lake, aren't we? But that's old news. You know what else I feel about? I feel like things are slipping away from me, out of my control. I feel you slipping away. I close my eyes sometimes and everything is gone: Susan, the forest, the lake, even you." Carol was finally struck silent. "I wanted to do something, but I didn't want to tell you guys about it right away till I figured it out. But my thoughts keep coming back to here. The smell of the flowers. The smell of the campfire. It sounds stupid. I've got to break through something, something has to change. I wanted to do something special." She moved closer to Carol. "Since you're so interested: I wanted to tell my cousin something. I wanted to grab hold of stuff in my head and hold it in place. I don't know, something. It was a stupid idea anyway."

"It was your cousin who died here?" I had been holding my breath until now. *You remember now.*

"Yeah. Susan. She was nice, but grumpy. She had long red hair and she drowned herself when she was fourteen." Nicky didn't turn away from Carol, but she answered me. I looked down at my hands, saw my fingers in sharp relief in the fading light, my knuckles and my finger-nails. The bending abrupt crooks of my joints.

Not so long ago, a woman dipped her hands in, trailing from the canoe, and I happened to be looking up then – so I saw her fingers – and let me tell you, her fingernails were painted with a blue polish, and with veins of white, brown, too, each nail painted to look like turquoise stone in all its gemmy glory – it must have taken great time and expense to have it done, I thought to myself at the time, but the concept thrilled me – beautiful, stones on fingernails rather than rings on fingers... Blue was a colour I liked to see looking up, too, blues, greens. Belles on her fingers and belles on her toes; she will make music wherever she goes. I'm sure you've guessed that when I first went down my fingers too were blue, but that has nothing to do with my preference for the colour.

"Yeah, I was six or so. I always felt really weird about it, it was just one of those things that stick in your head when you're a kid. There was no real reason for me to get so upset about Susan drowning, but I thought maybe if I try to exorcise it, then the other stuff I used to worry about as a kid will disappear as well." She paused, then repeated it: "The other stuff." This was Nicky's third long speech in as many minutes. She was breathless and tried to move closer to Carol.

But you can't exorcise her, Nicky, you can't. Because then she will float up and grasp the roots – her fingernails too will look like stones of turquoise – that's how beautiful she will be. And looking through the water all will be silver or yellow or looking down or sideways through it, green, blue, light chlorophyll fills her lids of eyes – they will say she thinks it is red, the hearts, throats of lilies. But she does not breathe or live blood anymore as the living, and she does not feel one way for the pulse of red, that is for the living and no harm for it, but she relaxes in blue, and she trails her cheeks in silver, and all the lilies drained of colour grasped by her are no longer white but clear, or green, or blue to her sight.

Carol looked at Nicky for a long time. She didn't blink. She had grasped her knees, sitting in a ball so that she was not touching anything at all. From the way Nicky's body leaned towards Carol, it still looked like she was asking something of her. "What kind of other stuff would disappear?" Her voice was ice-cold.

Nicky's head snapped up. "The stuff with Brett; some other stuff. And the whispering." Nicky looked embarrassed. "The whispering in the trees. Although sometimes I think I'm growing to like it. They whisper to me."

I thought Carol was going to burst out laughing or call her crazy, but she did neither thing, she just turned away.

"What do you mean, with Brett? Why are you always going on about him?" Now Carol was whispering herself. I watched her look down at the wooden slats of the dock and not the water.

"Because of all the stuff he did to me, Carol. The kind of stuff you won't even permit me to think, or dream about. The kind of stuff that wakes me up at night; the kind of stuff that you ignore. Sure, my cousin's death was tragic, and it comes back to me sometimes – very, very rarely –" even I thought Nicky might be lying at this point "– but not like your brother's horrible touching, his tongue in my ear that night we went camping when you were there, too, and you did nothing, nothing, to stop him –" Nicky's voice drifted off for me then; I could see the lake beginning to bubble and froth, the whole thing was churning like a cauldron. I stood fascinated and engrossed until Carol's voice broke through –

"Fuck off! Fuck you, you're such a fucking liar, you always have been."

"I'm not a liar," Nicky said coolly.

"You are!" Carol was on her feet, "You're a *fucking* liar! How can you suggest those kind of things about Brett? You, who've done everything but rape in your sick little games with me. You, who's trying so hard to get Ellen in them too, now – her grasp on reality is shaky at the best of times and you're manipulating her; you're the sick one, Nicky Barber!" Carol's voice was feverishly high and she was screaming there in the blood-coloured sunset, but every word she said came out slowly, like a tape recorder on low batteries.

Whereas I found myself resenting the implication that I was nuts.

It wasn't slow motion as Nicky rose from her crouch on the deck, but it seemed that way as her flat hand connected with Carol's cheek in a drawl of a slap. The moment slurred as I saw Carol flail and slowly lose her balance before her fall. There was another pause then before I realised the second splash meant Nicky was there with Carol and that she was carefully, almost lazily, holding Carol's head down under the water.

Blood or red or orange is what once pushed her down, though it's blue that has enamoured her by now, and it was beginning, too, even in her fall – for her heart was never beating fast, she enjoyed the fall...

When you go under the water the colours go –

When you go under the water the colours go –

13. Carol

Underneath the water is the hiss of some escape, like air that's being let out from balloons. You wake up in the middle of the night; can hear sounds against the bubbled walls, which in more alert states are wind and muted animal calls. Your eyes are wide open to a familiar conclusion: Nicky had told you the forest was drifting away, that you were trapped forever, yet still you see it stretched out before you. What does she mean, there is no forest? All you see is trees. Somewhere out there is a lake which is real. You wave your fingers through the water. There is a terrible pressure.

Your hair flows out in sheaths behind you; your hair grows out in white long strands through the water, *chalk hair chalkrocks,* your hair is white like chalk. You sometimes twist the strands within the fluid, rolling the hair in your palms. You have old hair now. There is no way out of the bubble, though you pummel, kick, gouge and carve at the wall of water encasing you. The mental scenes have grown quite marvellous, with well-developed characters, two girls: one strong and cruel, one kind and crazy. You place your knives away for now, you give up, you submit to sleep with a half-dream, half-memory of the forest. You feel the trees tug. Throat and body pulled. The wood is new and freshly bloomed. This pinning beautiful amongst the spruce trees, you can feel the trees within your chest throbbing, thrumming as you recall this. But they can't pull you back, you're lost...

Your lover appears in trees behind your private bubble, demands for you to throw out all your hair to waves. You do not wish to mermaid her. You are nobody's siren. It is strange how clearly you can hear her calling now. Though the white strands are farmed out, rapunzeled, whored, you are nobody's siren. You do not care terribly what happens. She steps through to you, and barely are you given time to pull her up on hair before she ruts on you. Her roughness, her lack of reciprocation are not so significant this time – your lover does not notice that you have withdrawn yourself. You do not want to come back. She didn't notice when you withdrew yourself from love, so why should she notice when you withdraw yourself from pain? She dries you up, she takes you far from flow, she mops up lubrication on your belly with your pale hair, rubbing the white strands in to soak up the fluid. You do not want the staling stench of sex on your hair. You don't want to be parched.

And these are sterile and calculated humiliations. Before she goes, your lover lifts your hair to examine it, remarking on its coarseness. But you know it is not truly coarse; it is strong despite the toughened scabbing on your scalp – or perhaps strong precisely because of this folded tissue. Strong enough to support her. You have always supported her and now you float weightless on the water.

The knives slash out again against the bubble. The first chip in the fantastic, the glorious first tender of the wall, the stone parts as if it were a lotion, it parts like a knife creaming through softened butter. First strokes of carve: the greening trees, curving them. Yes, and far below someone is calling your name, asking if your hair is long enough. This is the voice you must ignore. Knife is gouged into the wall; shape the creeks and wetness wrapped round the tower *wetness you remember well you remember wetness the marshes pouring sweat tears of marshes tongued saliva the warm flow of genitals cursing stolen blood from tiny cuts pus coaxed out from the scabs on your head forest water to your lips to freshen and quench relieve liquid etching vision the graves of children glistening locks*

knots of wood knots of flesh love gifts of fright the hiss of spruce for now you know what the secret is and what has been eluding you all along. Extractions of concentrates, deepest strokes.

Sex is dry. Someone's calling. Nothing yet. Did she check to see if you were wet and ready, every time? Often the only wetness on you was her own. Push her away, hand flat on her chest. No desire in it, says your lover, I will leave. *soft as water dry as bone dry kiss before she leaves, dry as air dry as fire-tinder*

so she does not call   she does not call   wonder why not   do you wonder why not

Stop. says your lover. Has tears in her eyes and says I don't know how I

Someone tries to call you back. Calls you back. You don't trust her; it always gets worse. Seeds of worse. You lean in now to kiss her; you are kissing those deceitful lips. Once again, you can feel your nipples erect as you move in on her. You are in control. Your lips are pink and it's your kiss. And she knows it, she knows you're there and in control. Her lips are pink and it's your kiss. Your cheeks so hot, the energy scalding underneath your facial skin. You can feel your body all over yourself, feel your skin from the inside. You want her to cup your breasts in her hand. You want her; you want her to touch and hold the curve of your skinny waist and your breasts. There and there.

The thrill she should feel as she feels your breasts and feels your waist and keeps feeling your breasts and feeling your waist. There is smoke, in the air, on the other side of the bubble. Making your view wince and waver, smoking up your eyes. Leaving a mirage, when you close your eyes, against your eyelids. Kisses through bubbles. *Kiss me through bubbles.*

You a cracked nausea-apple, one last time. You've let her climb up; one last time, you tell yourself. Mild headache and uglier cerebral monsters. You want the nausea; tie up the sick of it in skinny black spider-legs. Sex like an extraction; your head cracked open. It seems old. It is all cracked. Dry. There is little to replace her, not even a religion of romance. Rotted humans, wizened, crabbed, withered, mummy-like, papery-skinned, sinking, waning, ancient, fading, drying out,

Sick to your stomach. Sick in your head. Sick to the death of it and fuzzy at first. Comes in a little clearer, steering itself from the abstract to exact. You see a face, sunken in, sculpted from skin; it could be yours. *No,* this decides you, *you will not come back;* you drift off to the silent gash of sleep. A dream of the middle of darkness. You have been hung: your hair has you tangled in the bubble, suspended like a spider's pearly egg-sac between the extremes of sky and water. Neither feels familiar or benevolent to you, neither sky nor water, you want to keep on hanging comfortable. You are rocked and lulled, and swing gently, back and forth. *Come back, Carol, come back.*

The ropes of hair are twisting in your hands. The fibre winds so tight that it begins to burn your palms. Twisting, wristing, turning, burning, writhing, lithing, the strands of hair are wild fibre now, unwoven, waving, tripping in the wind. Something begins to rip and your hair falls away as if it were constructed of the filmiest threads of gossamer. The texture and sound become akin to the ripping of feathers. It is a frightening sound and a frightening texture. *Come back to us.*

And the water so beautiful, just lovely, so clear. Don't you damn kiss me back. Don't you fuck kiss me back. You are falling from the basket of hair towards the – you wake up. And you are with your deceitful lover, still high up in the tower. This will be the last dream you will have of hanging. That feels distinct, no precise touch of tragedy, not tragic. Just lying across from her, your own hair twined in your mouth like a rope-cable. *What are you choking on? Think, now.*

You are gasping on the dock. Nicky's lips pressed clinically against yours. It is dark, the sun has set, you are choking, you can only tell it's Nicky from her scent. Close by, you sense the worried presence of Ellen. But you're vomiting, you're panicking, there's something you've left behind, an answer of a sort, now it's being pumped away in breaths blown into you, and you've lost it, finally…

It is too black to see faces. The shadows work away at you to bring you back. They have no features and very little meaning. The lake, the ground, the sky, the loons which call, the creep of sylvan gods within the trees are dark, and dark, and dark.

14. Nicky

There were at least six rogue mosquitoes in the house: all buzzing irritatingly, all female, all competing vampirishly for blood. Nicky had slathered herself in a sweet poison of mosquito dope, but even the repellent didn't stop their incessant humming and she couldn't get them out of her head. Meanwhile Carol just brushed them away. Nicky considered walking over to offer the mosquito dope to her, but didn't. Ellen – wearing no repellent at all – was letting the insects feed on her just to see them fly away as red-gorged little balloons. Their bodies would swell up translucent with fresh blood; they were insatiable. Still, Nicky thought, they were sharp and pointed; they were not vague. They knew what they wanted and went straight for indulgences; they worked obesely. You had to admire the little gluttons.

"She's looking better," Ellen announced. "Her colour's coming back." Ellen had been conversing quietly for several hours with Carol, who lay on the cot set up by the stove. Way over on the other side of the room, Nicky leant against the hard dark wood of her chair and waited, feeling paranoid.

"Are you really crazy?" Carol was asking Ellen now. It was a blunt question, but like that really mattered after what had happened already today. Nicky squinted, trying to observe Ellen's expression as she answered.

"Well, I'm definitely eccentric," said Ellen. "And there's other things, too. I think the most they could ever conclude was that I suffer from hypomania."

"What's that?" Nicky asked from across the room.

"It's considered the mildest form of mania. It's characterised by optimism and euphoria."

Carol struggled to sit up. "Optimism's considered a disorder now? For chrissakes." Her face appeared healthy in the firelight, but the truth was, it was at its palest. Her roots were showing, Nicky noticed. She needed a bleach job. "Since when?" Carol was having difficulty croaking the words out. That was the reason for the secretive whispering between her and Ellen the last few hours: her throat was too sore from the vomiting up of lakewater. It wasn't meant to exclude me, Nicky thought with relief. She even felt a slight optimism, but certainly not enough to be considered a mania.

"The shrinks just want to make their money," she contributed in a slightly bitter tone. "That's right, through diagnosing *hypomania.*" She couldn't get the word out of her head.

"Really, Nicky? You seem to have the subject all figured out. Go on." Ellen sounded pissed off. Which was quite irregular. "Keep on talking, Nicky." Was it her imagination, or did Ellen's tone sound threatening? Nicky looked away. There was a strange smell in the cabin. What was it, just there on the tip of her tongue? Oh, yes. The taste of burning, spooling in her mouth.

Ellen was still waiting for her to speak.

"I figure that psychobabble mindset is geared towards finding pearls in the shit. How about that? You know how often that happens. Pearls in shit. You don't usually find one in the other. Unless it's the shit in the pearls. But maybe you should get a second opinion from Carol. She's the psychology expert." Nicky kept on talking and she couldn't shut up. What was happening to her? She sighed and watched Ellen raise one eyebrow, watched Carol turn her head away. Were they still listening? Couldn't she have hypomania like Ellen? Then, instead of flaws, she would see the good mixed with bad, flow and the pleasures of vagueness. But the good in the midst of the bad hadn't happened for years. It had been the other way around and that's what danger meant: the uncovered bad within good, beneath the fakery and masks.

"Feel better? Got a load off your chest now?" Ellen's voice was condescending. What the fuck, it was Ellen who was nuts, not Nicky. And she didn't feel better.

There was no talking of any type for a while: the fire they had fed crackled and blushed in the stove. Their clothes hung before it on the back of a chair, damp but slowly drying out. Nicky listened to the mosquitoes buzz. Now there were only two left – she had clapped her fingers shut on two, and Ellen had suckled at least an equal number. The light outside was finally turning; she figured it was nearing two or three and early dawn was coming. Inside the air felt warm and stuffy – the parts of flesh facing the fire turned uncomfortably hot. It was necessary to shift and rotate their limbs, like crisping oily meat upon a spit. When they came back from the lake, they'd had a good excuse to light the fire again, if just to warm the chill from their damp skins.

The drying clothes had not been thoroughly rinsed, and the smell of lakewater began to pervade the house.

Every time Nicky looked up she saw Ellen stroking Carol's hair, but Ellen stared wide-eyed back at her without comment. Nicky moved so that she didn't have to see Ellen gawping at her, but often found her gaze wandering back, and Ellen would still be staring at her with those round brown eyes. Eventually Nicky twisted round completely and watched the active charcoal decay of fire. Like little lapping suns, the flames left after-images against her lids. And Carol began lazy breaths of sleep; Nicky leant back against the stiff chair and felt herself begin to doze as well. Then she started to the sensation of a hand on her arm.

It was Ellen, though, not an untimely act of revenge by Carol.

"What do *you* want?" Nicky said, yawning and stretching and unnerved by the staring need in Ellen's eyes. The lake scent had invaded all corners of the room and it was creeping on Nicky's skin. Nicky waited for Ellen's answer and, when she grew tired of waiting, turned her attention back to the fire. Still, she remained conscious of Ellen standing only two or three feet behind her chair. One of the remaining mosquitoes flew buzzing by, and Nicky swatted at it, missing.

When Ellen finally spoke it was in a confident voice. "Have you ever seen anyone drown?" she said. The smell of the lake crawled up inside Nicky's nostrils.

"No," she answered finally. She turned around to face Ellen.

"Not even when your cousin died?"

"No!" Nicky snapped. "Not even then." The pair of mosquitoes were circling in on her, and she could feel the fire cracking, cracking, cracking –

"Well, guess what?" said Ellen, with a peculiar smile. She sounded proud. "I have. More than once."

"When? What are you talking about?" said Nicky, uneasily, shifting her position on the chair; her jeans were too hot. She had a weird feeling of *déjà vu* – Ellen's voice was too familiar. Then the feeling passed. But it made her think of other things. Alright, she'd be honest with herself: it made her think of what had just happened between the three of them down at the lake, and she had kind of hoped that they were all going to forget about what had happened and just move on.

"Well, one of the times was the summer just before I moved Outside."

Nicky's jaw muscles relaxed. It had nothing to do with her, then; she would have been twelve or thirteen when Ellen had left the state, more concerned with the intricacies of junior high school and her lack of friends. She feigned interest; anything to keep the conversation light. Or lighter – it was better to discuss a drowning that happened nine years ago than an attempt earlier that day. Jesus, even discussing Susan's drowning would be preferable. "Yeah? What happened?"

"Oh, just some girl got caught in clay and they couldn't pull her out. She was out walking in the inlet, or looking for clams, or something like that."

"Oh."

"She had just gotten married, and both her and her husband were real young, like nineteen or so; I think they were up from Reno on a honeymoon. Anyway, by the time they realised she had gotten stuck, the tide was already coming in."

Nicky watched the shape of the fire mutate into several guises before she commented. "Grisly. What happened?"

Ellen moved very close to Nicky. Nicky could smell the heat of her breath and it stank. As surreptitiously as she could, she moved several inches away from Ellen. "No, it wasn't grisly – it was just tragic. I was there watching from the beach. Her boyfriend or husband or whatever had been stuck at first, too, but he was free and managed to get one of her legs loose. But as the tide kept coming in, he realised he wasn't going to manage, so he left her there and waded back, got to his car and drove to get help. Somehow he managed to get someone with a boat, and a doctor and two paramedics, too. They had to take a boat out. By that time just her head was above water and she was getting really cold.

"The husband wanted the doctor to cut the leg off, but he and the paramedics refused to do it because of malpractice, so they gave her a straw to breathe through once the water covered her head, but eventually hypothermia got her and she just passed out, passed away, her hands got too cold to hold onto the straw, so they leant over the boat and held it for her, and then there was no grip in them and she let go and –"

"How do you know all this?" Nicky said sharply.

"Perhaps I've made it up," said Ellen. "Hey, I have a hell of an imagination. But still, think what it would be like to watch someone drown, Nicky. It would be horrible, wouldn't it, watching someone go down?" Ellen stared at Nicky unblinking.

"I don't know what your point is, but it's not a nice one," said Nicky in a low voice.

"Not *nice*? Sorry, did I hear you correctly? Come on, I'm trying to confide in you. I'm trying to say something important here. 'Not nice' – give me a break."

Nicky suddenly saw that Ellen was no threat: she was just a cocky little dyke who'd lived down in Seattle for far too long and who spoke sense only half of the time. She was upset about what had happened earlier, but Jesus, so was Nicky.

"That's right. It wasn't a very nice or very optimistic story. I thought you were supposed to suffer from optimism."

"Maybe I don't anymore," said Ellen, poking a stick in the fire and stirring the coals. "Maybe I've been cured."

"Don't stir the fire, alright. It's hot enough already."

"It's like that game, isn't it? Cold, cold, you're getting warmer, now you're almost there; you're burning, you're on fire!"

"What are you getting at?"

"I think you know, Nicky," Ellen said darkly. "You've almost got it. Think hard." She went back to sit down next to Carol and stroke her arm. And then Nicky had a sick feeling that Ellen was somehow connected to every fear she had ever had. She shook herself: that was crazy. Ellen was weird, not evil. But there was some recollection there, some memory that she couldn't yet dig out. Carol stirred, opened her eyes and sat up.

Yep, the firelight flatters her, thought Nicky, but I bet under her flushed cheeks she looks awful.

"I had the worst dream," Carol whispered out; her voice scratched against her throat. "God, it's too hot in here to sleep."

"Why?" Ellen asked. Her voice and stroking hands were gentle; Nicky stifled a wish for Ellen to *shove down* on Carol's neck and shoulders instead, *slam down*! A wish for Ellen to make sharp, quick movements. But Ellen was going soft now, too.

"Oh, I don't know; it gives me nightmares, I guess. Not like Nicky's, of course – but nightmares all the same." Carol suddenly jerked her head up and looked across the room. "Do you still get bad dreams when it's too hot, Nicky?" Carol's eyes were glazed and unfocused, but Nicky could still feel her mood surging out like a heat-seeking missile. Carol would never forgive her.

"Those bad dreams were directly related to your own brother and that one time we went camping. As discussed previously, down at the lake. Now can we drop it?"

"Which time we went camping, exactly?" Carol's brow wrinkled as if she were trying politely to remember something, rather than stirring things up all over again.

"It doesn't matter which time, Carol." Nicky tried to relax. She would be mature. She would let it go.

Irritatingly, Ellen got up and walked over and stirred the fire again, but Nicky had too much of an investment in the conversation to break it off and tell Ellen to quit poking at the wood. Though a mosquito was sucking on her upper arm, which she hadn't noticed till now, and a dead forest was crackling in the Franklin stove as Ellen poked away. *Remember, Nicky?* Christ. And a force of smoke poured down her throat again; she was nearly choking on its strong perfume.

"Well, I think you're making a mistake," said Carol, "You must be remembering something else."

"No, I'm not." Nicky said in a quiet voice.

"I can't hear you," said Carol. "Come closer, come over here by the cot."

Nicky walked over and sat in the seat Ellen had vacated. "I'm not mistaken," she said.

Carol pulled herself up to a sitting position. Now that she was away from the glow of the fire and had moved a bit closer, Nicky could see that her face was drawn; her long hair straggled from the freshwater residue. "You've been mistaken about a lot of things. But listen, I don't want to talk about you at the moment. I want to talk about me. Don't you want to know what my bad dream was about?"

"Not particularly," said Nicky.

"I listen to yours."

"Yeah, well, it's not like you take them into account." She was starting to get nervous in the early morning light. A glance told her that Ellen was still on the other side of the room, standing up and staring into the fire. Nicky looked out the window. The outlines of the trees were melding into branches and needles in the dawn, as progressively more of the trees became visible. The trees swayed; Nicky made another small prayer to them to keep her safe; to keep her safe from whatever now lay before her. But no scent of conifers ripened in her nose – instead she smelled damp decay and liquid rotting. She had made sure the door was shut firmly, but the lake was outside and she was a flood victim in the house, caught while it started to seep under the doors and batter against windows. It was uncontrollable and so was she. She wanted the wildness, but it frightened her. The mosquitoes kept buzzing.

She took a breath and held it. "What did you dream about, then?"

"Ropes."

"Ropes?"

"Ropes," Carol repeated, "ropes around my neck. Pulling tighter than your fingers did earlier today."

There was a pause. "I'm sorry, Carol," Nicky said, finally.

"That's just as well, because you should be." Carol lay back down on the cot again, exhausted, but there was a change in her: Nicky was going to be forgiven. She could feel it. Nicky felt the trees pierce her heart, and their honey-sap began to flow once more, revitalised and sweet. She realised that she had been holding her breath. Now she could exhale. She sent a silent thank-you to the trees outside the window; the lake was starting to recede and the trees themselves pinned out in stark, clear detail. From where she sat, she could see every olive-coloured spruce needle through the glass.

"Carol," she whispered, leaning over the cot, "listen, it's going to be okay, it's –" There was the unexpected hand on her shoulder again and she shuddered.

"Quite a little conference here," said Ellen. Her voice was petulant. "Anything you want to share with me?"

"Look, I'm sorry," Nicky tried to be patient, "but you know how it is – sometimes there's stuff that just me and Carol have to talk about, and –"

Ellen kicked the chair by the cot over. The violence seemed understated, not startling at all. "You've always left me out of it, really –

haven't you? Nicky –" she looked desperate "– I've tried so hard, as well. I really have. Remember? It was me helping Carol at the lake so she wouldn't die. You needed me there, too. The lake was where I was supposed to be. I needed to be there. She needed both of us to live..." Nicky found herself oddly fascinated. Would Ellen erupt now, too? Or would she remain as controlled as Carol – always hinting she would explode and then swallowing it back, always inevitably controlled in the face of all her internal fluctuations. *Remember? You better wake up.*

Nicky looked at Ellen for a long time, then put her arm around her. "You're right. I guess." She paused. "I need you." Maybe that would be enough for Ellen, just those simple words. But she didn't know how much longer they would need her for; maybe she and Carol could strike out on their own again, everything forgiven, just like before. Nicky gave Ellen's shoulder a little squeeze.

"So quit the fighting, right? It's hard on me as well." Ellen sniffed. The run of mucus down her nose disgusted Nicky; slime disgusted Nicky. "God, just relax, just for a little while. There's something I want to tell you, about the day your –"

Nicky interrupted. "We'll all relax." It felt ludicrous trying to mollify a woman in her late twenties. She would say what she had to say, for the time being. But things were going to change soon; Ellen wasn't necessary anymore. She was staring at Nicky, her eyes huge, her mouth open like she wanted to say something quite important, but Nicky continued, measuring out her words: "It – is – all – going – to – be – chilled – out. Right, Carol?"

Carol lay on the cot looking at them, but said nothing. After several seconds Nicky answered for Carol: "See? We're not going to fight anymore. So fucking relax."

Ellen opened her mouth to speak. "But –"

"Don't push it, Ellen," Carol finally commented. "Just drop it for the moment." Yes, thought Nicky, good, Carol was on her side again.

"Hey listen, go to hell," Ellen said, close to tears. "I'm not trying to stir things up. When I say what I have to say, it will all make sense.

Believe me. But if you really want me to be quiet, then I can do just that, too."

"Thanks." Carol looked pained. "Just let it rest. We can discuss these things tomorrow, once we've had a bit of sleep." Hell, when did Carol get so smart? Nicky wondered. She didn't sound like a bimbo at all, at least not at the moment.

Ellen thought about it. "Okay, maybe you're right – sometimes it's better to just let things settle. Okay, let's do that, then."

"Of course she's right," Nicky said, moving closer to Carol and blocking Ellen from touching Carol's arm again.

But Ellen still wouldn't shut up.

"Do you know what sacrifice entails, Nicky?" Ellen asked. She seemed increasingly agitated. "I doubt you do. But for me, I just may believe in the greater good. Perhaps I expect it in others. Maybe that's where I'm going wrong. You know, like in Carol's psych books. Projection," Ellen added, her face flickering into an adult and then back again.

Nicky gave Ellen an insincere smile. "Well, aren't we erudite tonight."

"I sneak a look at them from time to time, okay?"

"Then you know the concept is bullshit, tailor-made for people who go soft and let themselves get screwed over."

"Oh, Nicky, I don't think anyone could ever accuse you of being a self-sacrificing masochist." Ellen said, glancing briefly at Carol.

Sharp as high heels and sharp as the Shoes.

"Bitch." Nicky stated it flatly. Now that was nerve: Ellen had loved those games and now she was using them against her.

"Hasn't it occurred to you," Ellen said in a little girl's voice, popsicle-sweet, "that I might –" there, yes, Ellen's face had been caught in the frame of a woman in her late twenties again – the light wrinkles, the slightly loose skin around her eyes "– have my own reasons for being here today? I don't mean I've got a scam going on; I mean it in a real way. I believe in the three of us. I'd do anything for us. Ask Carol," Ellen nodded to Carol, but kept her eyes on Nicky. "Ask her if I hoped for this – the three of us together – even when she first came home with me that night in Seattle."

"What?" Nicky felt the colour draining from her face. "You guys slept together up there?" She looked at Carol, who was still not facing her.

"Don't be an idiot, Nicky," Ellen said. "Of course we did. Why else would I have ever phoned down to Oregon?" Ellen stared Nicky down. Nicky had been horribly, terribly wrong. Ellen was a threat; Ellen was experienced; Ellen knew exactly what she was doing; Ellen stood between her and Carol. Ellen was going to win.

"I feel sick," Nicky said, out loud. Ellen's face was suddenly serious: Nicky couldn't tell if she was looking at her with love or hate.

"Don't let the past rule your life, Nicky. You can let it go; you can forget about guilt. I know what I'm talking about, believe me. I watched the drowning. I was there –"

Nicky managed to dodge Ellen's staring eyes. "Yeah, you told me already. Nice story. Too bad it ended so badly. Remind me to always cut my leg off, if I have the chance."

"No, I mean that –"

"Just shut up, okay? You promised us you would." Nicky sighed. She felt weary. "I'm going to lie down for a while, too." She unfolded a second cot, which stood propped against the wall, and set it up next to Carol's.

"Is that okay with you?" she asked Carol.

"Yeah, fine." Carol said in a low voice, her face turned away.

Nicky lay down in the drowsy heat and started to feel better. Yes, this was a much better set-up; she was close, level to Carol now. They were a team. Though she didn't raise her head to check, she imagined Ellen sitting across the room, glowering by the fire. She didn't want to think about what Ellen had said. Ellen sounded like a crazy person; and it made it worse to think of Ellen and Carol alone together. Ellen and all her scheming, plotting.

So she lay there on the cot, smelling Carol's characteristic vanilla scent. It made her think of ripe things. Things opening up. Carol's sex opening up, like all the sexy, festering fruits in that Kahlo bridal painting. Nicky had seen a slide of it in Art History class at college and she had gone wet even then. Now, here in the cabin, she knew she was experiencing the same reaction. Carol opening up. Things were going to be fine. Eyes closed, lying on her back, breathing in vanilla. Fine.

Nicky put a hand on Carol's back. Fine. Carol didn't respond. She touched Carol's hair. So pale and so very, very soft. Something moved in Nicky's mind right then, a half-memory of something. *a kiss, a kiss a fluid soft kiss sinking in her cheek   her heart warm* Safe in the early morning, safe on the cot and safe in the trees.

Then she was on top of Carol, kissing her pretty and familiar face. Nicky was surprised but happy to find Carol had forgiven her so quickly, but Nicky was kissing her and over Carol's shirt Nicky had her hands on her breasts, which felt so round and full beneath the fabric. Carol so turned on and so attracted to Nicky – maybe even more so then Nicky was to her. But Nicky was turned on and horny, too. The fire crackled. In between and during the kissing Nicky's mind would flash on the glistening, possible look of Carol's pussy, a little shiver at the thought of wet cunt would run through Nicky. But that hadn't happened yet: that was a futurism, a possibility, the present was the pleasure of kissing Carol. Crackling. Nicky was still straddling her, so she began to pull down Carol's jeans over her legs.

A dream. It must be a dream. So why wouldn't her head clear?

Carol was just lying there, so passive, waiting for Nicky's reaction. Because Nicky was looking at limbs so thin, so skinny; they were skinnier than a child's and the flesh was taut over them.

Oh my god, she must be anorexic, Nicky thought. She didn't know what to do, but she knew she didn't want to insult or hurt her girlfriend. Nicky wasn't sexually disgusted in any sense, it was just that she had immediately forgotten to think about sex at all. She looked down at Carol's bare legs and realised that she was wrong, that Carol's legs were actually bare bone, bone that had the rusty, ex-fleshy look of chicken bones which had been mostly licked off and then dried, both the right leg and the left leg. Bones, perhaps, that had been soaked in water until the meat had peeled off. For quite a long while. And her joints, Nicky realised, were held together by twisted bits of wire, barbed wire, yes – how could anyone survive like that? You better wake up. But Nicky looked up at her and it was Susan. She was hopeful, and smiling.

"Get the fuck off me! What are you doing?" What *was* Nicky doing? She was on top of Carol on the cot, undoing Carol's jeans. *You better wake up.* Oh god, she must have been dreaming. Oh, Jesus.

"No, Carol," Nicky was stumbling to get off her. She had heard of sleepwalking, but this was ridiculous. "Oh, god, oh no, Carol, I'm sorry." Falling off the cot, had to get away from Carol, get away as quickly as she could. "I'm sorry, I wasn't trying to touch you or anything. I was having a dream, a weird dream." Nicky was talking too quickly and talking too much, her words bubbling from her lips. She was having a hard time breathing.

"Yeah, well," Carol had pulled herself up to a standing position, "You've got a hell of a nerve complaining about people molesting *you*." *Remember, Nicky?* She straightened the T-shirt and jeans she had been sleeping in and peered at Nicky, who was also standing up by now.

"Carol, don't say that. I thought we were going to try." *You tell her.* Nicky was very close to tears. "I really am sorry, Carol. I wasn't awake." She faced Carol now, and things were much more sharp in her head than they had been before in this room. Despite the heat, her head was clearing. She had nothing to hide. She pulled nervously at the sweater she was wearing, barely meeting Carol's eyes. "I didn't mean to. You must believe me."

Carol looked at her and it hit Nicky that Carol finally believed her. She was believed.

"Come here," Carol took a step forward as she spoke, and enfolded Nicky in her arms. *soft applesoft* "Come here."

And she was deep in Carol's arms and more safe than she had ever been.

But something violent and bright was in the house that night;

Nicky was shoved, pushed even in the middle of her safety. Pushed, and there was a great slow heat, a burn –

"Ellen, what are you doing?"

Ellen holding in her hand a wrist-thick log, its end already molten charcoal, its end vivid in its death and active. Not a passive stick –

"Get that the fuck away from us!" Carol ducked, and the fire stick came towards Nicky and Carol again, in all its blood-red glory and infectious burn. Oh, god. And Nicky remembered now her early fears of contagious fire.

Ellen was irate. "I'm not going to hurt you, Nicky. I just want you to step away from Carol. That's the ticket, slowly, slowly. All three of us have got to make it, not just me and you but Carol, too, Carol too and red-white-blue –" It was all going too fast –

"I'm not hurting Carol, Ellen, we're talking, see."

"Jesus! What the fuck were you doing in her cot, then? She didn't ask you there, it seemed to me. Just relax, you said, and then look what you did –"

"No, Ellen, I was asleep –"

"You're ruining it all for us; you're ruining it all! Deny it! Deny you tried to drown her in the lake."

Nicky couldn't answer that one. Ellen seemed to be moving slowly, as if she were exhausted. She waved the fire stick and Nicky and Carol both cowered. Nicky put an abrupt hand up to shelter Carol, who seemed shaky still and unsteady on her feet.

"Don't hit her!" Ellen screamed, and in the stuffy cabin the torch twirled towards them, like a flaming baton relayed by a practised fire artist. Nicky half-expected herself to suddenly snap out a hand and catch the sparkling log.

The stick passed by them, landing on the floor with a thump.

Carol's hair was on fire, blooming like a garden. Sparks were riddled in her hair. She pulsed, her hair turned red-gold, the air acrid. All the stars in heaven on her head, and she did not scream.

Nicky looked desperately around her for some water, anything, but only saw the two mugs of lukewarm vegetable soup. Douse it. *Faster.* Her brain was moving so slowly. She poured both mugs over Carol's hair and drenched the flames. Carol still stood there, seemingly catatonic and transfixed. The fire was out. Nicky looked at the torch on the ground, and threw the damp lake clothes on it, smothering the torch as if it were a small, malevolent animal. That done, she stepped back and looked at Carol. Grotesque, but compelling. Carol's eyes were as huge as ever, her hands stilled into claws, fragments of vegetables dripping from her hair. Instant, rehydrated vegetable soup. Bits of orange carrots caught in the loose, charred strands. Peas caught in the blonde fibres, next to charcoal stumps of crisp hair.

"God," Carol's eyes finally focused. "My god, that was close. That was quick thinking." She looked at Nicky, but Carol's eyes were already beginning to dilate again. It had all been very quick, hadn't it? Nicky thought.

"Don't worry. I'm not going to let you burn up. You're not getting away that easily." Nicky's voice shook. But she was aware she was the only one of the three laughing. It wasn't until then that she noticed Ellen was on fire, too.

15. Ellen

It was blue summer now. Blue as the blue-black water flowing in the lake is, blue as the muddy streams which feed it aren't, blue as lips starved of oxygen always will be.

It wasn't my bubbling, crackling new-red skin that killed me, though the possibilities of that grotesquerie will remain with them, I suppose. I caught flame, to be sure, while trying to protect and save. But I caught fire because I was already dozing, passing out. They beat my bright body for me, you see, to stop the fire, but a lethal amount of carbon monoxide had already polluted my veins, making emotions erratic, unpredictable; the round globs of poison (or so I like to think of it) already moving through me.

A small cabin with a fire-stove is in many ways a danger. With no proper ventilation it is the equivalent of the locked, stalled vacuum of a car that keeps its motor running. You're safe in shelter, but you're not safe. Nicky and Carol just managed to get out in time, really, when they dragged me out to stop the burning. And so, as Susan always wanted, I saved them. It would have been Nicky, I think, who would have suspected a carbon poisoning as opposed to fire burns, when they sluggishly confronted themselves for a reason why I wouldn't wake up. Their brains must have been working quite slowly then, too. But it would have been Nicky who insisted that they didn't go back inside.

Then I lay on damp grass and in the half-light I could still smell ashes, charcoal, the sour scent of burning feathers. I knew, you see, that I was not yet gone. But they didn't.

I wished I could reach out to either of them, as they cried, to comfort them, but I was in a comfortable paralysis. My eyes were sightless, but I knew how each of them would look, lying in the glittering dew of the grass by the trail that led to the cabin. Carol crying in her hands, the tears rolling fat and perfect down her face. Her hair burnt in clumps half-through, her scalp exposed as blistered red, shiny in some segments. She would be the physically weaker of the two, having already survived the previous onslaught on her lungs not so long before.

Nicky would be weeping, too: in sorrow, in frustration over misunderstandings. Over misunderstandings that arise from sorrow, and her frustration with them. More then Carol, it was Nicky I wished to comfort. I wanted to give some explanations and reconciliations for her grief. I never got to tell her what I'd witnessed. But a clarity hit my mind then, lying in the grass. And a certain peace hit me too, and I believed, still believe, that it wasn't time for Nicky to hear those words, not yet. The glass-dew blades of grass moved by me, the waves of trees shimmered above me. But one day there would be a time. Just not yet.

I was light within my body, soaring out. And I called out for Susan, but there was no answer. This time, I knew, it was not because she chose to ignore my calls. Susan was already and forever gone. Instead of discarded shells, I like the metaphor of a maturing snake. Snakes are pretty, magical creatures and their former skins retain their fragile paper grace. So this is how I like to see it, my twisting, curling into something new. My true self exposed again. *Something would touch the meat in me, soon, something would touch my raw and fresh softness.* My senses, thus exposed, soared. I lay on dirt, I crackled with heat, I swam through fire, up I flew.

When I was dead I flew above the world, ten thousand feet above. So natural, so rarely high for me – the lake dark-blue below was spewing ice. And the sky was clear and the water looked clear; and my heart was clear as a heart can be clear, and the trees were green – as they should look.

And near the first time that I fell, I lost the others painfully but soaring, shooting, scorching, hooting, soaking up. I've insaned a half-year's night and fifteen thousand nights at once and one night I rose above the water.

From up a branch of prickened bare, there were spruce trees too – a thousand feet of five times spruce trees tall and blueing eight times silver that of waterfall.

The skinny soar 8,000 feet of shoot, more slender than the higher trees. I was close to giddy/close to glitzy, elevated/high-elated; in a world so elongated my breath was silver-tongued and -plated. I didn't know I moved still on. I levelled off, looked off, looked down: the atmosphere was blushing blue.

Yet I wanted to be waterskimming, somewhere down within the lake. On that icy skin-blue lake, I'd drink her like I drew it in/the water warmer than/her mouth and streamed it out, but I fell off my bones to its very edges (lake). Darling, I'll share this deep with you – I saw a white carving of a girl who filled the deep of liquid's space.

> *A girl entire whittled out*
> *the whole statue underneath*
> *of something white*
> *would glow like teeth*
>
> *Closer scanning, dawned on me*
> *I had been down for quite some time*
> *I didn't feel the need of breath*
> *though prudent to dive up again*
> *I did so like the time in death*

So you see how when I was dead, I flew above the world.

16. Carol

You bury bundles of babies in your mind – small disposed bodies – and they are refuse in the bushes, fat cocoons thrown out the tower window, down into the brambles. Sedate until the teeth and claws of the forest tear them apart, before they disintegrate into: infants, larvae, faceless people, not entirely human thoughts, not yet.

There is no reason why you should go on. Not yet. Yet you feel you may find a reason, somewhere past the gate of absolute despair. It's because you are forgetting something you are supposed to remember, and somewhere there is a solution. You cannot remember what it is, so you lie in the centre of the trail leading up to the cabin on your back and try. As numb as you are, your thoughts bend towards remembering. You gain a curious solitude and peace in this manner.

The trail is made of stone slabs, cool to the touch; they are worn down by treading. Your back stretches against it, the stone cool; you feel your thighs, run your hand over the curve from your cunt to the outer sides of your thighs. You feel the sand grains on the stones press against your ass. You put your own hands there instead and let the images from your dreams come unfettered into your head: fruits and babies, even images of larvae float back into your eyes now. Germinating fruits and eggs, larvae, spider-sacs. Your hands on your buttocks. The smell of smoke is in the air.

This time you will keep this thought with which you are pregnant. Your body swells to savour it for the first time. Your stomach is a huge bright apple, the fruit held taut inside until it is ingested. Or spoiled. Sometimes fruit is not picked and it drops to the ground and rots; this happens even to previously germinated produce.

All you smell is sour, sour burning. You remember why, but you lie on the stone path and you try your hardest not to. Your eyes are swollen – you must have been crying, maybe even minutes ago. There is a residue of wet salt on your cheeks. Your face lies near dirt – you should be able to smell rich mulch, but only smoke is in your nostrils.

"Nicky," you say. "Nicky, can you hear me?" There is no answer. "Nicky, we've got to do something." You can hear Nicky crying. It was the second time in twenty-four hours she had tried mouth-to-mouth; this time, on Ellen, her own lungs gave out first. She is crying. "Nicky! Answer me!"

Her hand reaches out and touches your hair, white hair flowing coarse over your heavy bones, your freezing head, your recovering body, the fragile-boned skeleton of a thought that's not yet come. "It's gone," she says. "The forest's gone. All gone." *All gone*: those are your words, not hers.

You think you know what she means, but how could she know this story inside your head? This particular birth has a strange placenta. You know Nicky is thinking: your hair is too uncontrolled. Too wild. She wants it controlled, bound and braided in a long plait down your back. Rope.

God. This thought, too, is snatched from you and from your skull. Your knife flies from your hands as the child is torn away. So you curl what remains of your hair in a long braid around yourself and sleep in its spiral, oestrogen-tainted and heavy.

Controlled is safe. Nicky wants you safe. You are not safe with Nicky, and she cries until early morning. Over Ellen, over your burnt hair, over her own grisly desires, you suspect. Over gifts of fright that have all come true for her. If you could feel at all, you'd feel pity for her. But now you must rest on the cool stones, on the grass, the sky turning pale and light before your eyes. Then you both must get up and wait for Nicky's uncle's truck to come, too late, so he can take the body and both of you far away from this hot slaughter. But you lie dry-eyed and burnt till Nicky's cries blend to the eerie music of the loons you can just hear. From the lake. You slip in and out of stale dreams.

You're in the tower, intact, but you slip in and out of odd, disturbing dreams. You are expected to take your life. She wants you to jump and nothing seems clearer. You have been set up. Now you own the riddle's answer, but the question still evades you.

She wants you to jump. She cannot take your life directly. But you are wise enough to know that if people want to kill enough, there is no law on earth that will stop them. Not wanting blood upon her hands, she'd rather see you kill yourself. It would erase her blame; it would be your own fault. She has calculated to an infinite precision your isolation, and placed a window from which you'll jump. She's only bided her time. "Look, look at the young woman in the tower, in the bubble, in the shelter, in the skull," she says to everybody else, "she is safe, but she ages there; this will happen to you, too, when you transgress all my wishes."

She expects you to kill yourself; she waits to see if you will jump or not. You feel strongly sick. Vomit is pressing to your mouth. You think of the knife in your pocket with which you have cut your hair. You could have cut yourself with it. You have not yet maimed yourself.

You wake up vomiting. You would be so grateful for the amnesia that often follows sleep, but everything is still here in sickening focus. It is brighter – perhaps seven in the morning. You hear the chirping of a robin and not the more nocturnal warbling of loons. Day. Nicky lies not so far from you. She breathes. Ellen does not; Ellen is a cold lump of flesh. You are a burnt, damaged monster, your lips covered in sick, your teeth chattering. Just as quickly as your wakening, sleep is swarming in on you again, you let yourself follow into it once more –

A window to fall dangerously from. Braids of hair with which to strangle yourself. You breathe. A knife. A deep cut across your lips, your wrists, perhaps your throat, a deep cut across the labial lips, a tiny nick. She wants you to. You haven't yet. You breathe. A lonely bare grey room. No escape. A window to jump from. A knife to cut yourself but you've discovered – you've discovered –

Then you have it. A simple revelation of despair. A mixing of grief and joy in your heart, but that's beside the point; one cannot erase one's life, and now it can only go forward and forward and forward. There is nothing left now but hope and a means. This is a different revelation: you could have escaped all along; you could have used the knife to cut the ladder from your hair. Sheared hair and you are free. All you need and all you want. Now. The answer to the riddle. All you need to do is cut your hair –

You're walking on the beach. There's not supposed to be contamination on this stretch, but they've stopped commercial fishing for the summer here, too. Polluted fish you neither need nor want swim past in waves of gas and salt before you. You note the high, quiet plateau of Lady Julia across the inlet. Everything is so familiar, but you feel stunned. It doesn't feel like you're back for good; it's a respite. You're going to take off sooner or later. Otherwise you'll be trapped here too, in small-town strangulation. You're heading for a city next time. Alone. The thought thrills you momentarily, and you wonder if it's possible. There's still Nicky. There's Nicky to deal with.

She is somewhere up ahead on the sand, walking on the rim where water hits the pebbles. The tide is coming in. Kids in three-wheelers narrowly miss her, then carry on dodging the waves, shrieking over the motors. It's a very hot day, nearing the high sixties.

"Wait up, Nicky." And you catch up with her. "I couldn't find out much," you say, slightly breathless. "There are no relatives at all, and no belongings other than what she brought up with us. I called her bank, told them she was dead, and they put me onto her ex-housemate, Jackie, you remember –" You pause. They never met. "Anyway, Jackie was quite upset to hear the news. The bank said Ellen had cancelled her bank account – what little she had in it – before she even left Seattle."

"Seattle." Nicky says the word bitterly, and you wonder if this is due to grief over Ellen's death, or jealousy concerning your escape from Oregon up there to Ellen's arms. "That meant she was planning to stay." Nicky's brow furrowed, as if she were trying to work something out.

"What?"

"She must have been planning on staying when she came down to Oregon to see us," Nicky repeats.

"Oh." You hadn't thought of it that way. It makes you feel quite nice and warm; you're touched, but it also makes you feel responsible.

"Come on, let's go back." Nicky offers you her hand and you take it for a moment, before the kids come tearing back on the three-wheeler.

"I'm not sure if I like your hair so short," Nicky says. You're not sure if you like it either, but there are few alternatives when half of it is burnt off. And Nicky doesn't really have the right to give an opinion, you feel. If there hadn't been that business at the lake, then what happened later at the cabin could probably have been avoided, too.

Nicky reaches out one hand and lightly touches your hair. "I always liked it long," she says. You flinch away. Her hand feels callused, rough and sharp.

You have your ladder. The knife in your hand. You lightly touch your hair. You raise a small handful of locks up in your hand in front of the light from outside the wall of the bubble. You let hair after subsequent hair fall from your hand. You hold the locks up in the late afternoon sunlight and release, until one hair remains between your thumb and forefinger. You tug at it, it holds, and for a moment you feel a faint repulsion. You should be done by now, but your hand holds out this strand from your head, and you cut – and then the hair flutters down to the floor after that.

"Well, we should be there by now," Nicky says. You pass another group of adolescents on the beach. Only two or three years ago that would have been you sitting there, roasting hot dogs and marshmallows on malformed metal clothes-hangers. Now you only feel a faint repulsion as one of the boys eyes you up.

"Christ, did you see that?" Nicky is looking proud and pleased. "Did you see how that guy checked you out?"

"No," you say, walking more quickly up ahead.

You've let her get away with stuff. It's too evil to consider: Nicky faking her nightmares, mumbling shit about Brett. Inducing guilt, then taking advantage of you, then not even admitting her lies. It makes you sick.

"What's *your* problem?" Nicky says, catching up. "A year ago you would have loved that."

You cut another single hair with the knife, working more quickly with its blade than you had before. You then blindly use your fingers, pick out single hairs from your head, stretch them out until they are strung taut and pluck them out. You have been thinking so hard that you hear nothing. You've been: letting her get away with it. You've been: forced. Pushed down. Shorn again, shorn again. Your hair for your ladder for hair for your ladder is for your ladder. Taken away. Taken away. She leaves with your hair and locks the door again. You can hear the sound as she descends. Now you hear. She leaves to go.

"Quit dragging your feet," you say. "Come on, let's go."

The crematorium is cool and grey. Morbidly, you try to see if you can detect the smell of burning, but you can't. The room is cloaked in a fresh, flowery fragrance: they must go through cans of the stuff. It's just as well, anyway, the scent of anything burning makes you sick these days. You ponder for a second the irony of Ellen being cremated, but you know the answer: it was the cheapest method. Even the cardboard coffin (some pointless law that insists the body can't go into the incinerator uncovered, so you have to pay an additional fifty dollars for the box) has depleted the last of the money you've got from selling your car. You're at a funeral – of sorts – and you've been back in Alaska for less than a week. Christ.

Nicky has refused to look at you ever since you entered the small, formal building. You imagine she's scared, but this time you think, so what. You're scared, too. She reaches for your hand – you pretend not to see and shift both your hands behind your back.

Into the furnace she goes. Goodbye, Crazy Ellen. We hardly knew ye. Your throat is closing up and you struggle to keep calm. The doors shut with a resounding clang – perhaps it is your imagination – and the 'grief specialist' assistant steps back.

If you looked through those doors you would now see Ellen's body, this time entirely consumed by fire. No second-rate job this time around. Her limbs cracking, her cold dead brain bursting, her flesh becoming finally ash. Except you've heard that in truth not every-thing gets burned up, no matter how hot the fire is, and they've got some mortar and pestle mechanism that crushes everything properly before the little sealed plastic urn is handed back, as compact and packaged as a Big Mac. What's left over is called 'cremains', as it's referred to in the industry. You read that in that funeral book, back in Oregon. A six-pack of Cremain Nuggets with fries, thank you. You can feel yourself starting to vomit; you can feel it rising up through your throat. Not here, not now, with the immobile burning figure of a lover only doors away from you.

There is a room, a grey cool room. The walls are carved, and in the mid-dle of the floor lies the figure of a woman. The woman does not move. Lying close beside you, discernible in a moment of evening sun shimmer, are sev-eral very, very long strands of plucked hair, the ones that were left behind. And they are not enough to make a rope.

Nicky tries again to touch you, but her rapid movements are not enough to stall you. This time you are too quick to even have to resort to evasive tactics; you are already out of the crematorium and throw-ing up outside, into a flower-box full of blood-red Alaskan poppies. God. How awful.

You wake up in horror the next morning shocked, for the first time, by grief. Ellen is dead. You are sleeping in your old room at your par-ents' house. Nicky sleeps at her mother's house four houses down. It's like you're still kids and you've slept through a night full of night-mares. If only.

"Carol?" Your mother calls from downstairs. "I've got some blue-berry pancakes cooking. Do you want some pancakes, honey?" Yes. You can smell them and the butter sizzling on the hot griddle. The fatty smell of butter just so slightly sour, so you can just barely smell it beginning to burn, crisp up, char…

"No, no thanks, Mom. I'm not hungry."

"Oh." Her footsteps head back to the kitchen. Just another June

Cleaver clone. That could be you.

Later, the telephone rings. You can hear your mother picking it up. "Carol! Nicky's on the phone for you. Don't you want to talk to Nicky?"

You don't answer, pretending you're asleep. You can hear most of what she says: "No, I'm sorry, Nicky... yes, I'm so sorry, it must have been awful for you girls... ever since she came back here yesterday, won't even smile for her father... that's what I say... if you girls had just stayed here from the get-go, instead of that fire-trap cabin – oh, I'm sorry... Yes, I'm sure she'd love that, Nicky. Around seven? She could use some company. I think –" Your mother lowers her voice dramatically, but the final two words come out loud and clear: "clinically depressed." Great. And all you want to do is sleep. No nocturnal hallucinations can be quite as bad as what you feel in your gut the moment you wake up.

But then you dream your hair's been cut. You wake up in horror with it lying on the floor. Swollen. Bloated-neck swollen and dead. Splintered nightmare. The intensity of a sick dream. Drained, you lie unsure here in your parents' house. Another dead thought has been torn from you. You were so close to a type of answer, an escape – but it warped. You doze through the next two days – you do not want to be awake, when what is wrapped around you is so damn disturbing. Awakened from your stupor by a sound below your window, you assume that it is who it always is. Your lover, you think, rising to the window. It's Nicky.

"Your mom said I could come round," she begins.

"Fuck off," you say, and you spit on her. You are weak. *Riddle me, riddle me, riddle me weak.*

Below, your lover waves both of her hands in the air, smiling. Why? You are safe from her up here. Your hair will grow again, though it may take years. When that happens you will cut it off, make a ladder with it. Strength. Your lover's pleas will no more affect you. You go smugly to the window again, turn your head mockingly so that she might see that it's all cut off, the burnt patterns still showing cheetah-like on your blonde hair. She makes a gesture of resignation. Let down your hair. She screams, calls your name.

"Carol! Come on. Come on down, I'm serious." Laughing. But why would she be laughing? You feel a little confused, point to your shorn head again, retreat back into your own room again.

But what's this you hear, as you lie on your bed? The sound of the bottom door being opened, the key creaking in the lock. How heavy the footsteps seem this time! A rattling tread that you have not noticed before, perhaps in a hurry, you think. Or angry. And now the rattling of the gate on your level, and now the rattling of the turning of the key in the lock of your door. It surprises you that you do not care much. All you have to do now is wait for your hair to grow. Then the door is pushed open.

"Carol?" It opens wider. "Carol? I'm going to turn on the light for a second." Electric pain. You hide your eyes. "Carol? Nicky's waiting downstairs. She wants to talk to you for a minute, honey. I think it would be a good idea." Your mother comes closer, the little gold cross jingling at her neck. She smells of vanilla. It's too flowery, like the crematorium deodorant. You'll never use the scent yourself again. When you unveil your eyes to look at her, she's smiling far too brightly. "Nicky has the girl's ashes, honey. She thought you might like to scatter them with her." You are falling now, falling back into –

You have been very stupid. "Where did you get the key?" Curiosity momentarily triumphs over loathing. She smiles brightly, too widely at you. "You've always had the key, haven't you?"

She smiles at you as if ready to explain something to a very small and dull child and says, patiently, "No." But she is a liar, remember. She will not crack you. She places the key carefully in her pocket. You tell yourself to think rationally now, to not let yourself be provoked and panic.

"Don't you see," you say, "your coming here proves how dependent you are on me. Why don't you free yourself of it? Why don't you leave and free yourself of me?" But liars are adept at recognising manipulation. So her

answer is no. She loves you. A lie? The truth?

"Now I have come to you," says your lover, "and I am strong. Accept me. Accept all my little secrets. I will keep your hair so short. If you've secret knives with which to carve, then I will find them. I will find the loose strands of hair you save, hoping one day to make a fragile rope. Don't bother. Your hair will always be shorn; you will never again fear that you are snared and hanging in it. You will be safe. Safe within walls, within bubbles and shelters."

She takes a step towards you. "I can come now without you letting me in," she says. "And I like it better that way. I like it like this."

"Do you like it in this? I do," Nicky is saying, and pressing a little corked metal vessel into your hand. "I think it looks appropriate. I went through my mom's cupboard and found this. Is it alright?"

And *is* it alright? Good point. This little bronzed vase holds the pounded cremains of your mutual lover, who just two weeks previous was plotting sandwich-making in Oregon.

"Where do you think?" asks Nicky. Her face is tense and nervous, but you must steel yourself to her vulnerability. "I thought the lake would be nice, but if it bothers you too much, then maybe –"

"No." You break her off. "The lake's the only place it could be." For a second you think about scattering her in the ocean, or in the woods, but that doesn't feel right. You think about what Ellen said back in the cabin, that the lake was where she needed to be. You have a responsibility to Ellen. She put herself between you and danger, and the last time it was fatal.

"Tomorrow morning then, maybe?"

"Tomorrow morning." And that's that.

It is the kind of clear summer morning particular to Alaskan good weather. When you take a breath, strong clean air completely fills your lungs. Which is good, because you need ballast behind you today.

You walk over to Nicky's house and raise your hand up to rap lightly on the door. She must have been waiting on the other side of it, for she opens it right before you knock. Even so, chances are slim that you would actually wake Nicky's mother; from the door you can see her passed out on the couch in her muu-muu, a half-empty Absolut bottle on the side-table. Absolut instead of Five Star Brand? Hmm. Nicky's father must have been having some good months on the Slope.

"Just a second," Nicky says and walks away to the kitchen, to return carrying, reverently, the little makeshift urn. She steps outside to join you, quietly closing the front door behind her. You notice for a moment – but try to ignore – a needy expression of hope and eagerness in her eyes as she looks at you, which she is obviously trying to suppress due to the untimeliness of the moment. But it is there nevertheless. No, Nicky, you think. I don't think so. Sometimes it's lucky she's not prone to verbalisation. You'd have to be cruel to be kind.

Speaking of kind, your parents have generously offered you the loan of their car for the morning, so you pull out onto the highway to begin the drive out to the dirt road. There is silence in the car. Nicky holds the cork of the vase tightly, on the slim chance that it'll magically pop and its contents spill like so much cigarette dust. How did she decant it, you wonder? Maybe that's a question you don't want to know the answer to. Keep your eyes on the road and your mouth shut, Carol. That's right.

You try not to think about the specifics of your destination as the car bumps over the stones in the road. "I don't want to go up to the cabin," you say to Nicky. "I just want to go straight down to the lake." It is the first thing you have said to her in the car.

"Fine," says Nicky. "That's fine with me."

When you reach the homestead and park the car, you are careful to make sure that when you step out, your gaze does not climb back up to the cabin. Think of the lake instead, you tell yourself. *Think of the lake in summer.* The birds twittering, the green trees marbling it, the cool depths of it.

You walk down the incline together; Nicky is in front of you, gingerly carrying the vase. You wonder why you're not having a panic attack, nor a physical reaction of any kind, considering what happened the last time you were here. The smell of sweet spruce sap is already in the air: it's going to be a hot day today, too. And fortunately for your plans, a breeze is blowing, away from you. You concentrate on one step at a time. Left, right. Left, right, left.

Nicky waits for you at the bottom of the hill. Behind her is the dock. Funny how you can bear to see *that*, where stuff happened to you, but you can't look at the house, where stuff happened to Ellen. Still, it brings you no great pleasure to see the lake, either, it has to be admitted.

"I thought maybe we could scatter them from the dock," says Nicky. "Or is that a bad idea?"

"That's a bad idea."

"You don't want to go out on the dock?"

"Can you blame me, Nicky?"

"No, of course not." She looks crestfallen. She hands the small tidy vase to you. "Here, you decide."

You take the bronzed vase and are surprised at its warmth. Ah, from Nicky's hands, you think. But it's a nice fancy – Ellen's spirit buzzing through the container.

"In the lake?" Nicky asks. "Maybe we just put the vase in the lake and mix the ashes with the water that way?"

You glance at the cool blue-black water, thinking of it flowing into the container, becoming cold sludge. Cold sediment. Cold sentiment. For chrissakes, get a grip, Carol. "No," you decide. "Scattered over the lake, I think." You uncork the vase and pour a little pile of ashes on your palm. The wind is already lifting it, so you lean over the lake from the shore so that the ash is carried over it. It disappears like Tinkerbell's pixie dust and you prepare yourself to pour out the rest.

"Cup your hands together," you say to Nicky, and she does so.

"Shouldn't we say something?" she says.

You think for a moment. "'Take her and cut her out in little stars, and she will make the face of heaven so fine...' No, I can't remember the rest." You pause. "I'm saying sorry. How about you?"

"Sorry, Ellen," Nicky whispers, as you pour Ellen out into her hands, and then tip the rest into your palm, placing the urn-vase down. And then again as she lets her fingers separate and the dust fall through them towards the lake: "Sorry and goodbye."

You feel warmth towards Nicky despite yourself, but you step forward till your feet dampen and let Ellen slip from you. Some dust is carried off; some sparkles on the surface of the water like fallout from a tiny volcano. Goodbye, Ellen, you think. And thank you. Then you say it aloud.

For several quiet minutes you stand there, but your feet are getting cold. You know Nicky's feet feel exactly the same, but she will not dare to mention it.

You close your eyes for a moment and think of the warm brown flesh of Ellen's body against yours, the occasional lightness of her touch. The smell of spruce sap is powerfully sweet.

You snap your eyes open. "Okay, that's that," you say. "I'm going back up." Nicky looks miserable for a second, but for several moments she turns back to the lake and makes whatever peace she has to. It seems that she succeeds, for her expression is much lighter when she turns round.

You are already halfway up the hill, trudging through wet brush and avoiding Devil's Club, when she catches up with you.

"I want to go in the cabin," she says. "We've come this far, it's stupid not to take a look."

Your heart thuds, something sharp is twisting in it. You can even feel the burn again at your scalp and curls of quick, nasty fire. "Please, let's just leave," you say. "Let's just please leave."

You face her. Silence, a grip on your neck. "Please leave." Pause. "I said, please leave." It is a corner she has you backed up against. The useless knife. Remember it? Your hand grasps it and brings it forward quickly, towards her ribs – but not quickly enough. Your lover grasps your wrist and prises it from your fingers. You scream at her suddenly, hoping to frighten her, because you reason that it is more difficult for her to think if you are screaming. And she does hate to be startled. You hold the tone as long and loud as is within your power, but then you find that you cannot think, either. And she moves on in the surge of sound, if not unaffected, than at least not markedly slowed down. She's going to make you do whatever it is she wants. She has taken the knife from you. You can feel it at your scalp. Oh, not again. But there is only the tiny nick you have experienced before, the tiny cut you are familiar with, the smallest of pains.

You reach the top and you turn to face her. "I'm serious, Nicky. I really don't want to go back there. And you can't make me."

Nicky is looking at you strangely. "I *could* make you, you know." Oh no, not again. And you feel your knees weaken and your heart sink.

The knife has been placed inside your lover's pocket and she's furiously crying. Your heart sinks; there's no stepping back now. Her hand around your throat in fleshy pain; you are losing your breath. Not again. "We'll get rid of that knife now," says your lover, dragging you to the centre of the room by your throat. She leaves one hand on your throat and with the other throws your knife out the window. Your escape has been cut off. Summoning power that rapidly wastes, you bite her, you kick her, and this results in the greater portion of your energy being spent. It is not successful. Her physical strength is, as it always has been, superior to yours. She is saying words to you now, screaming things out, but you are not able to distinguish that she is speaking a language. She is speaking this tongue made entirely of growls, and a roar has begun behind your ears. A red roar the colour of blood; you know it is made of blood.

"No, you can't, Nicky. You can't make me do what I don't want to, anymore." A roar is filling your head; you're finding it difficult to concentrate on speech. Blood is filling up your eyes. Nicky's talking, but you can't make out her words.

Growl, gurgles your lover, gripping your shoulders and then releasing you. *Growl, growl.* You are rapidly losing strength. *Raughhhh,* snarls your lover. You cannot hear to answer; the roar is deafening you: not her roar, but the roar in your head.

Nicky steps towards you, grabs your neck and pulls you to her. It looks like she sees deeper in your eyes, past the blood.

"Bitch. You little bitch." You can hear her spitting it out. "What happened in the cabin is about me, too. I also need my funerals and my goodbyes, just like you do." She shakes you, and then raises a hand up to strike you. "Bitch –"

She hits you – fruitfully – and at the slap you recoil back and are prone. You lie damaged and limp in another corner, like a loose-limbed doll, thrown. Your lover rushes over and pulls down her pants and pulls up your skirt. Since she is quick to rush, she does not know if you are unconscious or awake. She suspects that you're awake. As a precaution she has her elbow pressed against your neck, with your head thrown back. She rubs at herself, feels for a moment the front of her thighs against the front of your thighs – the pubic hair bristling – and then she takes her hand and she enters you.

The fact that you are not aroused, curiously, arouses her. She feels she is unlocking a door, and she keeps battering against it, knowing she will eventually get through. And she does.

Nicky drops her hand before it makes contact with your skin. You are staring at her, breathing fast; your eyes stinging.

"Never mind," says Nicky. "I can come another time on my own. I think we better go now." You nod and walk numbly towards your parents' car. Here you are, anaesthetised once again.

Back at home after a silent car-journey, you encase yourself in your old room. The answer. The riddle. You've got to think.

There's a knock on your door. "Nicky's on the phone again," says your mother. "Don't you want to speak to Nicky?"

"Not now," you say. "No." And your mother's footsteps retreat.

You can hear a call outside of your window. You step over to it and look down at Nicky.

"Carol, listen; we've got to talk; the woods is gone; it's gone," Nicky is crying, saying nonsense, clutching her head as the tears roll down her face. You can't hear what she's mumbling; it looks like she's hard up for air.

The forest is still there, but your disbelieving lover clutches her head in her hands as she stumbles towards the window for air. She does not want to think on what has just occurred, she wants most to breathe slowly. She leans over the ledge of the window and draws great draughts of breath. She raises her head, just a little, and sees in the distance – it seems very natural – a forest, and it seems to her... the forest from when she was a child. Look! She can see the creeks, the curled foliage. She sees it so clearly she could lick out its greenness... and look, there it is, the lake! Of water... now of ice! Now of water! And ice again! She sees a deep woods; she knows where the paths are that lead to the lake, though the woods hide them. The forest hides everything. She feels wind rippling over what suddenly seems to be the very shallow layer of skin that coats her arms and face; it is the wind that clothes her instead; breezes cover her eyelids, thinly. In her nostrils is only the scent of many fires burning. Closer, the wind brings the scent of the wood-fires in, closer. She fills her eyes with the sight of the lake, so far away... There! If she could just touch it! If she could just touch it! She reaches fingers out towards it and leans far beyond the window... Ah... if she could only touch it... it's further away...

You walk away, and then look towards the window. No more Nicky. No more Ellen. No more parents. No more traps. No more men. No more rules, structures, imposed codes. You need to be free.

You look towards the window and see the clarity of the vision of the woods. I knew it was still there, you say to yourself. I knew she lied. You touch the nape of your neck. No hair with which to climb down. No knife with which to cut it off, even if there were still hair. You lay the back of your hand against the nape of your neck again. Rub your neck back and forth. You stumble to the window, and support yourself to look out.

On the ground is your lover's broken body. She has fallen and been crushed.

The decision comes quickly. It is as if everything else, all the years of the tower, have made the decision instantly. You will have her freedom. You will have her experiences. You know the question now. All the thoughts are extant now. You step up on the ledge and it is necessary to crouch.

"What are you doing, Carol?" Nicky's voice from below, worried.

Something delicately ecstatic peaks within your breast and breaks and spreads into something raw. Then you leap, you fall...

"That was amazing," Nicky says with admiration.

You are on the ground, unbroken.

You see that there is a forest, still, outside the tower.

You run off the path into the woods straight ahead, jumping over brush, running through the pools of wood-water accumulated in the moss, soaking your garments and not checking to see if you can hear behind you. The natural trenches filled with brown rotting leaves are ploughed through, your toes are cold and you do not care.

The woods taper off several miles from where you started running from the tower. You stop and feel: the wind blowing through your short hair, how out of breath and frozen you are.

17. Nicky

Several days after Carol's stunning jump into the unknown, Nicky hired a car for a day and returned to the lake. Carol still wasn't speaking to her, and this time Nicky had a feeling she wasn't going to change her mind. In fact, she had overheard Carol's mother telling her mom that Carol was borrowing money to take off again, soon, maybe to L.A. or even San Francisco this time. "Such a shame the two of them had to fall out," Carol's mother said, and then darkly, in reference to San Francisco, her meaning implicit: "I just hope she doesn't become – influenced." Yeah, well, a bit too late on that one, Nicky had thought to herself.

Well, she was leaving soon herself, anyway. She drove past a house where someone was smoking salmon in a old oil barrel, and for a moment the sharp familiar scent of ash passed over her again. Her dad had secured her the job on the spill and she was flying out to Anchorage tomorrow for orientation training. She should make a good bundle out of it by the end of the summer.

To her surprise she didn't feel as damaged by Carol's dismissal as she had thought she would. Sure, it was sad that they were breaking up, but she had accepted it, more easily than she would have predicted. Something had snapped in her, too, when she had seen Carol jump in ardent and feverish rage from her bedroom window – Carol wasn't the only one freaking out. It was a relief that she'd been fine; since there was no way Nicky could have caught and saved her – for starters, it had happened far too quickly. As it was, Carol had just stood up, brushed herself off and run into the woods without a glance backwards at Nicky.

There had been something cathartic about the incident. Nicky turned the car slowly into the long dirt driveway that led to the cabin, and reflected for a moment on the image of her calling to Carol from the ground to the window. There had been a whiff of Romeo and Juliet about the whole thing, or a fairy tale. Well, if that had been the case, she had certainly proved herself no hero, romantic or otherwise. She guessed that if Ellen hadn't collapsed when she did, she and Carol would have died then too, because they would have stayed inside a cabin whose very air was polluted. So if there was any nobility in the whole thing, that's where it rested, in Ellen. But it was a weird way to be a hero. No, she'd have to adjust to living in a world which contained nothing as clean-cut as heroes, love or explanations.

Nicky thought this as she walked up the trail from the parked car, up to her uncle's cabin. She noticed nothing unusual when she opened the door, other than a slight smell of smoke in the customarily stuffy air inside. There was some soup spilled on the floor, and when she lifted up her old sweatshirt lying on the ground, she found a stump of a stick, long since cold. The wooden floor beneath it was only slightly tarred, in a spot no larger than a fingerprint. Carol had been right; there was nothing left in this house for her now. Nicky closed the door to the cabin very softly behind her.

She walked slowly down to the lake. She had some things she had to work out for herself. Ellen had been trying to tell her something back in the cabin, Nicky realised that now. Something to do with another drowning, and not Carol's near-drowning, and not the woman who got her leg stuck in the clay. Something else that Ellen had witnessed.

No. Nicky grimaced, shook her head. That was stupid, probably impossible. But the suggestion was quivering in her mind now, and her teeth started to chatter. A memory was nudging at her: her uncle, showing a group of young teenagers around, the day Susan died. Ah hell, she had no idea, really. Everything from those summers when she was a kid got mixed up in her head these days. Even the stuff about Carol's brother. She hadn't been entirely truthful that night Ellen died: to be honest, she wasn't sure that Brett had touched her, though she had her suspicions. She wasn't sure. She wasn't certain.

Everything was shaky. She wasn't even sure how Susan's death really had affected her. It was just too long ago. Maybe it had just been an excuse for her, to keep her from dealing with her own cold self.

She gritted her teeth. The thing that frightened her more than anything was the thought that somewhere along the line, her brain and life had become stiff, as inflexible as rock. She had some other memories now, ones she must have forgotten along the line. Some of these new fragments were so clear she was sure they must be real: her uncle crying in the rain; her uncle teaching her the names and souls of plants the week after Susan died; her uncle showing a group of kids the shape of a fiddler's head fern; Brett's hand underneath her backpack.

But she *didn't* know: didn't know if Brett had messed around with her; didn't know if Ellen had visited this lake thirteen years before. Sitting on the dock, Nicky shivered, and then removed her shoes to dip just the tips of her toes in the water. She guessed she'd never really know. She was going to let her control mechanisms rest now and then. She didn't always have to know. And she didn't need Carol's acknowledgement of Brett's abuse, either. It was enough that *she* knew it might have happened. What other people thought didn't make it more, or less, true. She'd figure it for herself, eventually.

Nicky felt a surge of grief and began to cry, loudly. No one was here: no lovers, no dead cousins, no scary big brothers of friends. Just her and the trees. She cried until she was exhausted and after that she felt a little better. Her eyes were swollen and still wet, and her chest still tight, but she took a deep breath and looked around the lake.

Queen Anne's Lace grew from tubes of wild carrot near the lake. Out of nowhere, the names that had been lost somewhere in adolescence came back to her. Woody and ridged, the flora that grew off the stalks were also fragile and grey. She had forgotten about these plants; hadn't thought about them since she moved Outside. All of a sudden, she remembered her uncle making flutes. She remembered his hand on hers: kind, instructive. Maybe Susan had already died; maybe her uncle had been lonely, and that was why he was spending so much attention on a child. She couldn't recall clearly. But the memory of the flute construction came back to her, still sharp. Not *sharp*, she corrected herself. It was simply there, true or false, sharp or blurred. Would she still remember how to make them now?

First she broke the tubes off from the roots. Her eyes were still stinging, but she felt her tears drying up. She didn't want to be frozen again, high and dry in a shell of her own making. But her attention was on the flutes, now. The tubes rose up taller than she did, five foot six when in her stocking feet. She felt odd to herself, making flutes that once grew. There was the plug of seedpod, and now the mouth-hole towards one end while she measured the task of severing. A pocketknife would do it quickest, if she had one, but she ultimately clawed the hole out with her fingernails to further widen it. She even thought her nails liked the texture. She blew, letting out the clearest pitch, which also meant the highest pitch. More sounds were needed, so Nicky made holes for the fingers again, concentrating on making them small enough.

She made several flutes of different sizes. The funny thing was, the sounds rarely differed even with a variety of flutes and holes: she got several high tones, and naturally, just the mouth-hole sound, but the resulting music was eerily monotonous. Perhaps the tunes suited the water around her. The light in the sky had an elastic quality to it – it stretched while she played. Had Carol been here, the sounds would have irritated her, but this way Nicky could play her flutes for as long as she wanted.

The flutes would be easily crushed. In the car, driving home – maybe Nicky would sit on one in the car seat. There wasn't too correct an art of making the grey flutes, either – they were too temporary. Maybe her uncle had taught her that. Or even if he hadn't, it was something she had learned. Particular losses were vexing, but next time she could construct them again.

She let herself sit by the water, where she filtered certain thoughts:

how could fingerholes breathe and air come from her mouth through to the instrument, when she was herself open and gaping? Would she ever have the air in her to lay herself wide open and still attempt to push music through the gaps? She played out the sounds of a flute of wild carrot: highest tones, lower tones, on the cobbles.

The smell of sweet sap hit her while she played; the magic of the forest would return, though perhaps not with such precise clarity. The trees were blurred from where she sat on the dock. She was beginning to accept blurring as a way of thought. It didn't always have to be dead clean, and she didn't have to be wide awake and completely in control. She could accept the films that passed or overlapped before her eyes. The important thing, she knew, was the substances of the films, the blinds, the artifices. Once she knew their consistency, she could deal with her fears one by one, maybe even tolerate a few of them. Resignation was something new to her, and she was going to chew on it. Nicky wept for a little while, then picked up the tube. Then she lifted all digits from the flute and played, by the water, by the forest, the fingerless mouth-tones.

The lake is deep ebony-blue. Periodically the water supplants black for indigo and all the limited colours in between. While it is difficult to make a stab at its depths, I make a reasonable guess of thirty to forty feet. It is not clear what feeds the lake with summer water, but it is not shrinking. Leaves fall in bright zodiacs around the lake; some trees bend too far over and even offer the lion's share of leaves to the wetness for quick disintegration. Others keep their branches back, and the falling oranges and reds line the banks after their slow flights, turning at last a heavy brown. The colour is a heavy brown. The smell of smoke is in the air.

Chill sets in across the water, and the lapping movement of the waves stiffens into ice. The snow falls through lavender sky and the lake becomes a field of snow, covered like the earth itself in drifts of white. The ice is thick underneath for two or three feet; snow piles several feet above. It seems quiet and would be difficult to skate on, with such a bulk of snow. But there are not many who would try to skate. Reports shoot gunshot across the lake as the ice cracks into spring; the thick turns soft as mush of flesh and finally dissolves; the cracks deepen and eventually blinding sun rushes in to dank, untouched water below. It's best to be shielded at first. There is exposure to light as the sun bleeds in and the virgin depths adjust, but this happens quite, quite slowly.

There are three people by the lake. The season doesn't matter, as it is always the same. They are all adults; I am one of them. The two younger women are walking towards the lake and cannot be stopped. I'm watching what unfolds, gripping the branches of the spruce I hide behind. I'm calling out to warn them; my voice ringing like flute music across the lake. They're turning. And whether I dive down under, walk out towards, crash through thin ice or slip through mush, it always stays the same. I reach them in time; I hold their hands and save them; we walk on water, all three gliding on the lake. Safe. The ending never shifts.

More new writing from DIVA Books

The Diva Book of Short Stories
edited by Helen Sandler

"Big names head for the Diva list" *The Bookseller*

**Includes Kathleen Kiirik Bryson's new story:
'The Day I Ate My Passport'**

This anthology presents fresh work from familiar names – including Emma Donoghue, Stella Duffy and Jackie Kay – alongside the best from a new generation of British talent.

In tales of pride and jealousy, cruelty and community, the characters find themselves eating passports, healing horses, poisoning pets and proposing marriage. And when the gossip leaks out at a small-town party, the hostesses are forced to call the cops.

From random murder and sweet revenge to money-making scams and manic neighbours, this collection is as dark as it is funny. Get ready for the sea change in lesbian fiction.

RRP £8.95 ISBN 1-873741-47-2

Girl2Girl:
The lives and loves of young lesbian and bisexual women
Edited by Norrina Rashid and Jane Hoy

The only book written by and for young women
questioning their sexuality

In this lively illustrated book, girls from across the UK write from the heart about being gay or bi, coming out or falling in love:
• "The first time I kissed a girl I could have collapsed... it felt like I had always imagined a kiss should feel."
• "I don't remember when it was that I actually thought, Oh my god, I fancy the bridesmaid!"
• "People say bi-try is a big student thing – well it is, and I'm loving it!"
• "I asked my dad if he had ever considered sleeping with a man. He said no. I said, Well neither have I."

**"This anthology with its excellent resource section
is a must for any young woman"** *Time Out*

**"Fun reading and a lifeline to the young and isolated,
[a] very important book"** *G-Scene (Brighton)*

"Life-saving and inspiring"
Skin, Skunk Anansie

RRP £8.95 ISBN 1-873741-45-6

Emerald Budgies
Lee Maxwell

**"Great flocks of emerald budgies are flying
through your brain..."**

What I had to do was make amends, not write stupid lists. Phone
Martin and apologise, stop buying drugs, get a new flat, get out of
the Tracey situation without damaging her psyche too much (stop
thinking it would damage her psyche), concentrate on work, sort out
my future. Fall in love (either sex). How hard could it be? I had a
line of coke.

Ruth's got plenty to distract her from the grim secret that's worming
its way back into her brain – but before long, it will be too late to
make amends.

Lee Maxwell's first novel is a darkly comic tale of disintegration,
betrayal and revenge.

**"Great energy – so much chaos – and I laughed out loud a lot
too. This is a strange way to describe it, but Emerald Budgies
is really charming."** *Emily Perkins*

**"A book about addiction and destruction, so well written that
you get hooked on it and can't put it down."**
Reader review, Diva Blue Rooms

RRP £8.95 ISBN 1-873741-44-8

The Comedienne
VG Lee

"A very funny book"
Lesbians on the Loose

"I couldn't believe it at first – that Susan could switch from padded Valentines, eighteen inches high with 'Be mine forever', to not even stopping her car for me to cross on a zebra. If she hadn't recognised me with the added weight, she must have known it was my shopping trolley."

It's time for Joan to try her luck on the London comedy circuit. After all, everybody always said she was a funny woman...

"The Comedienne has an intrinsic truth that pulls you in before you know it" *Time Out*

"A sympathetic protagonist in the tradition of Lucky Jim – Grade A" *Girlfriends*

"An easy, feelgood, summery read, and a joy to behold" *What's On (Birmingham)*

"A touching evocation of loneliness and the complex relationship between an ageing mother and daughter" *Andrea Levy*

"Straddling the knife edge between funny and sad, it leaves you giggling, days later" *G-Scene*

RRP £8.95 ISBN 1-873741-43-X

Needle Point
Jenny Roberts

"The bruising and the torn skin were worse than I had ever seen before – even the most hardened users protect their veins."

Cameron McGill is on a mission: to find out why her sister, who never touched drugs, was fished from a canal with needle-marks all down her arm. Tearing through Amsterdam on her Harley-Davidson, Cam encounters radical squatters, evasive drug agencies and a particularly alluring policewoman. But it's hard to know who to trust in a quest that could claim her life as gruesomely as it took her sister's.

"Deserves to be read by more than a niche market... an excellently paced, well-plotted thriller" *Guardian*

"A fast-moving tale of revenge and retribution" *Time Out*

"Rivetting and well observed. Recommended!" *G-Scene*

"A very pacy mystery... we look forward to more" *Lesbians on the Loose*

RRP £8.95 ISBN 1-873741-42-1

And coming soon:
The second Cameron McGill mystery,
Breaking Point, in spring 2001